I0709305

ALSO BY WILLIAM COOK HAIGWOOD

Journeying the Sixties: A Counterculture Tarot

The Davenport Trilogy

A Time of Unsearchable Things

Songs of Surveillance:
Stories of Spying, Watching and Eavesdropping

Escape of the Alienated War Babies

AN UNEXPLAINABLE URGE

AN UNEXPLAINABLE URGE

william cook haigwood

Cooskie Creek Press

Printed in the United States of America

Published by Cooskie Creek Press

Library of Congress Cataloging-in-Publication Data

ISBN 978–1–7337262–4–5

Cover photographs © 2024 Willam Cook Haigwood

For Rick
A lifetime of shared stories

Table of Contents

AN UNEXPLAINABLE URGE

He had arrived late to his life's most rewarding destiny, appointed by the governor to the superior court of Sonoma County. He was 66 years old; the oldest ever named to serve on the county bench. The appointment surprised even the Judge who twenty years before was working days in a machine shop while his fellow judges were building their careers by becoming partners, clerking for the courts or administrating law. The judge worked his long days crafting gears and joints while at night he studied for the bar at a small East Bay business school.

Now there were no more ideas. The Judge was dead. Some thought, but could not prove, he died by his own hand. And while his death was a surprise, it was widely known that eighteen months prior the Judge had been censured and forced to resign. He was cited by the state Commission on Judicial Performance for stealing a small sculpture of a Greek god from the Pacific City Club in San Francisco.

The Judge had attended a dinner sponsored by the state's divorce attorneys to honor family law judges and, by his own admission, had succumbed to an "unexplainable urge" to take the figurine, no larger than three inches in height and cast in clay, that served as a paperweight on a table outside the dining room. An attorney phoned the Judge to tell him he had been videotaped taking the sculpture, which belonged to the Club and portrayed its corporate symbol, that of Pan playing on his flute. It was valued at around $80.

"He gave it back," said Mel, who still wondered why taking the sculpture was such a big deal.

"He mailed it back the day the attorney called."

Mel waited with his new acquaintance Furgie at the Mattole River trailhead. Mel had not thought himself a close friend of The Judge until Mel took an unexpected call from Furgie one afternoon.

"He's dead," Furgie told Mel over the phone.

He said The Judge had left a request that Mel join with Furgie and another specified friend to spread The Judge's ashes on the Lost Coast, a favorite backpacking destination. The Judge's request was written in a letter and dated shortly before he died in a car accident.

"Damn, The Judge? He's dead?" Mel remembered saying.

"Haven't seen him since…and the Lost Coast? Last time I was there with him…Fuck! He's dead?"

Furgie filled in the details and answered most of Mel's questions and though he described the circumstances of The Judge's death he was careful not to speculate about why he died. By the end of the call, Mel agreed to meet Furgie and another friend, a county judge named Galen, at the Lost Coast's Mattole River trailhead.

Mel was at first angry to be pulled away from his audition for a part in a TV commercial. But Furgie described his call as an emergency and when Mel heard it was The Judge, he left Encino that night to drive north. The Judge was a distant friend but a good one. And Mel had few good friends.

"Giving it back isn't the same as not taking it," said Furgie. "And, well, The Judge was a judge. Judges can't do that shit. And they know it."

It had been five minutes since Mel met Jerrell Ferguson, both by any measure relatively old men in their late sixties. But not as old as The Judge who was 72 when he died. They stood together in the dusty parking lot at the start of a trail that opened on to a long and windy coastline. They now knew each other but were not the friends each was with The Judge.

"I was a year behind you," Furgie said. "You probably don't remember me in high school. Saw you in the senior play. Some Moss and Hart comedy. You were good."

Mel accepted the compliment and retreated from his argument. They both knew Galen, the third and last of their assembling party and who had not yet arrived.

"Galen has The Judge," said Furgie. "I mean, his ashes."

Mel asked how far they were going.

"Spanish Flat," said Furgie. "You know. You've been there, haven't you?"

"Like two years ago," said Mel. "Gotta be ten miles."

"Eleven, actually," said Furgie. "We thought about coming in from the ridge and taking the dirt road up the mountain out of Honey Dew. Four miles from the trailhead, but the climb is vicious."

"Yeah, I've done it," said Mel. "Never again. So how do you know…I mean, I'm sorry, how did you know The Judge?"

"An old friend," said Furgie. "We went to Europe together in college. Only The Judge didn't come back. It was '67, I think. Yeah, the Six-Day War. He'd lucked out and had a draft classification that made no sense but that put him far at the back of the line. I came home that summer to keep my college deferment. It was a fun trip while it lasted. We did Morocco, Portugal and Spain on $1 and some change a day. I lost twenty pounds. Like I said, an old friend. We stayed in touch and ended up not far from each other. I teach at Benicia High School. When The Judge got his first job in the county Public Defender's office he called me. Camping up here became a once-a-year getaway until two years ago when the shit hit the fan. The Judge disappeared. Didn't want to see anyone for a while. And you?"

Mel turned away to see patches of puffy white foam ripped by the wind from the crest of an ocean wave.

"It's blowing out there," Furgie said.

"It's always blowing out there," said Mel. "The Judge was in my high school acting class. He was a senior. I was a freshman new in town and without any friends. He took me under his wing. Without his encouragement I'd never have become an actor."

"You're an actor?" asked Furgie.

The question usually troubled Mel who wondered why if millions of people saw him on television so few could recognize him.

"Television. *LA Justice*—ever see it?"

"Yeah…." Furgie's acknowledgment grew into a long, slow sigh.

"Hey, I remember. You played an attorney. Man, that was thirty years ago. What are you doing now?"

Mel dodged the question.

"The Judge was studying law when I auditioned for the show. He prepped me well. I got the part. Say, when is this other guy—is it Galen—when is he getting here? "

Mel returned to asking questions to which Furgie provided the answers.

"Galen Bridges, Sonoma County's longest serving justice. Helped The Judge get his first job with the Public Defender. Why? Because they went to grade school together, which is just about as close to nepotism as you can come without blood being involved. The Judge was more than a friend to Galen. He was essentially his sibling. Hadn't seen each other in fifteen years but I'm guessing they had one of those conversations where out of the blue you find some-one. And you can simply say a person's name and it's enough to gen-erate rueful groans or embarrassing laughter. That's a rare quality of connection. Galen loved it. And The Judge knew he loved it. Knew his friend was still his friend and, well, you know The Judge, when he saw an opportunity he grabbed it."

"Do you think he killed himself?" Mel blurted.

His question silenced Furgie, who waited nearly a full minute before answering.

"It was a weird accident," said Furgie. "If it was an accident. He'd dropped his wife off at a restaurant in Benicia and told her he would come back after parking the car. Then he drove downhill toward the wharf and didn't stop. Just plowed through a fence and into the Carquinez Strait. Took the entire night to retrieve the car and The Judge. Autopsy showed enough alcohol in his system to de-clare him legally drunk. But that doesn't explain shit. Did he hit the brakes? It looks like…I mean it could look like…"

"Like an unexplainable urge?" asked Mel.

Before he could absorb any intended irony, Furgie heard the sound of a vehicle behind them and the scrape of tires in the gravel roadbed. He turned to see a black Lexus SUV roll regally into the dirt parking lot across from the restrooms of the river's primitive campground.

"He's here," said Furgie. "Galen's here."

A large man wearing a straw cowboy hat and loose khaki overalls emerged from the driver's door of the Lexus. He turned toward the two men and waved. Furgie and Mel waved back. Galen approached slowly, his hand outstretched to shake those of his hiking companions. Mel felt the warmth of Galen's firm, solid grasp but noticed he gave Furgie a longer, more vigorous shake.

"Everyone ready for four days and three nights?" said Galen. "This isn't the way I'd have wanted us to meet."

He spoke with authority.

Galen's voice had an avuncular resonance that Mel imagined could reliably assert control of a courtroom.

"He loved this place," Galen added. "He knew we did, too. And if we didn't always love this place—'cause it can be a miserable, wet and cold wilderness sometimes—well, we still loved him."

Mel heard the words of a man accustomed to setting a tone that upheld and honored any action as ennobling and purposeful and even satisfying. Galen had the gift of gab and was the sort of person who could be called on by anyone at any time to offer homilies or encomiums.

As an actor, Mel knew how important it was to share in a consensus and how brilliant one had to be to create one. There was nothing reasonable about The Judge or his transgression or his death. But it was right to let an old friend take his leave and to honor his departure regardless the chosen exit.

2

"It's mid-March, what do you expect?" Galen said as he led his companions south, each carrying a full backpack as with every step they pushed poles in front of them through viscous, slowing sands.

"Wind. But no rain yet. Not in the last forecast, anyway, but you never know around here. It's wet, though. Plenty of storms this winter. We'll have to ford Four-Mile Creek. No doubt. Sunset at around seven. Would love to get to Cooskie Creek but that's a fierce ocean out there. Don't want to get stuck in the rocks. Let's check the tide at

Sea Lion Gulch and see where we are."

The men held onto their hats as they rounded Punta Gorda and fell into the whipping velocities of Windy Point.

"Shit!" shouted Furgie as his baseball cap blew out of his hand and flew into a tide pool several feet ahead. The fierce wind pushed the men along and, for all its biting cold, relieved their first labored steps through the dunes.

Galen was right about Four Mile Creek. Its waters rushed boundlessly though recent hikers had leveraged a floating log into place and buried it in rocks and sand. It offered a partial bridge across the coursing stream, leaving a shallow rivulet that could be crossed bare-footed. Which the men did, though Mel thought he could leap the shallows and kept his shoes on which were soaked when he landed a yard from the sand.

The abandoned Punta Gorda Lighthouse appeared ahead of them.

"Our first milestone," said Furgie. "The Judge and I always stopped here for our first and last beer."

Galen laughed.

"Yeah, no beer this time. Weight, you know. I'm carrying The Judge. But I do have some Japanese whiskey for a toast. It was his favorite."

Furgie and Mel had also brought whiskey that each carried in a pint flask.

"Then we'll have lots of toasts," said Galen. "The Judge would like that."

The men poured their whiskey into small aluminum shot glasses and then lifted them as they stood on the turret of the old lighthouse.

"To The Judge," said Galen.

Even in good weather, half the Lost Coast Trail was inaccessible at high tide. All three hikers knew the times of the tides and had planned the trip accordingly. It was why they did not meet at the trailhead until early afternoon. Low tide would arrive at exactly 6 p.m., which meant they would hike into the evening. Galen hoped they could reach Cooskie Creek before twilight and have an easier second day walk on to Spanish Flat. The coastal stretches north and south of the creek were slow and rocky and pushed up against a wall of steep mountains that shot up from the ocean and offered near certain death to any hiker caught like a bug in the vice of land versus sea.

When the men reached Sea Lion Gulch it was after seven. Galen stared at the spume whipped up by the distant, noisy waves.

"Not tonight," he said ruefully.

He pointed toward the weedy indentation of a nearby ledge.

"We're camping here tonight. The rocks and waves can wait until tomorrow."

No one argued. Even without his judge's robe, Galen ruled.

Everything was wet and dead limbs of trees and shrubs had to be peeled before they would burn. The men gathered what they could and got enough of a fire started to dry more sticks. Mel set his wet shoes and socks in front of the fire's flickering flames. All then threw up their small tents and searched their packs for provisions. Galen brought out a bag of instant chili that fed everyone. Another sip each of whiskey opened their minds and mouths. They filtered water from a trickling stream and filled their bottles. Their camp faced into the north wind, which sang a loud howl as it blew high waves onto the rocks. By mid-evening the ocean surged at the base of their subtle cliff.

"Damn, that's a loud ocean," said Furgie as he stepped toward the ledge. "Is it the wind that makes it sound so loud?"

"No, it's just a mean place," said Galen. "It's a hard stretch, but beautiful. Nature is a liar just like we are. What you see is not what you always get. It's a beautiful land. It's also deadly."

"You mean like The Judge?" said Mel. "The Judge was a liar."

"No," answered Galen after pausing to consider Mel's accusation and also to wonder why he made it. Perhaps Mel was a little drunk.

"The Judge was afraid. He was afraid he wasn't good enough, not strong enough to take his place in the world. I wonder if he really wanted to be a judge and if there was some relief for him in his censure by the commission."

"He never denied taking the statue," said Mel.

"Yes he did," said Furgie. "That is, until he was clearly and completely caught."

"You guys need to understand something," said Galen abruptly. "Nature is full of fraudulent display and perception. Butterflies that mimic the markings of another species to fend off the blue jays that feed on them. Birds that make the sounds of other birds to scare invaders away from their trees. Dogs that walk with a sham limp to gain their owner's attention. Little wonder humans have learned to lie with intention, to conceal, misinform, invent and create ambiguities. Fish that change sex to steal another fish's eggs.

"The Judge saw fraud every day in his courtroom, a menagerie of human deceit comprising everyone sworn to tell the truth and all trying desperately to lie better than the other. A court is another of nature's battlegrounds where the most convincing lie usually prevails. The Judge's problem wasn't that he stole the statue. It was that he got caught. Caught like a frightened rat in a trap."

"So The Judge was deceitful because he was afraid?" asked Mel. "Afraid of what?"

"If he feared anything, it was that people wouldn't like him," said Furgie. "He wanted friends. He wanted everyone to be his friend. In high school he would do anything for his friends. He would steal for his friends. And he did. I saw a paperback book of Beat poetry in the drugstore one afternoon waiting for the bus home from school. I mentioned I wanted to buy it but couldn't and when I sat down on the bus, Marshall handed it to me. He had stolen it. It was a gift, though from his typically communist perspective he described his acquisition of the book as an 'appropriation.' It wasn't stealing. It was taking from the rich, and it was impossible to steal from the filthy and useless rich what the people naturally deserved for all their unpaid labor. From that time on I called him Little Red Robin Hood."

"We're getting pretty fast to the core of this man's hard life," said Galen. "I thought it would take at least another six miles to get real."

Mel smiled but Furgie did not.

"He did steal," said Furgie. "He took things. Especially if he had been drinking. He'd appropriate the oddest stuff. Never stole from friends, though. I never worried he would take anything from me. He never did."

Galen pulled the collar of his jacket tight around his neck as if to hide from the wind. His wrinkled brow and shocks of unruly white hair gave him the look of a mad wizard.

"He was loyal," said Galen. "I liked that about him. It was one reason I wrote the recommendation to the governor that he become a judge. He never stole from me or for me, as far as I know. And he was the most damned dependable and hardworking court clerk I've ever had."

"So he was afraid and deceitful but also loyal," said Furgie. "Sounds like a literary character. Gatsby, maybe. Or Dimmesdale. A loyal dreamer with a bad conscience. It's the American way."

"Whatever it was, his wife couldn't manage it," Furgie continued. "She tried to stand by him at first. They were churchgoers, which surprised me because The Judge was an atheist when I knew him well. But a second marriage and the difficult birth of a daughter on the spectrum must have sent him looking for Jesus. I can see how his censure might have been too much. His wife was a regarded therapist in the county and she thought her association with The Judge was pulling down her career. So she left him. Or, at least, that's how I heard it. They stayed friends, though. She said the night he died they were going out to dinner to discuss their daughter's care."

"It was so public," said Mel. "I mean, I read about his censure on the London Times website. It must have covered the globe, at least for day."

"It was big local news," said Galen. "And the courthouse…well, it's a little world in our county. You can smell every fart. Everyone remembered Marshall's installation four years before, and the way his wife shook out his new black robe and threw it affectionately over his shoulders. He was an old guy who came up the hard way and it felt so good to reward him for his good work. He was a good judge. That is, until he forgot he was a judge. Forgot what that really meant about how he would have to live his life."

Mel was quiet, as if guarding a secret he was reluctant to share. Galen noticed. He asked Mel to talk about The Judge.

"I didn't live nearby," said Mel. "But I saw Marshall twice a year. This trip was one of our favorite adventures. We did this walk together at least a dozen times. So we talked a lot about our lives

with the kind of confessional honesty you share with someone who
knows you well but won't be around the next week to give you back
your guilt. He helped me through two bad divorces. I heard him
lament the struggles he faced making a life with June. And I heard
him complain about his career in law. I always had the impression
he had come to hate it. And he especially hated some of the people
he worked with. In his opinion the law existed only to protect the
rich. And while he had no expectation of ever becoming a judge,
he wanted desperately to mess with the gears of justice. He wanted
to halt all the mechanisms of so-called justice that made victims of
the already victimized. And he kept a list. He called it an enemy list.
It included people he worked with and that he thought were most
decadent and most corrupt, most deceitful and unfair."

"Who was on his list?" asked Galen, a query he delivered in the
dissembling, avuncular tone of a judge playing the good cop.

"I don't really know. People came and went on the list. There
was a time he didn't like you," said Mel.

He turned to look at Galen.

"Damn, you must be drunk," Furgie said to Mel.

"No…" Galen said after a pause. "The Judge and I had a rough
time once. I remember. But we fixed it. At least, I thought we did.
Mel is right, though. I rule for the defense."

Furgie relaxed while Mel spoke again and directly to Galen.

"Like you say, the universe is a malicious place of fiercely com-
petitive creatures all using every deception they can devise for survival. Much like a courtroom."

3

It wasn't that Mel thought truth to be unimportant. It was just that
it wasn't always interesting. He thought of his life, and that of The
Judge, as odysseys driven by their instincts to survive, to live and to
be free. A courtroom was a world within the larger world, but one
still wracked with serious fates and ruled by too many gods. Through
his ingenuity, inventiveness and labor, The Judge had climbed to the

top and taken charge. It was cruel he should be destroyed by a single, unexplainable urge. It was cruel and also classically comical.

The men rose and climbed into their tents, Furgie still trying to make peace between Galen and Mel, though neither was apparently bothered by Mel's honest words. And Mel knew he had nothing to lose. While The Judge had climbed in midlife out of his seemingly chronic loneliness and misdirection, Mel had fallen from his early years of success. It was if a wheel of fortune had turned for both in opposite directions, The Judge rising as Mel plunged, two trends merged in a reliable and, for Mel, embarrassing synchronicity.

Success came early for Mel, who before he was thirty had earned supporting roles in several daytime TV soaps. The money was good and he was happy but an agent suggested he audition for a new legal series with the title LA Justice. His strong jaw, good looks, and moody projection earned him the role of a junior law partner that, over six seasons, grew into a main character and a large paycheck. Millions watched him act every week, until the show was canceled in the early Nineties. Then very few ever saw him again.

For the next two decades, and through two divorces, Mel managed few TV appearances and even fewer film roles. Now in his late sixties, he tried persistently to sell his aging face and once famous voice to film but with limited success. Web commercials were limitless but not very lucrative. He had been auditioning for a laxative spot when Furgie phoned him about The Judge.

A year before, Mel was diagnosed with prostate cancer and at his age the race was on. He had made the fateful decision not to go under the knife, his doctor thinking it was the "slow" version of the disease. But then things sped up and now it was too late for surgery. He might have just a few good years left and no spouse or children with whom to share them.

"So I tell the truth now," he said to himself as he rolled into a ball inside his sleeping bag.

It was another kind of unexplainable urge, a compelling need seized directly and firmly from one flashing moment of revelation. And Galen had started it, with his talk of lies and deceit, which became for Mel a catapult for an uncontainable and probably ancient desire. He was a natural animal and he introduced what this trip needed but did not want: a bad mood.

"There's been a change in the weather," Galen said as he sat at the morning fire he created from dry branches kept next to him through the night. First Furgie and then Mel crawled out of their small tents. Heavy mist had become slender rivulets that ran down their rain guards and off the trees and soaked everything. The wind was down but the surf was up and higher than expected for an hour after low tide.

"We have two hours to get to Cooskie," said Galen. "The rocks are brutal and this sea won't quit. Once we're there, we should be able to catch the next low tide at dusk and reach the Flat."

"It's lookin' weird out there," said Furgie, who had hiked here more than the others.

Additional to his hikes with The Judge, Furgie at times had brought his son and friends down the coast. He preferred the south trail and its meandering path through the redwoods high above the sea. It was safer but also steeper and longer. The north trail was all ocean all the time. And that's what The Judge loved.

By *weird*, Furgie meant to say that the sea was fatter, its waves higher, its movement more glacial and threatening, than he had ever before seen.

"Change in the weather," he said, repeating Galen's words. "How would we know? We're long past a place we'd ever be able to hear a weather report."

All had brought their cell phones, which were useless so far outside a service area. And no one had thought to bring a radio.

After a quick breakfast of cereal and instant coffee, the three men set out, their hiking poles poking softly at the countless boulders and stones comprising the slender beach trail to Cooskie Creek. Going was slow.

"A mile an hour…we'll be lucky to keep that pace," said Galen who staggered ahead.

By mid-morning the wind had picked up and, at the mouth of the creek, physically blown Galen into the creek's gulch. His companions followed, holding on to their hats. At the mouth of the creek a dead whale floated, its body shaped into a massive crescent that rhythmically bounced with crashes of the ocean's increasingly intrusive waves.

"We made it," said Galen. "Let's have lunch."

"Damn, it's cold," said Mel, who experienced his first still moments without a fire or sleeping bag to warm him.

"North wind," said Galen. "And it's strong. Worse weather than predicted, that's for sure. No surprise, though. Weather here is almost always worse than advertised."

"And it doesn't matter now," said Furgie. "We're nearly there. No problems once we get beyond Randall and onto the Flat."

Furgie's optimism irritated Mel, who again brought up The Judge.

"A lot of work for a dead friend," he said.

"But we're his friends," answered Galen. "Is there much else we need to say?"

Burbling under the men's exhaustion was a wish of each to sell his distinct remembrance of The Judge. And however lofty anyone spoke of him, each would have to address The Judge's decision to throw away his professional life for a trinket. Mel acknowledged that Furgie and Galen spent more time with The Judge, but did not know him nearly as well. Any ceremony to scatter ashes would become a way for each to remember The Judge as they wished him to be. Mel, though, loved The Judge and wished to remember him as he was.

The men were quiet on the last lap of the hike to Spanish Flat, the ocean so loud their words could not be heard anyway. Mel wandered among his thoughts, acknowledging that self-deception was not unusual and part of the mind's normal functioning. He had compassion for The Judge and his miserably stupid choice though he knew enough about cunning to brand his late friend's weakness for what it was: a lack of wit to be crafty and underhanded. The Judge had put his toe into a familiar stream, not thinking that a shark likely would bite if off. It never had before.

The sky darkened quickly into the early evening and by the time the men scurried quickly up the trail south of Randall Creek, the ocean was lapping at their boots. All stood in wet shoes as they surveyed the Flat and Galen pointed out a distant beach.

"We can make it," said Galen. "The trail is well-marked and we're on the bluff now. We'll be at Spanish Creek in 45 minutes. We'll camp up from the beach. I know the spot."

"You noticed we haven't passed another hiker?" said Furgie. "Not one? That's very strange. The first day of spring is a week away. Always have people out here in March."

"Must have read a different weather report," Mel responded cynically. "This is a rough sea. Seems a lot rougher than predicted."

"Trip's half-over," said Galen. "We're doin' fine. Let's go."

"Wish we could see the moon," shouted Mel. "Wish the moon could see us."

No one responded.

"Really? He tried to pour mouthwash into her…into her pussy?"

Another hearty soup dinner and more shots of whiskey relaxed the hikers into a reverie of stories about The Judge. The conversation began while Galen recounted his discovery of a Facebook site that listed the members of their high school classes that had died. One was a woman named Wendy who had gotten drunk with The Judge after the senior prom and dragged him into an empty bedroom at an after-the-party party.

"It was his first fuck and he came fast," said Furgie. "Wendy freaked out. She reached up inside to get as much of his cum as she could. Then she dragged him into a bathroom looking for, of all things, a spermicide. All she could find was a bottle of mouthwash and, now this was what The Judge told me, she stood on her hands and lifted herself up while the judge tried to pour some of it in her… you know…. That is, until she screamed in pain. Then it was another problem, entirely."

"Well, I thought I'd heard everything…" Galen said with sagacious solemnity. "Don't know if I'd have sex again for a while."

The incident was funny but the men did not laugh.

"What killed Wendy?" asked Furgie.

"Uterine cancer…two years ago," answered Galen.

"Who else is dead?"

Galen recited familiar names and others no one else knew.

"Dozens from our classes are dead now," said Galen. "The smokers, you know, a lot of them went first. Then there were those with chronic diseases or who died in accidents. Big Jack Mumm, remember him? Huge guy who drove a motorcycle and bullied us all? He fell off his bike thirty years ago and spent nearly a decade in a coma. And a few guys died in the war."

Mel wondered if anything Galen said was verifiable. He had a strong distrust of what people said they remembered or claimed to know. As an actor Mel knew that most statements framed wishes and not facts. He had never heard Furgie's story about The Judge. And certainly not from The Judge who never again would correct or contest anything said about him.

4

If insights were excitements, each was real only for a moment. As they ate, each man spoke of his common love for The Judge while also delineating specific idiosyncrasies that might have predicted The Judge's fall. Galen again emphasized The Judge's loyalty and also his self-effacement.

"He was afraid to offend anyone," said Galen. "I told him a judge is not a social worker, however much he loves the common man. His sympathies were tested in Family Law court where angry, divorcing parents fought like pythons for the dubiously valuable custody of their children. He'd let them fight for a while and then try to speak for the children, but much too late. No one was listening. Once he needed two bailiffs to restore order."

"I'm surprised he ever wanted to be a judge," said Furgie. "Must have been the money. The Judge's childhood was spent in poverty. It was wrenching and secret, especially after his father left and took away his engineer's income. Wouldn't have anything to do with The Judge. Bad dad, though they made up later and The Judge ended up taking care of him until he died. Child support was always late, though. The Judge had bad acne and it needed treatment. His mother did her best. Is it surprising he would steal from time to time?"

"More than time to time," said Galen. "It sounds as if he was your class klepto. I mean, emotionally he had his reasons and politically he had his rationale, but it was stealing. And it sounds compulsive. I'm surprised he never sought treatment. It would have been much less costly all around."

"He never got caught," said Mel. "Until he was caught. The idea he was on camera never occurred to him, I'm sure. There are things all of us are capable of doing if we think no one is watching. At least he was close to retirement."

"Retirement?" shouted Galen. "He sacrificed a lucrative retirement. Retired judges make small fortunes filling in on busy court calendars. The censure prevented The Judge from ever serving again in a courtroom. He was banned for life."

The wind stopped and it began to rain.

"We are gonna get wet," said Furgie. "Time for bed."

The three hikers stirred and crawled into their tents, leaving wet boots under the rain tarps.

"Weather's a lot worse than expected," Furgie said again.

"No worries," said Galen. "We'll dump The Judge after breakfast and start back tomorrow afternoon when the tide starts to recede. We'll have our last night at the big creek and get up early for the hike out."

Mel could not fall asleep. He wasn't tired and the rain pounding on the flapping rain guard of his tent contributed to a concrete claustrophobia. He hated camping in the rain. He hated more his need to socialize with Galen and Furgie about the miserable demise of a dear friend. Lying came so naturally to human beings, and especially lying to oneself about oneself. Mel had made his living as a liar, acting genuine emotions he did not feel.

Yet he was convincing, and so sincere as an actor he lost track of what was genuine about his feelings and what was false. Others knew this about him. Two ex-wives could testify (and during fruitless psychotherapeutic encounters did) that Mel cheated and, to the degree he took advantage of their vulnerable love, behaved toward them much like a thief.

Throughout their friendship The Judge was notably empathic toward Mel's life of accelerating and ever more hopeless defeats. The Judge had cared about Mel's wounded heart and now Mel was determined to have his dead friend's back.

Rain fell through the night. The men stirred together in the first dawn light and shouted to one another from their tents.

"Rise and shine," Galen finally called and the men arrived together at a driftwood lean-to over which they hung one of the tent's rain guards.

"This wasn't in the weather report," Furgie said as he held his hand out to feel the steady fall of raindrops.

"Which report?" asked Mel, tired of Furgie's constant and useless weather updates.

"You mean last Tuesday's? Old news, man."

Mel's impertinence seemed to piss off Furgie who had hiked this trail many more times than Mel and had survived them all.

"Hey, I'm just sayin'…'" Furgie answered, irritation suddenly and surprisingly present in his voice.

"Don't matter, man," said Mel. "We're all here and accounted for. It's cool."

It wasn't cool. And the men knew it though as men they were legacy members of the world's largest liars' club. Where survival might be at stake, not one would share real feelings. Lies were usually attempts to make things simpler, so reliably for all of them things were fine, just fine.

"It's not the rain that worries me," said Galen. "It's that damned wind. And those waves. Supposed to be low tide right now and that sea looks anything but low."

Galen's avuncular tone eased the conversation toward breakfast, which featured apples and cold cereal as the men gathered around a slender, quietly roaring flame from Mel's propane stove. It was too wet to start a fire.

"How's Monica?" Galen asked Furgie who stopped chewing.

Monica was Furgie's wife and Galen's question was thoughtful, but also probing.

"She moved out last month."

Furgie spoke bluntly, as if trying to spit out a seed.

"Furg…" Galen said as if hearing sad news that was not a surprise.

"And the boy?" Galen asked, referring to Furgie's son.

"Gone to live with her," said Furgie. "She has the big salary and a cool condo in Glencove and he can drive her BMW anytime he wants. I'm just a fucking high school teacher with a nine-year-old Ford hatchback who grades papers every night. You tell me who wins that auction."

"That's fucked," said Mel, offering sympathy derived from his own rough life with bad lovers.

"What's more fucked is that she has a boyfriend. He's a local realtor who is also on the school board, which technically makes him one of my bosses. Can you believe that?"

Galen searched cautiously like a jurist, asking Furgie what he thought he would do next.

"Monica wants a collaborative divorce but I think that's just to save her money. I used to think we had an honest relationship, that is, until I learned she'd been telling me anything but the truth. About six months ago she began complaining to me that I was a bad husband and a bad dad to Pete. What she should have told me was that she had found a new lover."

Men who thought themselves wronged by women shared a vernacular that like a King's English was what every man was, or should be, speaking. Many men who loved a woman also had experienced her fury and engaged in a succession of battles that threatened always to become a war. So it was natural that Galen and Mel were drawn together with Furgie to defend him. He was a warrior and comrade and standing together in the cold rain they together were no different from doughboys sharing a trench in any of the past century's wars of industry, wars no different from the open field battles of the Scottish plains or the valley of Agincourt.

And like all modern or ancient soldiers they were a united band of brothers. Even Mel went along, as cynical as he was about Furgie and what he perceived as his temporary companion's neurotic antipathy. But any man victimized by an intimate enemy was easily Mel's long lost friend. A mother was a formidable force in shaping a man's hatred, but more formidable was the father that continued to instill attachment to the presumed values and perks of manhood, however irrelevant they were or had become. It was a bad lesson passed from generation to generation and that gave Mel little hope his species would much longer survive.

"Damn, why didn't you tell me?" Galen asked Furgie. "Do you have an attorney? I know some good divorce lawyers who…"

"I don't know," said Furgie. "She's a bitch, a fucking bitch."

Furgie was a bitter man consigned suddenly to solitary confinement, a prisoner of his own loneliness and one cultivated expertly by the lonely males he befriended in a long, tedious life as a high school teacher. The biology was clear to him from watching for years the emergence of boys and girls into men and women. And by the time a man realized he had been out-thought and out-managed by a contriving partner, he frequently felt lost in a suddenly directionless and chaotic new reality. How had he not seen this coming? How not, indeed.

A pause in the rain allowed the men to break camp. Their packs were ready as they stood together at the shore. Furgie dug a hole in the sand and Galen brought out a large oak box. An embossed label read *Marshall S. Weston*. Galen set it down beside the hole.

"He wanted this," said Galen. "It's why we're here."

Galen offered a few words that no one could remember. Then he opened the box and lifted from it a cellophane bag filled with the white, granular ashes of The Judge. Galen held a soupspoon from his mess kit and scooped up a lump of ashes that he tossed into a hole dug into the sand. Furgie followed and then Mel, who took two scoops of the Judge and threw them down hard until the last scoop, caught in the wind, flew as a rain of ash over all three of the gathered friends. Mel tried furiously to dust away the pellets of The Judge that landed in his hair and eyes.

The shoveling and dumping continued as each took turns until the bag was useless as a container and Galen held it up and shook The Judge's last grains into the hole as if they were crumbs from a potato chip bag.

"OK," said Galen as he surveyed the horizon and dodged an ocean wave as it rushed in and covered The Judge's hole.

"Let's get up to Randall. Tide should be going out when we get there."

The ceremony had been quick, Mel imagining it similar to the planting of the cross by a frightened explorer who after discovering a new and dangerous world needed to make his claim quickly before turning to hurry home.

5

A nearly two-mile return hike along the flat to Randall Creek took the three men most of the afternoon. Mel noticed the wind-whipped and white-capped waves far offshore seemed to converge steadily with the trail where the men would drop to the shallow beach.

"You think we'll have room to walk?" Mel asked.

"Still early," answered Galen. "Low tide is a little after sunset."

"I see someone," Furgie shouted. "He's waving."

The men scurried toward Randall but the "someone" seen by Furgie was a bleached tree branch stuck in a bush and that swung irregularly in the fierce wind.

A blotch of obscure sunlight fell away through distant clouds as the men climbed down to the rocky beach.

"You sure it's low tide?" Galen asked Furgie who looked at his watch.

"Half-hour yet. It's a ninety-minute hike to the big creek if we hurry."

Furgie looked north along the trail toward a wall of boulders that identified the next narrow point on the coast. He stared as if looking through a window without noticing the glass of rough sea in front of him.

"Rougher than when we came down and just about as dark," said Galen.

"So let's hurry," said Furgie and took his first long steps on the slender beach leading north.

Galen followed Furgie and Mel followed Galen. The wind bit into Mel and he stopped frequently to assess how Furgie managed the first narrow passage. Then he danced, as Furgie and Galen had, across the surf swirling briefly under their shoes.

Darkness was on them quickly and all turned on their headlamps. A second narrow point loomed farther ahead, approached across a field of sharp, slippery rocks.

Furgie charged forward, reaching the place of passage before Galen and Mel. He turned to see his companions emerge like shadows from the darkness. He waved them forward. He climbed a large boulder to shout at them. He turned his back on the sea. Mel saw the white spume of a powerful, approaching wave. So did Galen who shouted and waved his pole at Furgie. In an instant Furgie was soaked by the wave's furious assault and then gone.

Galen ran to the rock, climbed it and bent over to search for Furgie until the weight of his pack pushed him over the side. Mel also ran to the rock but removed his pack before climbing it. His headlamp illuminated an angry, white froth that lashed at the tapered edge of the large boulder. A hand appeared and then another. In a moment four hands and arms swam out of the water and slapped hard to grab whatever could be held. Mel reached for two and braced himself. He would grab the hand of each of his companions and drag them forward until they could get leverage with their legs and feet. He pulled hard, in a race with yet another large, boiling wave. Mel slipped but held on as the wave rushed into him and he used its force to push him and his companions over the boulder's edge.

The wave receded and Mel opened his eyes. Lying before him was Galen whose two hands Mel held tightly. Mel jumped again to the top of the rock and called out.

"Furgie! Over here! Furgie!"

He searched the surf but saw nothing until another, larger wave approached. Mel dropped back behind the rock and held on to Galen who was without his pack and did not move. Another wave washed over them and Mel squeezed Galen in his arms, his feet pressed hard for leverage within the crevice formed between the large boulder and two smaller ones.

A pause before the next surge allowed Mel to move Galen away from the point and on to a stretch of dry sand. Mel then ran back to the rock and timed his climb to miss another surge that was slower and weaker than the one before. The next was weaker still, not even reaching the top of the boulder where Mel cautiously searched the water for any sign of Furgie.

"Furgie!" Mel called again. He thought he heard a sibilant and distant cry farther out but saw nothing. He waited a few minutes as the surges became weaker and the ocean calmed enough for him to search the shore in both directions. He still saw nothing, but heard Galen moan. Mel climbed back down the boulder to attend to him.

"My leg!" shouted Galen. "My fucking leg…"

Mel examined Galen with his headlamp. He bled from a superficial cut to his head but there were no other open wounds. Mel struggled to help Galen to his feet and though he stood, Galen struggled to walk. Mel handed Galen his hiking pole and led him slowly to a higher, drier stretch of beach behind the rocks. He pulled a sweater from his pack and wrapped it around Galen before returning to the big boulder for another search of the horizon, another probe of the adjacent slender and rocky beaches. He saw nothing. Galen's pack was gone, and so was all of Furgie.

An hour before dawn Mel sent his last undeliverable text. His phone was on fumes and he had sent more than three dozen messages hoping even one might slip into some area of reception and alert someone, anyone, to the emergency in front of him. After accepting that Furgie was lost, Mel found a steep staircase chiseled in the cliffs that stretched like a high wall across the coastal trail. It led to a slender ledge where, after huffing and lifting, Mel placed Galen and wrapped him in his tent's rain tarp. He gave him water from his bottle to wash down two ibuprofen tablets and then fed him an energy bar. He also tried to keep him awake and checked him from time to time until Galen began shivering violently.

Mel asked Galen to tell him what was wrong. Galen's lips tried to form words but nothing emerged from his mouth. His eyes widened in panic and nearly a minute passed before Galen spoke.

"I'm so damned…cold…" Galen said weakly. Mel dug out his tent and wrapped it around Galen.

Mel had spent the night assessing his situation. Furgie was gone along with Galen's pack and poles. It was Sunday morning and the men weren't expected back until Tuesday night. Only Galen's wife would be concerned if they didn't arrive and it might be Wednesday before anyone phoned the rangers. Unless they encountered another hiker, survival for Galen was very much in question. He was an old man and, while fit, significantly wounded.

If Mel could move Galen to the gulch of the big creek they stood a chance. Staying where they were would be dangerous if not fatal. They had fended off one high tide but the next few might be higher. They needed flat ground and Galen needed to sit by a fire. In Mel's favor was that the rain had stopped, the wind had died down and with it the mean, angry sea. Mel estimated he and Galen were three-quarters of a mile south of Cooskie Creek with less than six hours before the next high tide. He recalled that a quarter-mile from the creek they had passed a small gulch that rose with the mountains. They could slip into the gulch if the ocean surprised them.

It was not reasonable to think Galen could walk even ten feet, not to mention three thousand, but the madman was not the man who lost his reason. Mel had already given up on what was reasonable and had nothing left to lose.

"Need you to walk, Galen. What do you think?"

"The knee…weight on my knee…shit!"

Galen had obvious trouble forming a sentence.

Mel gave Galen his pole and had found a long stick he could also lean against as he walked. He helped Galen down from the ledge and stood him like a tall box against the large boulder where Furgie last appeared. Mel handed Galen the stick and gave him a gentle push through a rocky gap and onto the beach beyond. Galen staggered forward and Mel looked at his watch and counted twelve steps in a minute. A steady pace would get Galen at least to the gulch. Mel decided to go for it.

Mel went ahead to clear rocks and debris. As they walked Galen found it easier to ignore the pain. Their pace accelerated until a ridge of rocks forced them to climb, which required Galen to use his arms and pull himself forward. They lost nearly a half-hour. At the small gulch the ocean lapped at their feet but the beach opened and by hugging the hills they could avoid the encroaching tide. At last Mel saw the wide flow of a creek and its receding gulch and at its mouth the still decomposing carcass of the large whale.

He pulled Galen up the trail and sat him on a log and gave him a bottle of water. They were alone.

"Just us girls," Mel said, trying to raise a laugh from Galen who, exhausted, could barely offer a smile.

The country was dangerous and also beautiful, though it held nothing. And for now the nothing of it was all Mel could comprehend.

6

Mel offered Galen another ibuprofen, which he accepted quietly.

"Furgie…" Galen muttered weakly.

Mel shrugged his shoulders.

"He might have gotten to another rock," said Mel. "Hope he made it."

Mel knew he hadn't.

Mel erected his tent and climbed in to spread his sleeping bag. He helped Galen inside.

"You rest now," Mel commanded. "We're safe. You take a nap and then we'll have dinner."

Sun broke through the late morning's heavy clouds and briefly heated the gulch. Beyond the creek's mouth the sea roared again into its livid rage, the wind spraying white foam across everything.

Mel walked down to the mouth of the creek and looked anxiously south. He stood on a log to see past the rocks. He searched vainly for Furgie, hoping to see him walk into view. It was an unexplainable urge and when it was not satisfied he returned to the gulch and opened his pack. As he thought, he had a package of powdered chowder, three apples, a bag of peanuts and two bags of chips, several packets of lemonade flavoring and a quarter pint of bourbon. Gratefully, he had carried the crew's water filter but did not have the propane stove though he had a pack of waterproof matches.

He also had a small first aid kit and enough painkillers for a few days. He had an extra sweatshirt and another pair of pants. It was afternoon and there were no decisions he needed to make. He had had enough of the ocean and would not test Galen again. He planned a full day of rest and divided his remaining food into portions that would last at least two days. He searched the creek's shore for handfuls of dead branches and with the help of a crumpled corner torn from a wilderness brochure got a small fire going with wood so wet it made more steam than smoke and very few flames. He searched vainly for dry branches and set the least damp beside his pitiful fire. In the late afternoon Mel checked again on Galen who had begun at last to stir.

"It hurts," said Galen as he sat by the fire and rubbed his knee. "Don't know what I did."

Mel rolled up Galen's pant leg to see his knee joint swollen to half again its normal size. The skin was bright red and wrapped in a patch of black and blue streaks. Galen tried to stretch his leg forward and moaned.

"Damn!" Galen muttered through clenched lips.

"No worries," said Mel who had nothing but worries.

"We're OK here. I have some chowder for dinner tonight. And a half-shot of bourbon for dessert."

"Where's Furgie?" asked Galen.

It was Mel's first hint that Galen might be having trouble processing his thoughts.

"He's back there," Mel said pointing south.

"Hope he catches up soon," said Galen. "He'll miss dinner."

Mel lied again.

"He's experienced with this coast," said Mel. "We just need to take care of ourselves."

Meaning had become more valuable than truth in a situation

where survival was very much in play. Mel did not worry about himself but Galen's state became immediately concerning when he asked Mel for his meds.

"Meds? You mean medications?" asked Mel.

"Heart pills. Would you get them for me?"

Mel did not know about the pills.

"Where are they?" asked Mel.

"My pack," said Galen. "Just go get my pack."

Truth was useless now. Mel considered how to avoid the truth or at least make it credibly false. He decided to ignore Galen's request.

"How about more soup?"

Galen stared off into the afternoon's sinking darkness.

"Soup? Sure," said Galen vaguely.

He said nothing more about his heart pills.

Among all unexplainable urges the urge to live was the most unexplainable, even more so than the unexplainable urge to die. Each increment of future life held both the promise of a pleasure but also the terror of its likely and inevitable absence. The past was typically a repository of reasons to keep on living. And his past seemed at least temporarily unavailable to Galen who, as a result, was also without fear. Once Mel grasped that Galen could no longer comprehend their devastating predicament, he began to plot their escape.

Low tide had returned but Mel had no interest in racing it north to Sea Lion Gulch and through the crevices and rocks of a sky black shore with the lame and apparently disoriented Galen in tow. Nor did he wish to wait for the morning low tide, which was a higher tide and one still influenced by the unpredictable weather.

There were choices. He could wait with Galen at the big creek for someone to come along or for the rangers to begin looking for them. But a week might pass before they were found. Mel could abide it but he worried Galen could not last. For a moment Mel considered and rejected the idea of leaving Galen while he scrambled up to the trailhead himself. The last choice was to climb back through the mountains. He remembered seeing on Furgie's map a dotted line showing a trail from the big creek to a mountain trail that climbed toward the high ridge and that fell back to the shore above Punta Gorda. Furgie had mentioned the trail on their way down. He wanted to walk it but always rejected it because it added three miles and 2,000 feet of elevation to the hike.

Night fell and Galen did not move from his place beside Mel's inconsequential fire. Mel handed Galen a pole and asked him to stand.

"How does that feel?" Mel asked as he helped Galen up and then stood away.

"OK," said Galen. "I'm OK."

"Can you walk?" asked Mel.

Galen appeared to have no grasp of caution and simply pushed his foot out in front of him. It landed hard on the ground and Galen wobbled briefly.

"It hurts," Galen said.

"Bad?" asked Mel. "Can you take another step?"

Galen staggered forward.

"Again," commanded Mel.

Belief in repetition was a form of hope and, as if he were guiding a child, Mel cheered Galen's progress as he took a dozen steps forward using the hiking pole as a third leg to drag his wounded leg behind him. It was slow but it was doable. Again, Mel calculated the some three thousand steps per mile needed to traverse the mountain's trail to the point. Galen would need to make more than ten thousand steps. How long would that take? It would take Mel a few hours. It might take Galen as many as two or three days.

"We'll start out in the morning," said Mel. "You rest now."

Mel settled Galen back in the tent and slid under the tent's outstretched rain guard. It was a tight squeeze but Mel would stay dry. A patter of rain bounced off the tent as Mel tried to sleep, all his fears drawn from a repertoire of past possibilities.

Mel awoke from a dream about The Judge. For the first time in his memory he missed the past. In his dream Mel was clearly and cleanly connected with his old friend. They were hiking again, walking the familiar and dramatic trail of this lost coast, and The Judge was laughing as he announced he would not return. Mel did not understand as he watched the laughing Judge disappear up a gulch and into the bulbous and grassy foothills. Mel took the dream as a sign he was right to break all the rules. He was swept up in a mystery (and perhaps an ancient one) that held him in awe and that might even offer an epiphany. He considered the dream an omen of a safe passage he might not have otherwise found and another affirmation of an unexplainable urge that violated the first rule of wilderness survival: don't move from where you are.

"Let's go," Mel said as Galen stood by and Mel folded the tent and strapped it onto his backpack.

Mel had found the slender line of bare dirt that marked a trail along the swollen gulch of the creek. Above them was a patch of blue sky.

"We're going that way," said Mel and pushed Galen in front of him who stepped hesitantly forward.

"When do we get home?" asked Galen. "I'm hungry."

"Soon," said Mel. "Soon."

Galen did well climbing the gulch and by noon Mel had identified the intersection of the creek trail with the coast's ridge trail and confirmed with his compass the next steps north. Galen had traversed half a mile in four hours. Mel wanted to push them farther north before nightfall but at the apex of a high hill the wind blew Galen over and he fell hard, grabbing frantically for his injured knee as he wailed in unbearable pain.

Mel knelt to soothe Galen and pulled up his pants leg to look again at his knee, which was still swollen and still fissured by bulging blue and black veins. Mel knew that one of his strengths was the way he could conceal his fears from himself. Had he not been able to do this he never would have maintained his authenticity through years of acting out the fears of others. It was helpful to think of Galen as a character in a script. He again considered his own fear to be something of value.

By Mel's calculation it was Tuesday morning and he and Galen were still far from the trailhead, perhaps farther than if they had stayed at the creek. It would be at least another 24 hours before anyone would consider them late to return, not to mention missing. Mel jumped off the ground and shook Galen awake inside his tent.

Mel opened their last bag of nuts and fed a handful to Galen who chewed vigorously.

"Can you stand?" Mel asked as he helped Galen out of the tent.

Galen stood on his good leg and grasped the hiking pole to pull himself up on the other.

"Can you walk?" Mel asked.

Galen obediently pushed the pole in front of him and followed with his bad leg.

"Yeah. Maybe."

The trail away from the creek still climbed toward the ridge. And Galen still struggled, but going up was easier than going down.

Mel folded and packed the tent.

"Let's go," Mel said and filed in behind Galen who trudged like a sullen zombie up the hill.

They were out of food and had a quart jug of water between them. Another cold night might finish Galen whose condition continued to deteriorate. And Mel had seen more bear scat in the hills than he had seen anywhere else. So spending the night on the mountain without a fire was out of the question.

By noon, they had marched another 2,000 steps and the trail began to slope down toward a steep gulch. A furious wind picked them up and again blew Galen over.

"I can't. I can't," Galen cried as he choked back tears.

It wasn't true. Mel knew that truth wasn't a given. Truth was made. And he would make Galen walk.

"Almost there," said Mel as he invented their desired outcome. "We're so close. I can see the beach."

"Where's Furgie?" Galen asked. "Will he meet us?"

"Yeah…" Mel answered instinctively. "He's waiting for us. We have to hurry."

From a lip of the gulch Mel viewed a hundred yards of coast he calculated to be just south of the Sea Lion rocks. He also saw two hikers slip briefly across the sand as they walked south. Mel screamed and waved his arms but the hikers were quickly gone.

The dotted line that was the link to their survival lived on a map Mel carried in his mind. He reminded himself that he and Galen were not lost but only stranded. He realized the lie he told Galen was a way to tell a larger truth. Mel also knew another night in the wilderness might kill Galen whose wandering mind at some point would persuade him to sit down and never again stand up.

It appeared for an alarming moment that this point had arrived and Galen would not again walk anywhere. But rain began to fall and like a grumpy sunbather Galen stood to find a way out of it. Mel led him forward, promising every few minutes that another several steps would bring them closer to the trailhead and to the comfort of Galen's Lexus and that Furgie would be waiting, in fact, was waiting now.

Hours passed as Mel kept up the ruse of proximate arrival and reunion and finally as the sun appeared through grey clouds to hover just above the horizon the two hikers dropped down to the beach north of the old lighthouse.

Mel faced the last obstacle of their journey: the turbulent rush of Four Mile Creek. He searched for the log they had crossed coming over. But it had been loosened and sent tumbling into the rocks on the beach. Several days of rain had increased the creek's volume and velocity and while a healthy hiker might forge the creek's broad mouth at low tide, Mel knew it would be impossible for Galen to hold his balance or for Mel to hold it for him.

Mel led Galen back to the empty lighthouse.

Look," Mel told Galen. "Our own bed and breakfast."

Mel guided Galen into one of the building's empty, windowless rooms, the scent of urine strong under a twisting, iron staircase. He tucked Galen in a corner out of the wind and found a few sticks left inside that were dry enough to make a fire. He started a blaze on the building's shallow cement porch and fed it with driftwood from the beach.

"Where's Furgie?" Galen asked.

"Not here yet," said Mel. "Anytime now."

Again, Mel wrapped Galen in his tent's rain guard and set him in front of the fire. Galen's eyes were closed but his breathing was steady. Mel squeezed in next to him to provide further warmth. Galen's survival wasn't assured but it appeared more likely. A day of cunning and chicanery had given a severely wounded Galen shelter from the storm. Life depended on the success of deceitful enterprises, on the impetuous innovations born from an unexplainable urge.

A new dawn brought more rain. The fire was out and it would be hard to start another with no dry wood and just two matches left. Mel checked Galen who was still breathing and still warm. He thought to wake him but decided against it. He might have to explain why Furgie wasn't there. But then Mel worried that Galen might sink into a coma and so shook him vigorously until he awoke.

"Where's Furgie?" Galen asked.

"Not here yet."

It was all Mel could think to say.

"What's for breakfast?" asked Galen.

"It will be late this morning," said Mel with no plan in mind and only hope to guide his next move.

That hope dwelled on the idea that it must be Wednesday and that someone should now realize that something was wrong; that Galen, Furgie and Mel had not returned when they said they would. It was an anxiety born from the discouraging truth that Mel had told no one about his trip north, largely because he had no one to tell, and that Furgie's estranged wife likely would not care or notice he was gone and that only Galen, married for nearly fifty years to his one true love, extended a tendril into the world of the otherwise caring and living who might reliably cry out for help.

At noon the rain started again and Mel dragged Galen into the lighthouse. The sound of thunder roared out of the north until its peculiar and rhythmic continuance alerted Mel to a thought the thunder was, in fact, a plane engine. He ran outside to see a helicopter swing twice over Punta Gorda and return to hover over the lighthouse before turning and flying south. Mel gave chase, waving his arms. When the copter disappeared, Mel turned back to see two tall, white jeeps descend along the old Windy Point Road and splash through Four Mile creek. In a few minutes, rangers and medics surrounded him as Mel pointed toward the slumping Galen.

Within two hours time Mel's world was recreated as the scene of an accident. The wilderness was an open wound that had injured Galen and killed his companion, though it was clear from the quiet whispers of the rangers that most on scene thought the men had brought it all on themselves.

"Did you check the weather, the tides?" asked a Mountie-type who called himself Ranger Drew.

Mel nodded.

"This turned out to be a one-hundred year storm. What brought you out?"

"A friend," answered Mel. "It was his last request."

The ranger appeared puzzled but dropped his line of questioning.

"I don't doubt it," the ranger muttered.

Galen was put on a stretcher and airlifted to a hospital in Santa Rosa. Ranger Drew said the copter had found a backpack washed into the rocks south of the big creek but no sign of Furgie. Later, Mel would learn the backpack belonged to Galen. All evidence of Furgie's existence had vanished without a trace and likely forever.

Mel ate a K-ration in the cab of the ranger's truck before declining a ride into Eureka. He was fine and would drive to Santa Rosa to be with Galen.

He arrived in the late evening and found his way to Galen's hospital room. Galen slept quietly. He was wrapped in warm blankets, his limbs sprouting the tubes of several IVs. His wife Angela sat nearby.

"You saved his life," Angela said after meeting Mel.

She was a sweet, short woman with thinning white hair curled tightly in ringlets spread weirdly over her forehead. She wore jeans and a sweatshirt as if she had just been torn from her garden.

"He's a tough old guy," Mel said as if to deflect her attention. "How's he doing?"

"They think it was a stroke," said Angela. "Too soon to know much. But he did see me and recognize me. And he smiled."

Tears formed in Angela's eyes and Mel gave her a sturdy hug that released a flood.

Mel's cellphone rang and he answered to hear the voice of Ranger Drew.

"Wife of your missing friend would like you to call her," he said.

He gave Mel the phone number.

"You don't have to," said the ranger. "She sounds pretty freaked out."

Mel said it wasn't a problem.

He hung up and dialed the number.

"You were one of the last people to speak with my husband," said the voice that answered.

It was a woman's voice and she was not frantic though it was clear to Mel it took great effort for her to speak.

"I just need to know…I mean we need to know…his son…"

Mel waited as he heard the woman's voice take a deep, unsteady breath.

"Did he say anything or leave anything?"

Mel reported that, no, the husband had left nothing and that all his belongings appeared to be lost with him. But he did speak. He did talk to everyone.

"And what did he say?" the woman's voice asked.

"That he loved his wife and his son. He said you guys were having some problems but that he hoped things would work out. He said he loved his boy and his family more than life itself."

"Those were his words?" the voice asked.

"The words I remember," said Mel. "He said he had a great wife and a wonderful son and that he wanted to help everyone find their happiness, whatever that might be."

Mel heard the voice on his phone crack into a million pieces as it tried hard to mutter the words "thank you" before abruptly ending the call.

Mel could tell whatever truth he wanted others to believe. He had trained his entire life to play the role of a stranger. And to someone in pain he could dissimulate cleverly because he knew so well what every character he ever played could never bear to feel.

IT WAS AN ACCIDENT

Giselle took great pleasure from putting people into homes. As a realtor she confidently managed the frontier that existed between the buyer of a home and its seller. Some deals proceeded like a walk in the woods, both buyer and seller meeting amicably to share the departure of one and the arrival of the other. Some required a treaty negotiated at a neutral site, in a demilitarized zone created at a restaurant or in a title office. And some frontiers were killing fields of resentment and disappointment that like all failed negotiations usually ended in a useless and costly defeat and no sale.

Through a dozen years of attentive selling, Giselle had become good at her work. Her first smart decision was to decide herself what family would succeed with its offer and to refuse to represent sellers whose assumed property valuations were as unrealistically large as their egos. The latter was a difficult choice in hard times when she faced the truth that if she did not list homes she would not last. But when times were good and home values surged she could pick her clients and, as the years became decades, her reputation for ease and success grew, establishing her as the complete package, a smart and caring and tireless representative for anyone buying or selling a home.

Giselle thanked her father for her discipline and success but not for the reasons he might have thought. He was long dead but at times in her mind as present as he ever was and sitting in front of her.

"Things happen for a reason," he said, which she understood finally to mean that things happened because he could think of a reason. Giselle never liked her father's reasons and especially what he told her were the reasons for her accident.

"If you hadn't left the church before the service ended…" he said repeatedly.

Giselle had left early, had left just as her father the minister was winding up a fierce sermon on God's command to Abraham that he slay his son, Isaac. Her father loved that story and loved its lesson of unquestioning allegiance to an angry god.

"It's possible God was angry with you," her father said.

"Then I'm pretty pissed off with God," Giselle had answered. "What good God calls out my disrespect by taking the life of a young, innocent child?"

Her father could not answer the question Giselle barely had the strength to ask.

Giselle long ago concluded that God had nothing to do with the accident, had done nothing to guide Giselle to look away just at the moment a toddler slipped out of its mother's grasp and ran into the street toward an escaped, bouncing ball. She still felt in her arms and legs the dull thud of her car hitting a small body. At first she thought she'd caught a vagrant squirrel and felt bad enough about that. But then she pulled over to check her front end and saw the tangled limbs of a small child in the street and cars swerving everywhere to miss it. She watched the hysterical mother running madly toward her, screaming in horror as she picked up the limp, lifeless body of her little son. Giselle slowly and with an incomplete and unwilling awareness absorbed what had happened.

"Oh, my god!" Giselle remembered screaming and wondered— even after nearly 15 years—if she had sounded like some stupid and surprised Valley Girl. Giselle had run toward the mother who turned to shield her baby.

"I'm so sorry," Giselle recalled shouting at the sobbing mother, words her attorney would later seek to have struck from the record because they suggested his client was admitting guilt.

But Giselle was guilty. She had been guilty for all her life since the accident and while the court did not convict her of a crime, she still bore its disgrace. Accident or not, she was a killer.

"You have to phone him," Charmian shouted over the phone to Giselle.

"He gave you his card, honey. Maybe he wants a house. But maybe he wants you."

Giselle heard her friend's enthusiasm bubble at the other end of her phone call. She heard Charmian penetrate the perimeters of Giselle's successful but restrained life. She was the only friend Giselle allowed in. She was Giselle's only friend.

"Get out of here," answered Giselle. "He said he'd phone. If he wants to buy a home, I don't dare call him. ..."

Giselle hesitated to get personal. She hated to reveal herself.

"That would be worse. I don't know anything about him."

"You said he was cute," Charmian responded. "You really liked him. You liked the color of his eyes so he must have looked right at you."

Charmian also lived alone. But she had been married once and so had more experience with love than Giselle who since her accident had avoided all potential human intimacies, especially with men. She rarely considered a reason for her avoidance of intimacy with others thinking sometimes she found most people boring though she worried frequently she was, in fact, the bore.

"Damn, woman, you don't have to be in love with the dude just to give him some time. Coffee? Ask him to coffee."

Giselle knew her friend was trying to be helpful while also imposing her own version of pleasure. It had been years since any man had expressed an interest in Charmian, much less given her his card or asked to see her again. Why wouldn't Giselle want this? Why wouldn't a woman her age want any chance for an elusive, even unrequited, pass with love?

Giselle didn't argue with Charmian and kept her reasons to herself.

"I guess I don't care anymore," said Giselle. "I'm too old for all that stuff."

Giselle wasn't old but she was not young. At age 39 she succumbed at times to the certainty some part of her life was over, indeed, that she faced fewer tomorrows than yesterdays and that all her important choices had already been made. And she convinced herself at these times that she had no regrets. Her investments and her long career in real estate had created for her substantial wealth, enough to assure a comfortable life as well as something left over to gift her community with charitable donations and bequests. Her parents were dead and her one sibling had followed her father's path toward God, a path that left Giselle far behind. She did not believe in God, even for a minute. It was a fact of her experience she had not shared with anyone, not even Charmian.

Giselle hung up the phone, alone with Charmian's reverberating words and the idiosyncratic and neurotic rationalizations she used to justify her celibate existence. She knew this about herself, that she was an outlying singularity, at least in the opinions of others. She did not care. And yet on some nights alone in bed or even during some days when she would follow a happy or bickering family around while they toured a property, she was stung by an absence from her life of what she imagined must be a kind of unconditional fellowship. There was enough of an echo of this from her childhood to arouse in her a nonspecific melancholy. But not enough to instill anything approaching regret.

As a young child cautioned at every turn by hovering parents, Giselle wondered what it was out "there" that required so much caution. Quickly she learned it was her own wandering in the world that made it a danger for her and others. It was why she gave so much of her money to charitable causes, why she wrote checks like a tithing saint to almost anyone who asked. And why for every four dollars she earned free and clear she squirreled three away for herself. She was rich by any community standard though not by any of the larger world's measures. She was a hometown millionaire, even if just barely. But it was enough to raise her visibility as a successful realtor and a visibility very good for business. She was good at business and as she opened a bottle of excellent Chardonnay she toasted herself before fixing her dinner.

Later, she sat alone in the living room in front of the television. She watched with the sound turned off so she could hear the phone. She waited in a flow of sudden, real feeling that became suddenly a tap of unmanageable tears.

Giselle waited for a call from the man who had given her his card. It likely was a call that would not be made. The symmetry of her denial was at once brilliant and disarming. She could feel the gravity of deep disappointment and, by the strategic intercession of her fear of attraction, also enormous relief.

2

A crisp morning alerted Giselle to the arrival of fall's deepening presence. The season's first days had at first been warm, even hot. But for the evening's earlier arriving darkness, she might not have noticed any change, that is, until housing listings began to dry up and sales slowed. She had one house sold and another in escrow and thought another sale might happen before Christmas. The New Year would bring a presidential election and Obama, her favorite president ever, was mounting his last political campaign.

And would he win? Giselle already was budgeting what donation she could give to the county's Democratic committee to help get out the vote. She had taken calls from the committee chair inviting Giselle to its annual fall barbeque in an exclusive redwood grove west of Occidental.

And Giselle was rich, and even richer than expected in the wake of the Great Recession which had been an enormous challenge but that also took down much of her competition. Now, as housing prices soared and sales boomed, she was a lucky survivor. Though she knew luck was not a factor. She just worked hard. It was what she did and what she did better than all the other things she did not do well or at all.

"Ladies and gentleman," said the Rotary president as he staggered half-drunk towards the club podium.

"I give you the founder of our feast and the funder of our scholarships. Please give a big hand for our favorite realtor and citizen, Giselle Sayers!"

The Rotary dinner was organized to honor Giselle's reliable contributions to the club's several scholarship programs. The crowd of dining, drinking Rotarians and their spouses stood together to applaud wildly. Giselle waited at her place at the head table and behind other seated guests as she was waved toward the podium.

"I guess I have you to thank," Giselle said awkwardly. "I've really tried my best to be a good resident, a good citizen. You are good people. You do good things."

Her tone was chilly, even if her sentiments were warm. Speaking in public was among the many things Giselle did not do well. The audience, quickly deflated by her apparent and very cool reluctance to engage, offered up another cheer and then let her go. She wandered back to her seat as the business and pleasure of Rotary continued. Everyone was now oblivious to her and she to them. Later she would curse herself, as she frequently did, when she considered her many failings. And she saw them all and everyday, having no one in her life to tell her otherwise, no one other than Charmian to see her and to remind her she was nice and even likeable.

All that mattered now was that she was rich. The house on Nob Hill Terrace she purchased for $112,000 in 1985 was now worth six times as much. And she owned two other properties on Petaluma's east side that together brought in $2500 in rent every month. Before retiring that night Giselle calculated again her accrued net wealth and fell asleep without arriving at the total. It was enough. And it was enough that it was enough. In the rest of her life there was very little she could think of as enough. Money was always welcome because it was something that did not talk back. But despite her presumed abundance she was still deeply and achingly hungry.

The next Tuesday her favorite president won re-election, giving Giselle a glorious, televised respite from the fears much larger than herself. She was free again to move about the cabin of her common, ordinary fears and to mingle with their insistent noise.

"It's for a good cause," said Charmian, as she tried to persuade Giselle to join her for another cocktail reception and fundraiser, this one for the local food bank.

Charmian loved to drink socially and while Giselle also liked to drink, she was too easily depressed by alcohol and nearly always sorry when she found herself tipsy in a room full of people.

"It's hard enough for me to hang out with strangers," Giselle told her friend. "It's really hard when I'm drunk."

"These aren't strangers," shouted Charmian. "You know all of them."

Yes, she knew everyone who would attend the local food bank's pre-Thanksgiving auction. And they knew her. But it did not mean that any were her friends. Giselle gave generously to the Food Bank. Following her accident she had sought some sanctuary from her guilty grief by serving food to needy families and for two years after the accident found comfort in her weekend stints at the Food Bank, sorting food, soliciting donations, and standing at a table to serve a Sunday dinner to hungry residents.

The accident had stolen her faith in herself and all that saved her during those nameless days after killing a small, young boy was that life itself was stronger than her love for it. The Food Bank eventually rewarded her with kindness and regard as she applied all her energy and educated skills to its management and success. Until one Sunday before Christmas she lifted a ladle from a tureen of vegetable soup and as she poured it into an outstretched bowl, looked up to see the mother whose son she had killed.

The woman's at first confused gaze surprised Giselle who greeted a worn and weary face, also pale and plain, but that suddenly opened into a full moon of horrific recognition and bore into Giselle like the crushing walls of a shrinking room. Giselle dropped her ladle and stepped backward. Later, she was told she had run away. She could not remember that but did learn the woman, whose marriage ended shortly after the death of her daughter, was broke and homeless. A deep freeze once again formed for Giselle over the powerful regret that now reigned within. She knew fear well, even if she could not open any part of herself to sorrow.

"That's him?" Charmian whispered vigorously to Giselle.

"He's a fucking hunk!"

Giselle blushed.

"Get outta here," said Giselle. "He's OK."

"Are you going to approach him?" asked Charmian.

"I'd rather not. I'd rather he approached me.

"Then get your ass up there, woman," Charmian urged. "Let him see you."

Giselle walked slowly toward the wide buffet table, already embarrassed to be putting herself on display. She hated the experience of her visibility. She did not like to be seen or noticed and yet she waited constantly for contact and attention. Where business was concerned, she had few worries about barging forward to forge a link. She clung to the idea that the man currently in view had already initiated an interest by giving her his card. She pushed herself up next to him to catch his attention and when he turned she looked directly into his eyes.

"And you are…?" the man asked as if trapped and flummoxed. He balanced a plate while sliding down the buffet.

"Sayers," said Giselle firmly.

"Giselle Sayers. We met last week. You seemed interested in one of my properties?"

It was already troubling for Giselle that she needed to bring up the reason for their previous meeting, a connection the man standing before her had clearly forgotten.

"Oh, yeah…" the man said fumblingly while Giselle examined him closely. He was tall and a tapered blue suit gave him the appearance of attractive thinness though Giselle could see the hint of a small potbelly exposed under an unbuttoned jacket.

"We met last week, remember?" said Giselle.

The man did not remember.

"Jeff," he said obliviously. "I'm Jeff Walters."

"I know," said Giselle. "You gave me your card."

"Oh yeah…" he said again. "Property, right?"

"Real estate," answered Giselle.

She could not say exactly why the man's foggy remembrance irritated her.

"So are you still in the market for a new property?" Giselle asked.

There was a long pause as Giselle watched the facts she had brought to their meeting congeal behind Jeff's eyes, eyes that did not look into hers.

"Oh yeah…" Jeff said again and looked away. "Well, it's all on hold right now. Thanks."

And then Jeff looked away again.

"Will you excuse me?" he said as he waved toward a woman at

the end of the buffet.

Giselle had no choice.

"That was shit," Giselle said when she again found Charmian. "He didn't even remember me."

"Men—what's wrong with them?" Charmian offered.

Both knew what was wrong. Both remembered the last time each had been alone with a man and how long ago it had been.

Giselle spent Thanksgiving visiting her brother's home in Vallejo. She was usually welcome by his family though she girded herself for the prayers and scripture that would punctuate the turkey dinner. She loved her niece and nephew who seemed to enjoy her and the gifts she always brought them. She was generally careful not to drink too much or to engage in any conversation about politics or religion. And whenever she left their home at dusk, soporific and stuffed, she usually carried a plastic container of leftovers intended to get her through Friday but which she often stretched into the weekend.

Only this year she arrived home agitated, even angry. She went outside and threw the container of food into the garbage can. She returned to sit in a big chair in front of her window from which she could see the moonlit outline of Mount St. Helena. She counted her blessings and then broke into uncontrollable sobs.

Later, she phoned Charmian.

"Well, Happy Thanksgiving, girl," Charmian said.

"How's the family?" she asked.

"They're fine but I'm pretty fucked up," answered Giselle. "Say, how would you like to spend a week with me in Carmel?"

"Carmel?" asked Charmian. "You selling something down there?"

"No, woman. I want to party," said Giselle.

"Damn," said Charmian after a short pause. "I love to party."

"Then pack your bags," responded Giselle. "My treat."

Giselle's life was a daily resurrection of the ordinary and as she stood at the hotel's wine bar she congratulated herself for her choice to live now and not to wait even a little more. She remained a conscious atheist and easily accepted there was nothing for which her life was meant, no purpose that in its completion would assist her slide over into some vague and unmapped afterlife.

"Those guys keep looking at us," Charmian said, pointing across the bar toward a table where two men in suits and loosened ties laughed, smiled and nodded. Both appeared nonspecifically middle-aged and shared pours from what Giselle knew to be a pricey Pinot Noir. One appeared slightly plump and jovial. The other was gaunt and wiry. Both smiled when Giselle's eyes found theirs.

"Want to say hello?" asked Charmian.

Giselle was drunk enough from an hour of wine tasting to have missed cues to which Charmian was always and attentively aware.

Charmian waved at the men, while Giselle blushed and turned away.

"We just got in," Charmian said to the shorter man.

His name was Willy and with a wide smile he offered the women two empty chairs at their table.

"We've been here for a couple of days," said Willy's companion Roberto as Giselle dropped down next to him.

"I mean in Monterey. Not here at the bar."

Charmian and Giselle shared a naughty laugh.

The preliminaries were obvious and, if all weren't at least a little drunk, probably embarrassing. Willy and Roberto were software engineers finishing a company retreat in Pacific Grove. The women were, as they said at once and together, "in real estate." Charmian furtively checked the men's hands for wedding rings and finding none, winked briefly toward Giselle who had no idea what she meant.

"We're leaving tomorrow," said Willy.

"We're here for a week," said Giselle.

"Well, would you lovely ladies like to have dinner with us?" Willy asked fearlessly.

"Sure," the two women said suddenly and unexpectedly at the

same time.

It felt too eager and foolish and Giselle regretted that the wine was now talking for her.

The laughs continued over dinner at a small Italian restaurant, provoked at first by Roberto's goofy perusal of the wine list and his imitation of a snotty connoisseur as he at last ordered a Tuscany Primitivo. Dinner then became a parade of bread, oil, salads, and richly sauced pastas and main dishes and all shared with ripping, riotous and ultimately ribald conversation that carried everyone into lovely, whimsical and silly recesses of imagined experience. By the time the tiramisu arrived and Willy persuaded the women to try a shot of grappa, they were all good friends though Charmian was closer to Willy and Giselle, by both her proximity and increasing and affiliating interest, closer to Roberto. The men insisted on paying for dinner and split the check on their business accounts.

Leaving the restaurant the men and women walked together the four blocks to the beach, separating at last as Charmian strolled to the shore on Willy's arm and Roberto guided Giselle to a bench hidden in the moon's shadows. There was a conversation Giselle could never again recall though she remembered how their opening words were followed quickly by touches that were expected and so deliciously familiar in a way that took Giselle back into her life and back farther than the accident, farther back to when her fast beating heart harbingered pleasure and not fear.

All agreed Willy would take Charmian back to the men's hotel room for a nightcap and Roberto would return to the women's room for a drink and conversation with Giselle. All knew what they wanted so it was surprisingly easy to negotiate the outcome.

"If I need to come back I'll phone you," Charmian had said to Giselle during their last visit together to the restroom.

"If you want me, phone me. You ready for this?"

Giselle, drunk and nourished, was never more ready. Both women carried condoms in their purses though Giselle worried momentarily that the one she carried was more than three years old.

She accepted that her fear was potentially false and if she did not address it directly then all her future would be like her past. For a moment in her conversation with Roberto this became too apparent, her head briefly above the waves of a terror that, like the tide, rushed in and out of her every day.

"Tell me more about yourself," said Roberto as he settled into a chair in Giselle's hotel room.

The line was an old one but a still comforting opening for Giselle who found it hard to resist an urge to tell her story.

"Real estate has been my life," she said directly. "My parents were poor and religious and I decided while I was young that, whatever I did, I would run as far as I could from both poverty and religion. I've done that."

Giselle poured a glass of wine for Roberto and looked out the window where she caught a view of the stars. A lover for a night might become her lover for a year, or never be a lover at all. In any event, for 12 hours she could hide anything from herself, anything that might interfere with a welcome opening to pleasure, one she had not until this moment acknowledged. She wanted the taste of a sweet little death just at a time when her fearfully boring life appeared to her as at best incoherent and at worst despairing and scary. For this one night, this one night only, she would trust herself and not seek a safe escape from either the joy or the pain of experience.

In the morning she recalled the previous evening's engendering words and the lowering lights of the hotel room until there was no light at all and no more words. Roberto's was a tender and deliciously unfamiliar touch, one she knew derived from a wider experience than hers. His caresses melted her. She recalled coming, perhaps unwillingly the first time until she felt excitement rise and come over her again. She fell asleep in his arms, comforted in an imagined intimacy which would have been perfect as the morning broke through the room's broad windows, perfect but for the apparent absence of Roberto.

Giselle had no idea when he left, at first thinking he might be in the bathroom. But there was no sound anywhere, only the crinkling of her sheets as she sat up on her pillows and the raspy sound of her breathing through a stuffy nose. Had she snored? Suddenly embarrassed by an enveloping carnal memory, Giselle did not bother to call Roberto's name.

She stood to search for any remnant of him, any tendril or evidence of attachment but all she found was a used and wrinkled condom stuck against the inner side of the bathroom's wastebasket, which she covered with a wad of toilet tissue after she blew her nose.

Giselle showered, dressed and put on her make-up. She phoned Roberto's room and there was no answer. She walked downstairs to the hotel's dining room and saw Charmian sitting with Willy as they ate breakfast together. They were absorbed in an animated conversation and neither saw her as Giselle slipped out a side door into the parking lot.

She did not know how far she drove, only that she had traveled south through hills and steep ridges along a savagely surging ocean until she arrived at a long yellow beach where a few cars were parked off the highway. She stopped and wrapped herself in a parka stored in the trunk. She walked out toward a long and grassy bluff. Below her a few people strolled across a wide swath of smooth sand exposed by a receding tide.

Who was she? What was she trying to be or become? As she walked, Giselle wondered if she needed to start therapy again. It would be cheaper than traveling to Carmel for a dose of intimate rejection. She begged herself for a way out and into some placid place of rest. Death came to mind but that was not what she ever wanted, even as she wrestled with her guilt as one of death's agents…and was she? Was that what this was all about?

Giselle made a point of returning to Carmel after the hotel's checkout time. The men were gone and Charmian was angry with her for leaving and not telling her until she heard about the vanished Roberto.

"He left with Willy after breakfast," Charmian reported. "He didn't know where you were."

"He likely didn't much care," said Giselle who shared with her friend the awkward facts of her morning.

"Well, that's men for you," said Charmian.

"How do they do that? How can they fake such kindness and

pleasure?” asked Giselle.

“There isn’t anything fake about their pleasure,” responded Charmian.

4

Dreams were a way Giselle had of playing hide-and-seek with herself though the dreams she experienced during her final days in Carmel were dazzling in their color and detail. The shock of Roberto’s craven departure disturbed in Giselle a hornet’s nest of other jolting distresses that blazed a trail through her sleeping and undefended psyche. Clowns wearing jewelry lifted her into the air and threw her into the sea. A man with dark eyes lingered somewhere in the background of a brilliant noise and when she turned in her dreams to see him, he vanished. Her father returned with a desperate plea for attention though his words were incomprehensible.

During the days left in Carmel, Giselle and Charmian shopped and ate and in the late afternoons drank margaritas by the pool. Willy phoned Charmian regularly just after noon, her giggles ultimately unbearable for Giselle who finally chose that time to go to her room where she could masturbate and nap.

“He seems to like you,” Giselle said at last over dinner in a gallery café.

“It’s silly,” Charmian demurred.

“Don’t play it down on my behalf,” said Giselle. “All men aren’t jerks. What do you talk about?”

“We had a good time,” Charmian answered vaguely. “He wants to do it again.”

“You mean, like, he wants to do you again?” asked Giselle cynically.

Charmian appeared hurt.

“I don’t know,” Charmian answered guardedly. “He’s coming to Petaluma to see me. Next Saturday.”

“He’s coming to see you?” asked Giselle, and then answered her own question.

“Sounds serious. You go, girl.”

Giselle knew that Charmian had been alone so long she had become an expert at feeling like a stranger. Giselle knew many unhappy women living with difficult partners, but not one willing to trade that partner straight across for a life alone.

"Do you think Willy is for real?" Giselle asked intemperately.

"C'mon, Giselle…" whined Charmian. "Give me my good time. Maybe it's just for now. Maybe just for today. Maybe it's silly. But he's been sweet to me and I'm going to go with it."

"You'll like us," said Pete as he prepared to introduce Giselle as his guest. "We may be the smallest Rotary club in town but damned if we don't have the most fun."

What "fun" was for Rotarians did not register for Giselle. She had no experience with clubs of any kind. Fellowship had been mentioned, but "fellow" was a man's term for other men and so Giselle could not guess to what she was committing. What interested her in Rotary was its membership of town leaders and public servants. If she were to sort out her needs from her wants she would accept that socializing was not something she enjoyed but, clearly, something she would need to do if she hoped to climb a ladder to the platform of community service.

She returned from Carmel with a desire to give more to her neighbors, to play a larger—a very big—part in alleviating the suffering of others. Unspoken was her hope that such an effort might further relieve her own suffering. She contributed much of her money to many good causes but now she wished to contribute her time.

On the drive back from Carmel, Charmian had taken another call from Willy but sensing Giselle's resentment, said she would call Willy that evening.

"He'll take a call from you at night?" asked Giselle.
Charmian nodded.

"Well, that's a good sign," said Giselle.

"It is?" asked Charmian.

"It means he's probably not married…"

Charmian visibly recoiled.

"Willy is my business, Giselle," she shouted. "Butt the fuck out."

It was a shattering comment that Charmian regretted instantly but one Giselle assumed she deserved.

Giselle apologized, her eyes moist with incipient tears.

"I'm a fucking bitch," she said to Charmian. "Little wonder no one will love me."

Charmian said she loved Giselle but nothing in her words or voice gave Giselle any assurance. It was not enough for Giselle that anyone loved her. The entire world could love her. But it would not matter at all until she could love herself.

Charmian had introduced Giselle to Pete who, as a new member of Petaluma's Sunrise Rotary club, knew of Giselle's success as a realtor and her generous contributions to local charities. The club had honored Giselle's community service and now Pete invited Giselle to join. The club met Monday mornings at 7 a.m. in the back room of Abe's Café, a diner north of town near an exit to the Highway. During her introduction as a club guest, Giselle noted that three-quarters of the some thirty people in attendance were men, and some of them quite old.

"It's one thing to think that someday I'll be the oldest member of the club," said Pete. "It's another to think it might be in two weeks."

It was a joke too close to the truth for Giselle to think funny. For Giselle to engage with Rotary she would have to spend time with a lot of old men, some older than her dead parents.

Though she might enjoy being the center of their attention. She was not unattractive, despite how Roberto had left her to feel. She was a mistress of detail and could function well at high levels of organization. And if this club needed anything, it needed management. Members came and went through a porous membrane of club inattention and neglect. Giselle saw instantly an avenue of service.

"I think I can contribute," she said to Pete after breakfast. "The club rituals are kind of weird but I like the idea of service above self."

Pete was grateful. He would be able to exchange his red badge for a blue badge by bringing in a new member.

"We're a fun group," he said again.

Giselle didn't care. She wasn't looking for fun. She never seriously looked for fun. Her search, unknown to her, was for salvation and there was work to be done she knew she could do.

By Christmas Giselle had wrestled with the rituals of club membership, owned the obsequious chores of a red badger, and emerged at last as someone reliably launched into the world of civic service. She settled, as she usually did, on the issue of human hunger, becoming the club's representative on the board of POPS, an acronym for Petalumans Organized for People's Services that served free meals to poor families referred by the county's human welfare department.

Giselle was determined to take POPS higher and farther. She donated $2500 from a recent sales commission to the purchase of supplies that would allow for mobile distribution of food to people living on the streets. She organized an emergency food bank for homeless families and created a discreet and anonymously supported "hot lunch scholarship" for undernourished students at the city's junior high school.

"Our goal is simply that no Petaluma child will ever go hungry," she announced at the Rotary Club's holiday dinner.

She received standing applause and, Pete told her, had she joined the club six months earlier would probably have been nominated for Citizen of the Year.

Giselle had found her charitable voice, even as she wondered if she were truly sincere. Sincerity, she hoped, would be something she could feel and that would arrive eventually as an epiphany.

Her beliefs about her dreams were no less wishful than the dreams themselves. And if she thought too much about her character, she became a caricature, an imitation of her own imitation, though no one else could perform her conscious or unconscious desires. Her thoughts made her wonder what other people thought and felt and how "other" they really were.

5

Giselle knew that loss and its unspeakable wounding set the limits of her intended charities. Loss was a stubborn fact, as were the boundaries of her compassion. Her work with POPS gave her the feeling she thought she shared with good surgeons whose skill at saving lives was strengthened by an attitude of cool detachment from their patients. Even so, she wished desperately to help alleviate misfortune on a more personal level. Giving from her daily life, and not just from her wealth, was now the driver of a new hope.

Charmian arrived late for her first Rotary meeting. She was Giselle's guest and while Charmian did not technically qualify as an owner or a manager, the usual requisite for Rotary membership, the Sunrise club was small and constantly in need of new members.

"Sorry, hon," said Charmian as she scooted noisily into the empty chair next to Giselle at the club's head table. After the Pledge of Allegiance, Giselle introduced Charmian as a local real estate executive and county native.

The past Sunday had been Valentine's Day and Charmian had spent it with Willy, driving up Monday morning from his house on the peninsula and, as she confessed to Giselle, "nearly forgot about the club today. I had to haul ass to get here."

After the meeting, Charmian showed Giselle a pendant set with a lustrous emerald that Willy had given her.

"This is getting serious," Giselle said awkwardly.

She continued to resent the presence of Willy in her friend's life, a presence that aroused Giselle's hardest opinions of herself as a person detached from intimacy and burdened with a rejection that was beginning to feel more like a quarantine. The club's old members made passes at Giselle, which she laughed off with cool and sororal deterrence. But the more Charmian's Carmel fling took the shape of something real, the less Giselle could accept it. She was surprisingly vulnerable to the grief grown from loneliness.

"He's a real darling," said Charmian, trying to suppress her obvious elation.

Giselle observed her friend's frisky delight, born back from her weekend with Willy as a gift at least as valued as the pendant hanging from her neck.

"Three months and counting," added Charmian. "It's an anniversary present."

Giselle reached boldly for Charmian's neck and grasped the emerald pendant between her fingers.

"I like the way he keeps score," said Giselle.

Charmian reached out and pushed Giselle's hand away. She heard her friend's cool, nearly withering sarcasm.

"Will you ever accept that Willy is something very important and real for me?"

Charmian sounded annoyed.

Giselle changed the subject and asked Charmian if she'd like to join the Sunrise club.

"We do a lot of good things."

"Sure," said Charmian. "What do I have to lose?"

What Charmian had to lose was Giselle's friendship. During her first month in the club, Charmian missed three of five meetings. She also failed twice to show up for Giselle's Saturday food drives and left one weekend when Willy arrived early to pick her up.

"I need some time to get organized," Charmian said weakly when Giselle confronted her.

"The club needs your commitment," said Giselle.

"I'm sorry," said Charmian.

"It's this damned Willy, isn't it?"

Giselle's question popped like a hurled stone through the earpiece of Charmian's office phone.

"I'll have to get back to you," said Charmian.

She didn't.

Within a week the club president phoned Giselle to ask why Charmian had resigned from the club.

"We all liked her," he said. "Did something happen?"

"No," said Giselle. "Some can and some can't."

Giselle apologized for Charmian but it wasn't necessary.

Giselle phoned Charmian who did not take her call.

After a few more tries Giselle gave up calling her friend and accepted the stubborn fact of this latest loss. Giselle's ingenuity depended on a capacity to turn her losses into gains. It was the sinking feeling of something dead or dying that continued to prompt the further development of her resources.

Giselle counted eight other women in the club and had been able to enlist just two into her POPS outreach. One was an insurance agent named Gertie who talked compulsively and mostly about her grandchildren, and the other a supervising nurse named Lauren who worked at the local hospital. Both were within a decade of Giselle's age and this allowed them to relate together to relevant old music and popular celebrities. Though their conversations rarely extended much farther than the limits of their past and both women were married, had been married for a long time. So they were reluctant to include Giselle in their social lives or respond to any of Giselle's invitations to join her away from their homes.

"You've been nominated for the club board," Gertie confided on Saturday as she helped Giselle distribute food to families at the homeless shelter.

"Don't tell anyone I told you."

Duty rewarded Giselle and pleasure not at all. Pleasure mystified her, even the kind of pleasure to which she felt entitled. Her orgasm with Roberto was intense and different from the ones she gave herself. Often she thought of him, rat that he was, when she was just about to make herself come. Giselle could grasp why Charmian put Willy, a boyfriend for a few months, ahead of her, a friend for more than fifteen years. She did not like what it said about Charmian, but even less what it said about herself.

Giselle first saw the story in the newspaper. A kindergarten student had bolted out of a school playground just as his mother arrived to pick him up. As the mother parked her car she watched helplessly as her child, legs and arms driven wildly by the happy sight of his mom, plunged in front of an approaching van. It was later determined that the van, driven by the parent of another child, was traveling well under the school zone speed limit. But it was enough speed to bump the boy into a trajectory that threw him several feet and into the path, and under the wheels, of another approaching car. The other driver jumped out and pulled the boy from under her car, grasping his shaking legs to drag him hard against the asphalt, his shirt still held by her car's left front wheel. The driver that first hit the boy ran over to help. Last to arrive was the boy's mother, who had driven her car up onto a sidewalk, just missing a group of third-graders walking home from school.

A playground monitor also ran to the scene and after several moments an ambulance arrived. Someone had alerted the office secretary who phoned 911.

Freak accident leaves Windsor child with grave injuries was the headline of the story. The details brought time forward to the moment in which the story was printed and that Giselle knew was much farther in the past than the moment she was reading it. She went on-line and found the paper's website. An update of the story announced the child had died.

That night Giselle's dreams choreographed the accident she read about in the news. When she awoke she knew the positions of all parties, could see the unlucky boy hurtled through the air, could grasp the shock and grief of all involved.

No one else knew what she knew about such a senseless death of a young child. She could heal these people. All of them. She had the resources and the confidence and while none lived in her town it did not matter. She had the knowledge and the love and the power and she could travel. She would phone an acquaintance she knew who belonged to the Windsor Rotary club and gather up the accident's facts and names in a healing harvest. She would find the door for which she already had the key.

6

"It's a devastating loss," said Jeff, the Windsor club's secretary.

"But why do you want to get involved?" he asked Giselle.

"Don't you guys have enough to do in Petaluma?"

"I have my reasons," answered Giselle.

"So this isn't club business?" Jeff asked sharply.

"Well…yes and no," answered Giselle, surprised by Jeff's question but aware that without her Rotary connection, Jeff likely wouldn't even speak with her.

"I want to help and I'm bringing it to the club."

It was a lie. Were there a mission of mercy it was entirely the work of Giselle whose distributions of charity had no emotion until now, until the loss of this family's child shook something loose like a clot in her brain, something that blocked all rationalizations and wrapped her in wordless, arousing empathy.

Jeff knew two of the women involved in the accident and through a business connection was acquainted with the father of the dead boy. He described an existing animosity between the volunteer yard monitor and the mother of the victim.

"Her son bullied the child who was killed," said Jeff. "You can imagine how she feels, since her job was to keep all the kids on the playground until their parents arrived to pick them up. She says she didn't see Josh bolt from the yard until it was too late. I don't think Josh's mother believes that."

The two women drivers who each hit the child were long time friends and did not know Josh or his parents.

"They are really shattered," said Jeff. "The club is helping them organize a fundraiser for Josh's funeral."

"So what are you and your club thinking about doing?" asked Jeff, warming to the idea another club might underwrite some of Windsor's charitable costs.

"I'll have to get back to you," said Giselle. "Need to take it to the board."

"Sure," said Jeff.

He understood.

Giselle did not ask Jeff for the addresses or phone numbers of the women, nor would he have given them if she asked. Grief as public as that caused by the boy's fatal accident was still the private business of its suffering survivors. Even so, Giselle counted herself a member of some imagined inner circle and one who should naturally be allowed into any family's suffering because she knew it, grasped it, and for most of her life had lived its incompleteness and sorrow fully and thoughtfully.

She knew herself uniquely qualified to penetrate the bitter veil of all involved in the boy's death. She was the one—perhaps the only one—whose studied suffering of loss could now inform, enlighten and finally lift the pain of loss for all involved. She understood as no one else the nature of guilt and its limitless capacity to inflict deep pain. She would intervene. She knew how to help. She knew all anyone needed to know. She knew everything about loss except all the things she did not.

Giselle did not know why the drivers or the yard monitor did not answer her e-mails or pick up her calls. She had learned the women's details from a Facebook entry she traced after reading their names in the newspaper's second story about the accident. She could not imagine why the two mothers whose cars hit the boy would not want to tell their stories, would not want to tell the truth of their innocence, would not want to stand up for their full atonement in a way Giselle regretted not doing. Giselle wanted to control all the interpretations of this sad accident without any awareness that, greater than her risk of failure, was the danger she might succeed.

Her first clue of trouble emerged when she phoned the police for more information about the accident.

"How do I give a gift to the bereaved family?" Giselle asked, trying to sound ingenuous and caring. Her deeper hope was to learn the address of the mourning parents so she could contact them personally.

The police were not cooperative.

"Are you family?" asked the answering officer.

"No," said Giselle.

"Then who are you?"

"A fellow victim," said Giselle urgently.

The officer ignored her enigmatic answer.

"Give me your name and phone number and I'll pass it along to the family," he said, sounding bored and impatient.

Without speaking again, Giselle ended the call. She did not want to give herself away to anyone but the mother who had suffered so deep and sad a loss.

It took a search of Google and a Zillow map to confirm for Giselle the location of the victim's home in a small subdivision just west of the town's center. A street view confirmed the address and Giselle studied a page of recent property listings in the area to give her a reason, as a realtor, to park on the street where the home was located. Giselle wanted to watch the house to determine when the dead child's mother was at home, but also to know how the mother appeared, what she wore and how she moved around.

Giselle had good news for the mother, could tell the mother a restorative truth Giselle alone knew and could explain. In a world made from accidents there was nothing to identify as salvation. Only a human being could save another human being.

Giselle spent three afternoons parked at a corner from where she could view the front of the victim's sprawling, one-story residence. Each day she watched the mailman stroll the quiet street that ended in a cul de sac and, as soon as he passed the house, Giselle saw the dead boy's mother emerge briefly to check her mailbox. It stood on a post at the end of the front walkway bordered on each side by a flat, green lawn that filled the yard. Giselle watched the mother gaze up and down the street before turning slowly to walk back inside her house. The mother was small but slightly heavy for her diminutive height. Her dark hair was straight and short and she wore sunglasses even though the late winter sky was consistently grey and overcast. Her steps across the walk appeared labored and she seemed reluctant to re-enter her home.

Once the woman stared directly at Giselle as she sat in her car, causing Giselle to squirm and scoot down in the seat. Giselle sat back up in time to see the woman enter her house and close the front door.

On the fourth day, Giselle decided to make her move. She had written a check for $3,000 from her business account and put it in an envelope. The check was made out to the mother. Giselle had purchased a flower arrangement of lilies and dahlias seated in a tall, pearl white vase, all wrapped in clear sturdy cellophane that was held in place by a decorative blue ribbon. Giselle imagined how her gift would raise the sad woman's spirits and relieve her sorrowful dependence. Giselle would embody the love of someone who understood deeply the nature of the mother's despair.

Giselle waited for the woman to check for mail and then walk back up the path toward her front door. Giselle then left her car and ambled toward the house carrying her envelope and flowers. She stood on the front step and pressed the doorbell, hearing inside a rhythmic, extended chime. She waited more than a minute and heard nothing else.

She rang the bell again, hearing the chime repeated. And again, no other sound. She rang the bell a third time.

"What do you want?" a woman's voice shouted from behind the door.

"Can you open your door?" asked Giselle.

"No!" shouted the woman. "You've been spying on me. What do you want?"

Giselle realized her visit was not the surprise she hoped it would be.

"I'm here to help," shouted Giselle.

"No!" shouted the woman again. "Go away. We don't need help."

"But you do," Giselle shouted insistently. "You don't know it but you do need help and I'm the one who can give it. I understand. I know. I can explain."

"For the last time," shouted the woman. "Go away. Now!"

"Please…" Giselle pleaded. "You don't understand but I do. I caused such an accident once myself. I understand your suffering."

"You what?!" Giselle heard the woman shout.

And then silence while Giselle waited for the door to open.

"Are you there?" Giselle asked after a few minutes of silence.

"Hello? Martha?"

She called the mother by her name.

Giselle heard the screech of tires and turned to see a police car barrel into the house's driveway. Two officers emerged from the front seat and ran toward Giselle, who turned to face them.

"Can you help me?" Giselle shouted at the officers as they slowed to a walk. "I'm trying to…"

"Step away from the door, ma'am," said the first officer to arrive at the steps. "We need to talk to you."

The second officer grasped her arm and firmly guided her back down the walk and toward the street.

"What are you doing to me?" shouted Giselle.

She tried to loosen her arm and dropped the vase of flowers that shattered as it hit the walkway.

"Shit!" shouted Giselle. "Why did you do that?"

The first officer ignored the vase.

He asked for Giselle's ID and after studying it for a minute spoke its details into a microphone attached to his lapel.

"You really don't understand what is going on here," Giselle stated emphatically to no response from the officer.

"People are suffering here," she continued.

"You're clear local," the officer said to Giselle after hearing something back through his microphone.

"You're being questioned because we received a call from a resident that said a woman was on her property and harassing her. We arrive and find you. What are you doing here?"

Giselle told her story, how she had read about the accident and her unique understanding of the woman's loss and that Giselle herself had caused such an accident as a young woman and knew uniquely the woman's suffering. Giselle explained her desperation to offer help. She had money and flowers to give to the mother of a dead child.

"The resident says you've been stalking her for days," said the officer. "It that true?"

"I parked at the corner to watch her," said Giselle.

"Is that a crime?" she asked.

"Could be," said the officer. "Stalking is a crime. So is trespassing. So is unwelcome harassment."

Giselle was quiet.

"You need to leave," said the officer. "You need to leave and not come back."

"But she doesn't understand…You don't understand…"

Giselle struggled for words.

"Or we arrest you now and take you in," said the officer.

Giselle's hubris subsided, lost again under the incessant wake of her unpardonable guilt. She turned and stooped to pick up her broken vase and scattered flowers.

"Leave it," said the officer firmly. "Leave it and go. Now." Giselle turned and, trembling uncontrollably, walked toward her car. As she started her engine she saw the second officer stand at the woman's door, which the woman opened slowly to admit him. The officer pointed toward Giselle's car moving away from the corner. Giselle saw the woman nod affirmatively.

7

Giselle sat in her quiet living room and weighed the perils and ecstasies of dependence and risk. She wanted to phone Charmian. Giselle would describe the violation by two policemen of her forbearance and kindness. But as she thought about it, Giselle knew that Charmian would not understand or not be willing to understand.

Giselle could not believe in God but did believe in fate. She might still intervene and thought a letter might be enough. Martha could read in a letter from Giselle the vast and important truth that would release both Martha and Giselle from their suffering.

For the first time, Giselle admitted that reaching out was as much for herself as it was for the boy's mother.

She spent the evening typing a letter to Martha, one that began as a short appeal for an audience but that grew by the late evening into several pages of what she thought compelling rumination. Every thought Giselle ever had about her accident landed on these pages. Her words were heartfelt and detailed and rich with her years, her decades of cultivated suffering. She read the letter back several times and embraced it as a curative offering for both her and the mother.

On the way to Monday's sunrise Rotary meeting, Giselle pushed the letter through a mail slot at the post office.

"She'll have it tomorrow," Giselle said to herself, confident her fluent words would at last touch and move the mother to grasp Giselle's loving kindness and to accept its wisdom, not to mention her check.

Giselle parked in the lot of Abe's Café and entered the restaurant to stand in line for the Rotary Club breakfast. She was about to grab her badge when a small, young man approached from the lobby.

"Are you Giselle Sayers?" the young man asked.

"Why, yes…" Giselle said, flattered at first to be recognized by a stranger.

"Are you here for the club meeting?" Giselle asked quickly before the man handed her a manila envelope.

"Have a nice day," he said and departed.

"Were you just served?" Pete asked Giselle.

"Served? Served what?" asked Giselle.

"A summons? A court order? Are you being sued? That was a court service," said Pete. "I recognize the guy. See what it is."

Following the club's pledge of allegiance, Giselle opened the envelope and read a court order restraining her from contacting in any way Martha Fimrite or any member of her family. The court document ordered Giselle to stay at least 100 yards away from Martha Fimrite, the members of the Fimrite family, and the Fimrite residence. Giselle was to make no contact, written or personal, with the Fimrites. The order stated that Giselle had 48 hours to contest the order, which she could do at a window in room 327 of the Sonoma County Courthouse in Santa Rosa. The hours and location of the room were described at the end of the order.

"You OK?" whispered Pete. "You need an attorney?"

Giselle folded the document, slipped it back into its manila envelope and stood to leave. She ignored Pete's query and went home and stayed at home and did not answer her phone.

Thursday morning Giselle was scheduled to join a realtors' tour of newly listed properties. Instead, she stayed in bed, the surest comfort she could have until finally her weary thoughts raced to know something about the world she had abandoned. It had been days since she left her house. She ate a light lunch on her back porch and basked in a burst of early spring sunshine. After eating she looked again at the restraining order and began to cry.

As sunlight faded from the cloud-burnished sky she heard her work phone ring.

"Is this Giselle?" a woman's voiced asked cheerfully.

"Yes," answered Giselle.

The woman said she was a reporter for the Press-Courier and had some questions. As a prominent realtor Giselle occasionally was interviewed for business stories and she had no reason to think this was otherwise until the reporter asked her first question.

"The family of the boy killed last week in Windsor says you're harassing them. Are you?"

"Am I what?" asked Giselle.

"You know, harassing them. Bothering them," answered the reporter. "The mother says you spent days spying on her and that you tried to enter her house. She said she had to call the police. The police report says you were told to leave and resisted until threatened with arrest."

"There's been a misunderstanding," Giselle said from behind a sudden flush of panic. "I wanted to help them. I don't think the mother understood."

"How could you help them?" asked the reporter.

"I have money to give them," said Giselle. "I know their pain."

"Is that because you were involved in a similar accident nearly 15 years ago?" asked the reporter.

Her voice felt to Giselle like the penetrating edge of a sharp knife.

"What?"

Giselle was incredulous to hear the return of a feared and distant past, even though it had driven nearly all her life's daunting considerations.

"It was an accident," said Giselle.

"One that got you arrested for reckless driving," responded the reporter.

"I was innocent," shouted Giselle.

She shivered with fear and nearly dropped her phone.

"The charge was dropped. I didn't go to trial."

"That's true," said the reporter.

"So I know how it feels to have such a loss," Giselle said, filling a silence she thought was the space left for her to tell her truth.

"The police have a letter you wrote to the mother," said the reporter. "You seem to have violated a restraining order against you.

Is that right?"

Giselle ended the call.

It was all an accident. Her life was an accident. The lives and deaths of children were accidents. There was no creation. Only accidents. And when her accidental life ended she would be free of the care that did not exist before she was accidentally born.

A sheriff's deputy stopped by Giselle's house around dinnertime and asked her about the letter. He left satisfied the letter was mailed before Giselle was served with the restraining order. He recorded her promise to comply. Afterward, Giselle waited silently in the darkness of her living room, and for what she could not or would not say. She was finished with good will and good deeds and doing the right thing but almost always for the wrong reason. She tried to feel gratitude that the whole episode might be over.

But it wasn't.

Friday morning Giselle stepped into her driveway to pick up the newspaper. She had ignored the news for days but Friday's edition ran a classified real estate section that featured color photos of the weekend's scheduled open houses. She leafed through the paper while eating her breakfast and saw on page three a photo of herself. It was the photo she used in her real estate advertising and for which she had paid nearly $200. She loved the photo, and it had appeared in the paper before, but not in connection with a news story.

Next to it was another photo of her, one she thought was lost and gone and one she never would see again. It was the police photo of her when she was booked for reckless driving after her accident. A headline over the photos read *The Too Good Samaritan. Family of Windsor student killed by car wants no help from local realtor involved in similar accident years ago. Accuses realtor of harassment.*

The story occupied a prominent space and was framed by a thick black line that appeared to box the story at the top of the page. Through several paragraphs the reporter that phoned Giselle recounted the circumstances of the Windsor boy's death, described the despair experienced by the family, and then introduced Giselle as an insistent meddler, determined to push her life onto the family without regard for their grief.

"No, we don't want her gift," said the victim's mother. "Obviously it's a gift for no one but her. She wants some kind of ghoulish credit. She can't know what we're going through or she wouldn't even try to do this."

Giselle's few words to the reporter were quoted out of their context, including the phrase *I was innocent,* which the reporter framed to sound like a frightened, self-absorbed denial of responsibility.

Without saying so much in words, the story concluded that the "too good Samaritan" was, in fact, no Samaritan at all. She was a needy perpetrator who waited ghoulishly for opportunities to advertise her supposed kindness, which was not about others but only about herself—her needy, lonely and remorseless self.

Giselle sat back in her chair.

"Is this who I am?" she asked.

Yes, it was who she was today. And it was drawn from the Giselle she was fifteen years before. All the time between was like an unremembered dream she had lived as if she were asleep until awaking in this moment. The hard words of the story, some of which she herself contributed, were a reckoning with her opened heart. And it was a heart that, as a maker of another's loss, did not actually beat for others. Others would now know that and not be fooled into serving Giselle's needs, which were highly evident and recklessly self-absorbed.

Giselle collapsed at her table, a recipient of truly bad news. It was her news for everyone to read though it reported also that she was still alive and could still think of herself as alive. She was alive and she was free. She could leave or she could stay. She could go again to Carmel. No, she would travel to Puerto Vallarta. She would book a flight tomorrow. This time she would not invite Charmian.

PANDORA'S FLASH DRIVE

It had never occurred to Jeannette it might be possible to enter another person's world without becoming a part of it. She watched butterflies and wondered about their magical aerodynamics. She could see a sad and tired mother on a bus and imagine herself similarly exhausted and depressed. But she could not embrace the reality that lurked within other living things, or grasp any way she could know or understand it without a conscious and informing connection.

"I always have too many questions," she thought to herself.

And no matter how specifically she asked a question, Jeannette knew she would never accept an answer until she fully grasped it. The time was past when she could ask her husband about those of his secrets that were now starkly within her view. Even if he were willing, he could not answer.

He was dead.

The most preoccupying of his secrets was contained in a small wooden box the size of a paperback book, which Jeannette had found at the back of a locked desk drawer, a desk used exclusively by Jefferson during their life together. Jeannette had nearly given the desk away to Jefferson's adult children by a previous marriage and if she had, they would have been the ones burdened with his secrets and not her. Instead, the desk's key was attached to her husband's keychain, one of the last items found in the pockets of his tattered pants when his body was pulled from the ocean.

"Would serve them right," Jeannette said to herself.

May was the name of The Twins' late mother, given to honor

the brilliant and warming month of her birth, which belied May's neurotic depressions and alcoholic anger. May died in a drunken car wreck that nearly killed another driver and Jefferson's children—described by Jefferson with a tone of detachment as The Twins—thought at the time their father would now leave all his wealth and property to them alone. When Jeannette entered their father's life and became first his lover and then his wife, The Twins fell apart.

"You can't marry her," Lena said as she stood during an awkward breakfast at which her father and Jeannette announced their engagement.

Recovering quickly from the shock of his daughter's sudden presumption, Jefferson stood up and waved a champagne glass threateningly.

"Lena?"

Jefferson spoke his daughter's name as if he questioned her existence.

"You will want to think carefully about what you said. You owe my lovely fiancée a sincere apology."

Jeannette remembered sinking deeper into her chair and turning to look exclusively at her future husband.

The other twin Tad also stood but too late to interrupt Lena's aggressive assault. Instead he escorted his sobbing sister out of the dining room as Jeannette and Jefferson watched.

"You'd think four years of college and a free pass into the wine business would be enough for those ingrates," Jefferson muttered to Jeannette.

"They're just like their mother. May was the queen shrew of our family and Lena thinks she is heir to the throne."

Since his children were at least half May's, Jefferson had as much reason to resent them as to love them. But even Jeannette knew these were the wrong words at the wrong time and in another lifetime she might have ended the engagement and returned to her career as a nurse practitioner at a local hospital. She was too far along with Jefferson and too invested in their spoken dreams to sound a retreat.

Now Jeannette considered the secrets she knew and The Twins

did not, wishing the situation was reversed and that she was the one in the dark. She never wanted to open the box and it might have been thrown out were it not for the word on its cover scribbled in fat black marker ink.

May!

The word's big, chunky letters were clearly in Jefferson's hand and meant as either a reminder or a caution. Whenever it was written it was likely during a time before Jeannette might be imagined as the one who would read it. Though as a result of The Twins' bad behavior and their exclusion from any inheritance, it fell to Jeannette to choose what would become of her husband's ill-hidden secret.

It had been nearly two months since Jefferson's fatal accident. Returning from a day at sea, he was one of three fishermen thrown from their boat by a violent sleeper wave. Two of the men were found and rescued but not Jefferson, whose body floated up on Doran Beach the next day. Jeannette's sorrow and shock concealed for a while her anger with a new husband who chose the second week of a tempestuous and cold March to fish for fresh salmon he could have otherwise purchased at the dock.

After her divorce from a failed and foolish young man, Jeannette had stopped looking for love. Seven years of childless marriage to someone who needed constant support in all ways emotional and financial was a mistake Jeannette would never repeat.

But Jefferson found her. On a Sunday afternoon he was wheeled into her hospital's emergency room, garrulous, half-drunk and with a leg broken by a wildly awkward slide into second base during his winery's annual picnic and softball game.

"Were you safe or out?" she asked him as a physician set Jefferson's leg.

The procedure took twenty minutes but it was three hours before Jefferson was cleared to go, time he spent talking up Jeannette who was assigned to watch and care for him. He said he would phone her the next week and Jeannette stifled a chuckle. The drugs do that, she thought. But he did call and asked her to join him for a lunch at his home where she could help him figure out how to use his crutches.

He offered to pay her.

"I don't think it's ethical for me to freelance with a hospital patient," said Jeannette.

"Our secret," said Jefferson.

She accepted the invitation but would not take a fee.

It was the first of several visits that turned eventually into dinners and evenings together and then became evenings and mornings and then, very quickly, weekends. It was two months before The Twins, who each had their own apartment in town, figured out what their father was doing and, even if they really thought they could, too late to intervene.

Jeannette wanted a baby and she and Jefferson were trying, though it had been more than a year without success and she at last persuaded her new husband to see a doctor since her own doctor visits seemed to confirm her fertility.

"I've already made two kids," Jefferson said resentfully. "Shouldn't be hard to make a third."

It was, apparently. Jefferson died two days before a scheduled battery of tests at the UCSF Medical Center.

It appeared that all hope was gone though Jefferson no longer bore any hope or care. His trust generously left everything to Jeannette: the wine business, the property, the home, the full measure of Jefferson's wealth and his potential for wealth. She was the boss of all his employees and two of them were The Twins who were left nothing from Jefferson and would get nothing from his estate until Jeannette died. Or, if she had their child, the child died, which as far as Jeannette knew left The Twins with only their jobs to tide them over.

Jeannette could have written off Lena and Tad forever. Instead, she began distributing to them the mementos and furnishings of their father's life in a way to suggest that, if they could open their hearts enough to see her and accept her, more would be forthcoming.

Jeannette was not a gold digger and Jefferson's death deeply saddened her. She loved Jefferson and his sudden death, at first a numbing shock, in passing days grew into the swell of a deeply disabling loss. She also realized it likely was the end of her dream to become a mother. She was not vindictive and respected that The Twins had grown up in an atmosphere of great marital discord and despair; parented by a mother they could not love and a father who would not love them.

Jeannette could have disposed of the wooden box she found in his drawer. For a week after finding it she obsessed over its possible contents. What was it? What did it contain? Whatever it was, it was something Jefferson wanted to keep a secret. And May? Why May? Jeannette hid the box behind shoes stored on the top shelf of her clothes closet and tried to forget about it. Jefferson's parents were dead and he was an only child, leaving just The Twins as his blood relations.

A brief memorial service was held at the Burgundy Oak winery and attended by enough employees to fill a purposeful distance between her and Lena and Tad who continued to eye her with suspicion. The next week, Jefferson's trust was read and The Twins learned they were no longer their father's immediate heirs.

"At least the bitch isn't pregnant," Jeannette heard Lena say to Tad as they whisked past her and out of the attorney's office.

But Jeannette was pregnant. Even if she did not yet know it, she had her suspicions and the following week they were confirmed by the doctor.

"I'm guessing about eight weeks," said a doctor.

The guess was based on the time of Jeannette's last period. Jeannette then recalled the last sex she had with Jefferson, the result of her warm and insistent arousal the night before he left to go fishing.

2

The secret held within her husband's small box tantalized Jeannette. But amid all the chaos that followed Jefferson's sudden death the box's cryptic arrival was enough to warn her off while she wrestled with the bigger task of gaining at least an understanding, if not control, of all she needed to do as the one and only heir to everything.

More than a year after leaving her job at the hospital to marry Jefferson she was now the owner and president of a venerable local winery and, together with her growing fetus, the owners and only residents of a large country estate.

Her first work was to identify whom among Jefferson's vast staff of employees she could trust. She settled after a week on the winery's CFO, a woman named Virginia who sought her out to sign payroll checks and who then lingered to explain with sharp clarity and surprising frankness, the significant ropes that tied together Jeannette's new possessions.

"I'm at your disposal," Virginia told Jeannette in a way that sounded both whimsical and deferring. But as the first days passed, Virginia attended to details while giving Jeannette daily appraisals and assessments.

"You're in good shape," Virginia said. "The winery is profitable. The house is paid for. Your husband was a Scotsman and never spent more than he earned. His children have their jobs as long as they want them but not enough responsibility to do any damage."

It was the end of winter, said Virginia, and a good time, if there were ever a good time, for Jeannette to learn quickly how to run the gantlet of a wine business.

"It's just agriculture and, of course, you could always hire someone to do it for you," said Virginia, though she made it clear she wasn't angling for the job.

"And The Twins?" asked Jeannette. "What do they do?"

Virginia was slow to answer, uncertain how to address the question.

"Are they good employees?" Jeannette asked again.

"Tad takes care of the crush and Lena runs the tasting room," said Virginia.

"Is that important?" asked Jeannette.

"The crush is critical and Tad seems to get it. The tasting room, well…it breaks even."

Jeannette heard in Virginia's voice a concern she didn't yet wish to vocalize.

After another week, Virginia accepted the position as interim CEO of the Burgundy Oak Winery, giving Jeannette time to deal with the disposal of Jefferson's belongings, among them the curious small box labeled May!

Of course Jeannette opened the secret box. But not without feeling treacherous and guilty. She at first shook the box, hearing the sound of a light rattle. Whatever was inside was small and singular. Was she dishonoring her dead husband by opening the box? Was she at the threshold of an irrevocable betrayal? How does one betray the dead? When the box revealed its contents she was at first confused. It contained only a single small flash drive, a short stick of black plastic shielded at its tip by a clear cover.

A minute passed before it occurred to Jeannette the flash drive might contain some secret about Jefferson's first wife. Were these documents? Were there photographs? She took another day to imagine all that might be recorded and what she might find. But nothing prepared her for what she encountered when, at last, she inserted the drive into her laptop computer.

It was evening and she was alone in the bedroom. Jeannette set the laptop on the bed where it sprung to life with a whir of recognition, displaying a file that, when opened, showed a long list of other files. Some were thumbnails too small to identify. She clicked on one. A live scene expanded to fill the laptop's screen. It took her a moment to recognize the motion of two people rocking naked together.

Porn, she thought. Did Jefferson watch porn? But the drive had said May!

Jeannette heard a quiet litany of groans. These were syncopated with the motions of a woman seen only from the back and who straddled a man whose legs supported her though his face or hers could not be seen. Jeannette watched, transfixed by the wobbling bodies and the richly evocative sounds of hearty and shared sexual pleasure. A few moments passed during which Jeannette became lost in the congress of these subjects. She watched intently and felt surprisingly aroused until a fury of thrusts signaled the scene's climax and the woman fell across the man's body. Jeannette watched as the woman moved off and the man struggled to his feet before disappearing out of view of the camera. It was Jefferson. And the woman, still reclining on the bed, was his first wife May.

An hour passed quickly as Jeannette discovered the drive was brimming with such scenes, held in a series of files. If this was Jefferson's work, and she had no reason to think otherwise, he had separated the encounters into categories roughly aligned with particular proclivities that ranged from oral sex to costumes and blindfolds and, to Jeannette's surprise, scenes in which Jefferson spanked May or May tied up Jefferson and teased him. Much of their sex was nothing like what she herself had experienced with Jefferson, who was always tender with her and comfortingly conventional.

The last tape, date-stamped in the frame, was three years old and, by Jeannette's calculation, filmed a few months before May's fatal accident.

The scope and intimacy of these intimate recordings at last overwhelmed Jeannette who pulled the drive from her laptop and threw it across the bedroom. She did not need to know this. She had no business with her husband's intimate past. She hated Jefferson for leaving this artifact and then hated herself for watching it. She tried to sleep but could not, realizing before dawn she was really more curious than angry.

And now that the lid had been lifted, she would need to look. In an odd way it was her last living memory of her husband and she wanted, even needed, to see it all. By morning she felt a surprising frisson—that she was doing something forbidden, that she was taking some historical pleasure of her husband into her own hands and that she would take for herself what she could no longer give.

Why would Jefferson and May—why would anyone—spy on themselves? Yet she now had to recognize herself as a spy implicated in a story she had unwillingly entered. And what was this story? Was she a witness to the couple's pleasure or their audacity? The day ahead was not her own and Jeannette unplugged the drive and slipped it back into its box which she locked in a drawer of Jefferson's vast, mahogany desk. She placed it next to a DVD that held a professionally edited video of her and Jefferson's wedding, until now the only video she knew existed of the man she had loved and admired.

Jeannette's day grew from a schedule that Virginia had devised to give her boss a productive morning of business and meetings that would allow her time to rest in the afternoon. Evenings were designated a quiet time when Jeannette retreated back to the large estate built above the rolling hills of Chalk Creek a hundred yards from the winery.

Today's meeting involved a discussion with Lena about the tasting room and Burgundy Oak's hospitality programs. It had become obvious it was the weak link in the winery's marketing outreach.

Lena frightened Jeannette who would never forget or forgive her rude behavior. Lena was tall, strong and athletic. Her voice boomed with conviction. Jeannette could not imagine how she would ask Lena for anything; much less tell her what to do.

3

For a week Jeannette left the flash drive in a locked drawer. Winery business filled her mornings and morning sickness her afternoons back in the big, empty house on the hill. It was spring now and mustard flowers bloomed their yellow earthshine from the vineyards in an awakening display of the season. Evenings restored Jeannette's energy. It was the end of the day when her life seemed to begin and when she could best tangle with the shifting and incalculable consequences that formed from her refusal to obey her late husband's dying wish.

One evening Jeannette went back to viewing Jefferson's videos. To distance herself from their power over her, she decided to watch them chronologically, as if approaching them along the path of their creation might offer her a more orderly experience. Jeannette was wrong. Too many feelings, including and especially her undeniable sexual arousal, pushed her deeper and farther into an uncanny warp of time and desire.

The first several were without sound, leaving Jeannette to imagine what Jefferson and May were saying, sighing, screaming. Abruptly, sound was heard with a new format of recording and conversations in the bedroom that provided the first clues to the time all this was happening. Casual and spousal, Jefferson and May's quiet words mentioned the children first and spoke worries, always worries, they would not succeed. And if the children did not succeed, that they then might not leave.

The sex was profound, violent, loud and stunningly creative. Jeannette marveled at postures, dramas, words and positions that defied her sense of how a couple typically made love. May, frequently tipsy or even drunk, seemed to initiate sex though Jeannette suspected it was Jefferson who turned on the camera. Date stamps appeared on the first sound videos beginning May 13, 2009 at 10:07 p.m. and from that point forward Jeannette knew when they had sex on Christmas Eve or an anniversary or after a night spent with friends that had elevated May's besotted interest in fucking Jefferson or vise versa.

Jeannette estimated the number of videos at around two hundred and filmed over perhaps seven or eight years. A few episodes lasted less than ten minutes and some went on for more than an hour. All were filmed in the bedroom though Jeannette found it curious that the angle of view changed on occasion.

As she watched, Jeannette remembered a time Jefferson told her a few things about his sex with May, enough to arouse Jeannette in ways she could not explain. Now it was all in front of her and Jeannette was surprised after a few nights of watching to discover her deeper interest in May, deeper after awhile than her interest in Jefferson whose sexual response she knew well and who always presented May as some kind of doomed loser when, in fact, it was May more often than not who appeared more sexually confident and assertive. May had gumption and drive. On one occasion she called Jefferson on his shit in such a way that Jeannette nearly fell over, remembering a time she wished she could have said as much.

Once Jeannette made the decision to watch the videos, she began looking forward to evenings she could view them, promising herself to watch only for an hour but frequently not switching off the drive until after midnight. Jeannette also decided she would masturbate only when she stopped watching. She thought she treasured her own fantasies more than what she saw, though there was no question that what she saw dramatically influenced her. And Jefferson was still a central feature of arousal but in a cluster of weird, lovely and newly unexpurgated ways.

May had wit and, on occasion, Jeannette would pause the video to write down something clever she had said. Specific scenes were unforgettable. Some that were goofy and loving, she watched again. Some, rich with the intimate flavors of neurosis and resentment, she would never again view. In some videos one was obviously in the mood and the other not. There was a video of May alone and masturbating that led Jeannette to wonder if, in fact, May might have been the driving force behind the videos. There was a particularly chilling scene in which Jefferson consented—in fact begged—to be tied up while May teased him, sucked him, offered her vulva for him to quickly and slavishly lick, continuing to tease him until Jefferson writhed in delicious sexual terror while May taunted him and stroked herself to an intense orgasm.

Jeannette now lived her days for night. She let Virginia march her through the mornings and afternoons and trusted her to spend her time wisely. By the collision of coincidence with consequence, Jeannette ruled a small and currently profitable fiefdom. And though it was uncomfortably co-occupied by the venal children of her benefactor, Jeannette was the queen. Jefferson might have been more decisive and, as the founder, more stubborn. Jeannette still barely understood what was needed to sustain the success of Burgundy Oak's big red wines, other than to make more. But thought enough was in place so that she might grow her husband's unintended legacy as she herself grew into a better understanding of his intimate past.

That is, until sometime during the second week of watching videos it became apparent to Jeannette that Jefferson was looking toward the camera and May was not. In one sequence Jefferson stood before the camera and waved his hand at it before May entered the bedroom. As well, May was on full, and often unattractive, display: her hair uncombed in the mornings, her eyes blotchy with mussed eye-shadow, her changing body perpetually on display as she romped in the bedroom, picking her nose or scratching her crotch. All her sexual moments, whether reluctant and uninterested, or ravishingly urgent, were on display. What woman would consent to such an exposure of so many protected vanities?

The angling of the camera also provoked Jeannette's interest. In early videos it appeared at bed level, perhaps from a camera propped on a dresser or bookshelf. In later videos the view appeared to be from a higher placement, perhaps the ceiling, causing Jeannette one evening to pull out a step stool and to examine the walls and fixtures above the bed. She found nothing.

But that she searched was enough. Jeannette's new morning began with the certainty May had no idea the videos were being made. They were Jefferson's design to satisfy his own heedless proclivities. And what did this mean for Jeannette? Did he tape their sex as well? The curiosity and arousal grown from her first investigations of the video now collapsed into a fear, and then a fury, that Jefferson might have so used her. And if so, where were the tapes? Where was the flash drive? Was it in something she unwittingly passed on to The Twins? Was it somewhere still in the house? Did it even exist anywhere other than within her tempted and suspicious mind?

"We have a security system here, don't we?" Jeannette asked Virginia during their morning meeting.

"Yes," said Virginia.

"Cameras?" asked Jeannette.

"Yeah," said Virginia. "Around the winery…I can show you."

"And in the house?" asked Jeannette.

Virginia didn't know about the house but gave Jeannette the phone number of a security firm in Santa Rosa that installed the winery's system.

"Jefferson liked the owner. Name is Sam," said Virginia. "If anything is installed at the house, Sam would know. Are you worried about something?"

"I'm alone up there most of the time," said Jeannette. "Maybe so, in a general way. I'm nesting, you know."

Virginia's smile was all business.

4

It surprised Jeannette to learn that the owner of Sam's Security Solutions was a woman.

"Samantha. Of course," Jeannette said when Virginia introduced her to Sam at the entrance to the winery's business office.

"You installed the security cameras?" asked Jeannette.

"Not all of them and not by myself," said Sam, a tall, fit woman in her forties with bright hazel eyes and long, blonde hair tied into a ponytail.

"But I can show you where everything is, how it all works, and if you want upgrades or…"

"We'll see," said Jeannette.

Sam nodded and Virginia left for a meeting.

"What was Jeff worried about when he installed the system?" Jeannette asked.

"There had been some thefts," said Sam. "Nothing really big. A few cases of wine went missing from time to time. A bunch of oak barrels were left outside and taken one weekend. He was curious about people coming in from outside, especially when his daughter started winery tours about two years ago. He had a $60 Pinot Noir on sale he thought was selling pretty well until he figured out people were grabbing bottles from the display and slipping out with tour groups."

"Was anyone arrested?" asked Jeannette.

"People were stopped and told to put the bottles back," said Sam. "Jeff was too nice to call the cops on visitors."

"I'm not so interested in people coming in from outside," said Jeannette. "I'm more interested in what's going on inside. The people who work for us: how do they do their jobs?"

"Let's have a look," said Sam.

The winery's surveillance system comprised seven cameras, one in each of the facility's key areas: the cellar, the winery lab, the tasting room, the retail bottling and storage area, the business offices and a last camera above the entrance that viewed the outdoor parking lot and picnic areas. All cameras fed their captures to a central computer that sat on a desk in a neglected corner of the business office.

"It can be checked anytime but I don't think anyone's doing it now," said Sam.

"Images are recorded for a week and then the system is reset. But if no one checks it, the system just tapes over the previous captures."

"Who should be checking it?" asked Jeannette.

"You could," said Sam. "Anyone you trust could check. It's easy but it does take time, especially if you don't know what you're looking for. Which is why some people who install a system end up never using it."

Sam showed Jeannette the system recorder. She brought one of the cameras up on a video screen. It showed visitors clustered at the tasting room bar.

"Looks busy," said Jeannette. "That's good I guess."

"You bet it is," said Sam. "You can check this anytime."

"Were any cameras installed at the house?" asked Jeannette.

"Not by me," said Sam.

"Could you check for me?" asked Jeannette.

Jeannette walked Sam up the hill and into the house. From room to room Sam's eyes searched ceilings, fixtures and walls for cameras. She went into the master bedroom and gazed at the ceiling, searching again the fixtures, walls and wooden trim at the doorway and above the bed.

"What's that?" she said.

"What's what?" asked Jeannette.

Sam asked for a chair to stand on which Jeannette pulled away from her vanity. Sam moved it near the wall above the bed and climbed up to peek behind a ledge of molding that bordered a vent.

"Looks like a lens," she said. "I see it."

Jeannette's heart raced though she was not surprised.

"But where is it connected?" Sam asked herself.

Seized by a professional urge to solve a problem, Sam jumped off the chair and walked the length of the bedroom knocking on walls before disappearing into the hall. The knocking grew louder until a scraping sound pulled Jeannette out of the bedroom where she saw Sam, deep in the back of a hall closet. Sam emerged and called

Jeannette over. Pulling away a raft of hanging coats she pointed to a panel she had easily jimmied and removed to reveal a shallow, hidden shelf. Sam pointed to a black, flashing box.

"There's your recorder," said Sam. She reached farther to touch a finger of black plastic protruding from the black box.

"Feels like a flash drive."

Jeannette turned away from Sam who sensed immediately that the camera's existence suggested other, bitter and uncomfortable truths that had in some way crushed her client.

"I didn't do this," Sam said quickly. "This isn't my work."

Jeannette walked toward the stairs.

"I can pull this out," said Sam, her voice pitched high by her new awareness of what the camera was, how it likely was used and what it said to Jeannette about her husband.

"I can have it out in a half-hour," Sam nearly whispered. "I won't charge you a dime."

Sam's earnest desire to help only further embarrassed Jeannette.

"I think you should go now," said Jeannette.

Sam slipped away, the front door closing slowly behind her.

For two days Jeannette did not leave the big house.

"Blues, I guess," she told Virginia on the phone. "Need some time alone. Baby stuff, you know."

Virginia did not know, having never had children. But Virginia knew the source of her new power and graciously honored the needs of Burgundy Oak's newest boss.

"Call me if you need anything," she told Jeannette. "Anything."

Jeannette thanked Virginia. She had much for which to be thankful, including a big house she did not need to leave, a house perched above the winery her late husband had gifted her. In life he had figured as a boundless source of security and the creator of her fulfillment as mother. In death he loomed as a specter and a thief that took pleasure from stolen intimacies and that now haunted Jeannette with a suspicion that another thumb drive existed that both featured and exposed her.

At last on the third day Jeannette pulled the flash drive from the hall closet's recorder and plugged it into her laptop. She opened it.

It was empty. She found nothing. The drive wasn't even format-
ted. She fell back into her chair and weighed the numbing aggregate
of both relief and exhaustion.

Jeannette tried to understand her late husband's videotaping
through his obsessive love of entertainment. Parties, special events,
adventures, the activities of his own life that thrilled him about himself, that gave him a feeling of being alive, that would, in Jeannette's
words, become Jefferson enjoying himself enjoying the sunset. It was
why buying salmon in the winter was boring and going fishing for it
in a storm was not.

He lived as if constantly intoxicated by the search for every potential source of sensation. It was at first thrilling for Jeannette, who
was so quickly swept up into the upper chambers of her husband's
delight until, at some difficult point— during the wearying effort to
become pregnant, perhaps—she understood that Jefferson's life was
fully and always and only about him.

For an afternoon Jeannette relaxed with the idea there was no flash
drive that featured her sexual intimacy with Jefferson until inevitably she wondered why. Was he a respectful husband to her or was
Jeannette's sexuality too boring? Did Jefferson not enjoy her as much
as May or even enough to record their lovemaking? Was love the
issue? These unanswerable questions quickly returned Jeannette to
the source of a deep, unshakable fear that a flash drive did exist of
her and Jefferson. It existed and it had been misplaced or, worse,
unwittingly given to Tad or Lena.

5

Jeannette floated at Burgundy Oak in a lucky bubble of wealth and
inheritance. She had lived with the expectation Jefferson would rule
his kingdom while she worked in a garden and raised for him a new
family. But now she was both kingdom and family.

With Jefferson gone, she assumed she had no real power until she realized that the power of surveillance, whether or not it was used to expose her, also existed for her to expose others. Being in the right place and at the right time, however, was not a substitute for happiness and Jeannette was not satisfied to be the incompetent, rivaled, perhaps even hated proprietor of the lives of people she might not like or even abide.

She wondered when she married Jefferson how she ever would live without him only to find she *would* live without him, would bring his child into the world without him, would live without him as she had lived without her parents, her brother, her first lovers, her first husband. An endless progression of seemingly compulsory losses defined her.

The morning Jeannette awoke without nausea she beheld a life that felt as if it was being lived without her. She stood naked before the mirror, aware that the better she felt the more she showed and, at three months, had passed through the first trimester of her first and likely only pregnancy.

She now deeply missed Jefferson who for more than a year had stood between her and the formidable business of earning a living. She missed his management of their affairs and the wall he maintained between the winery and their home. Now it was her winery and she knew she had not ventured far from the house due to her uncertain grasp of how the mysterious big factory took grapes from the field and then crushed them into cash. She had only a vague idea how that could possibly happen.

"I'm sorry for being so long away from you," she said awkwardly at her first management meeting, arranged by Virginia to connect Jeannette with the small army of supervisors that now worked only for her.

"I have a lot to learn," she added meekly, seeing Tad and Lena who sat together at the far end of the conference room and who together nodded furtively in trenchant agreement.

What would she do with them? Jeannette thought. They were Jefferson's children and also his disowned heirs. Here she was, the sole proprietor of their late father's winery and busy creating another heir to take its place ahead of them.

She promised to meet with everyone within the next few weeks and to listen to all suggestions and concerns. But, she cautioned, it would be at least a year before she could take full command.

"I'm having Jefferson's baby," she said directly. "It's a prized vintage."

Mild laughter rose from the conference room. Tad and Lena rose to leave.

Jeannette followed her doctor's advice and enrolled in an on-line group of local pregnant women, all with due dates a few weeks apart in late November and December. Once a week the women met at their homes and occasionally met at Jeannette's home above the winery. It was odd for some to come to a winery for their discussions of their pregnancies since none, including Jeannette, could or would drink alcohol.

During one of her weeks she stage a Saturday picnic that drew everyone: mothers, fathers, siblings and any available relative. Jeannette insisted there would be no restrictions. All were her guests with a full run of the property. It was delightful and, as Virginia reported, it was no surprise that the tasting room had its best weekend of the year.

Jeannette made friends among the mothers and learned three were planning to have their babies at home, an intriguing idea as she considered how the big house had become both her refuge from fear and also the source of a good portion of it. She still searched compulsively for more of her husband's unrevealed secrets, pulling out drawers, rifling through closets and boxes, even searching the pockets of his coats, pants and suits before disposing of them. She met with Sam again who showed her how to activate and use the winery's surveillance system.

"Would you like me to remove the recorder in the house?" Sam asked.

"No," said Jeannette. "I want you to show me how it works."

Surveillance might become Jeannette's salvation. Cameras might provide her with insight and a way to see without the interference of being seen. Acknowledged but unspoken was the promise that surveillance could also turn all life into a host of expanded and very interesting sensations. Her husband knew this and had employed a version of surveillance in the pursuit of his own pleasure. Jeannette's goal wasn't pleasure, but rather to extend her understanding of everyone else living and working around her.

Those who up until now existed for her as functioning strangers had performed work she could not understand but work vital to her continued security and comfort. They all could be unknowingly observed and thereby give up the secrets and strategies that created Burgundy Oak's wines and accrued its wealth. More compelling was the possibility she might come to know the secrets of those two nemeses of her life with Jefferson: Tad and Lena. Jefferson's children continued on as winery employees and why? They hated Jeannette. Why didn't they leave? Was there something they knew that Jeannette did not? She sometimes allowed herself the thrilling worry they possessed an incriminating flash drive that they thought might compromise or destroy her. It was one reason she did not try to fire them. She would not be destroyed. She would not allow her baby to become a victim of her late husband's selfish, angry children. Whatever loomed, she would need to see it coming long before it arrived.

"That's why we call it security," said Sam on the phone. "You want to feel secure. And to feel secure you need to know what's going on around you, especially where your business is concerned."

Sam told Jeannette her instincts were correct and that having the winery's security system anchored in her home would allow immediate access and give her total coverage of the entire property. And, of course, upgrading the quality and resolution of images, and extending their archiving, would provide even more security. And, of course, it would be a big job and Sam was happy for the work.

"Are you afraid of something in particular?" asked Sam.

"Surprises," said Jeannette. "I don't want any surprises."

Sam nodded knowingly.

"I'll give you a quote tomorrow," she told Jeannette.

"And don't tell Virginia," Jeannette said. "I don't want her involved."

Sam understood.

"This is your baby," Sam responded with a smile.

"This is for my baby," said Jeannette.

Jeannette knew her insecurities bespoke a deeper disability. She thought herself naïve and also blind. What she saw of the world rarely appeared in its full range of hues. From a young age there was safety in not registering the complete visible spectrum and seeing, or at least pretending to see, only the vast white blank spaces among and between. She was happy to be an easy read, unlike her girlfriends whose mascara and rouge projected fleeting urges and harsh, perhaps impenetrable masks. It never bothered her to be the good girl and not the nice one. She could earn her love by being obedient. But was it love she ever earned? Did Jefferson love her? Or did he use her, as he had used his first wife, May?

When Sam arrived with the quote for a new security system, Jeannette pointed out a small room on the second floor. She gestured broadly toward the window, which offered a view of the winery's roof, barely visible beyond a crowded crest of hills.

"As far as anyone there is concerned, I've asked you to pull the system out."

"You don't want them to know they're still being watched?" asked Sam.

Jeannette nodded without looking into Sam's eyes.

"You sound worried," said Sam.

"I'm always worried…and it's always something," answered Jeannette.

Sam created a plan whereby the system's existing cameras would be switched out after work hours and replaced with smaller units that would fit invisibly into discreet recesses of the winery's interior architecture.

"This could cost you," said Sam. "Are you worried it will show up somewhere as an expense item and raise eyebrows?"

"I have a house allowance," said Jeannette. "House expenses rarely get scrutinized. As far as anyone is concerned I'm pulling out the winery system and replacing it with one for the house. They all think I'm a little strange anyway. They'll imagine I'm just scared and self-absorbed. They'll be happy with the idea I'm pregnant, freaked out and staying out of their business."

Sam pretended to laugh.

"You'll learn what's going on, that's for sure," she said.

"I'll learn the wine business," said Jeannette.

6

June's first lulling heat opened the vineyards' blooms and buds. The rolling hills behind Jeanette were still green and as she climbed down from the house and towards the winery she noticed her once striding gait had become more of a tentative lurch. She was visibly pregnant and felt the new size of herself, the curving and still expanding shape of her lower abdomen as it stretched up and out to accommodate its rapidly growing occupant.

A month of the new system's surveillance had, from the comfort of Jefferson's old office, given Jeannette a perpetual and virtually limitless view of the winery's life and enterprise. She knew all the actors, if not in person at least by name, and at times surprised them with an affable and intimate greeting.

"Hello, Ted," she shouted at a flummoxed cellar rat employed to transfer barrels of Chardonnay to the bottling room and who wondered how the owner knew his first name and where he had ever met her. When she visited the winery, Jeannette was now a knowing goddess descending from her Olympus with intimate knowledge of nearly everyone below and a prescience of all their fates.

She was strengthened by a prevailing impression among her employees that the winery's old and barely used surveillance cameras had at last been dismantled. Though in recent weeks Jeannette had come down the hill to make certain unclosed doors were locked, that cellar workers who took after hours tastes from the barrels were admonished and sent home before closing, and to tell Tomas the winemaker he could sign a contract with a grower who had ten acres of Petite Verdot, a critical constituent in a red blend called *The Gleaner* that Burgundy Oak intended to make in the fall for spring release. The specially named wine was to honor the memory of Jefferson and to be offered for sale around the first anniversary of his passing. The wine was Virginia's idea and Jeannette loved it, indeed, had adopted the Gleaner project as a top priority.

There were other unsettling video discoveries, including petty theft from the tasting room, evening sex in the cellar and other slips and infractions that Jeannette could not discuss in detail with Virginia without revealing her surveillance. Instead, she brought them up as "vague concerns" in a way that earned from Virginia a pledge to investigate.

"A winery is a family," said Virginia. "A winery is a kind of half-way house inhabited by farmers and artists. Like the wine they make, the people who make it need a place to breathe."

"But what if they steal?" asked Jeannette.

"It's not what they steal," said Virginia. "It's how much. An unfinished bottle from the tasting room? I'd let that go. A case? That's another story. Still, we build loss into our calculations. Do you have a specific concern?"

Jeannette did but could not discuss it without giving away her surveillance. She had seen Lena pass out bottles of wine to her friends in the tasting room. She had seen Lena open the cash register several times without making a sale.

"What can you tell me about Lena?" Jeannette asked. "I sometimes think she uses the tasting room as an after hours open bar for her friends."

Virginia appeared puzzled, if not by the suggestion Lena was stealing then by what it was that aroused Jeannette's suspicions.

"I'll check on it," Virginia said cautiously. "I'll check and get back to you."

Jeannette imagined catching Lena stealing and then using it as an excuse to fire her. A crime would be the only grounds for dismissal that would have a chance of pushing Lena out. Legacy notwithstanding, a theft—one reported to the police and that resulted in a criminal charge—would be enough to get rid of Lena. Jeannette wanted Lena gone and her surveillance of the winery fed Jeannette's expanding hubris of ownership. The life of the winery had become her life, her soap opera and her clever experiment in remote management and control, not just of a business but also the lives that transacted it.

She watched surveillance videos in the mornings and the evenings, sometimes late into the night. She watched these videos as she imagined Jefferson watched his videos of sex with May. She watched, she told herself, with a pride of ownership. She watched, also, with a notably prurient interest in the actions and proclivities of everyone who worked for her. Jeannette now thought herself as all seeing. But she wasn't, not quite. Despite her confident and almost arrogant remote patrols of the winery, there were still things she could not see and could not hear. At the borders of her reconnaissance there was always a formidable potential for surprise.

Like a *flaneuse* drawn down a darkened arcade, Jeannette wandered extraneously each day and night among the rooms and offices of the winery. And what she saw on video strengthened the power of her detachment, though it was a detachment that at times polluted the truth and that, without authentic feedback, might lead to a bad decision.

One afternoon she watched as Virginia pulled Lena into her office. The two women laughed together amiably, which shocked Jeannette.

Are they friends? she thought.

Lena left for a moment and returned with two bottles of expensive vintage cabernet. She handed them to Virginia who slipped them into a carry bag she kept under her desk.

"Our little secret," Lena said as Virginia nodded and laughed again.

Is *Virginia* stealing my wine? thought Jeannette.

She had not imagined that Virginia and Lena could be friends. The idea frightened Jeannette and her busy mind formed immediately a variety of potent, even if logically improbable, conspiracies.

"What are you doing here?" Virginia asked, startled to see Jeannette in her office and standing behind her desk as she searched its drawers. It was early morning and Virginia had arrived before eight to complete a weekly sales report.

Jeannette jumped away from the desk. Her hands shook as she blushed the color of a sturdy red varietal.

"Something," Jeannette answered weakly. "I've forgotten."

Virginia was silent. It was apparent Jeannette was spying on her. And because Virginia thought she knew why, she said nothing.

"Have you been able to find out anything about Lena?" Jeannette asked.

She thought she was changing the subject but the word Lena tipped Virginia to a larger question as she, too, considered the possibility she was being watched.

Virginia did not speak and simply shook her head as Jeannette bolted nervously past her and out of the building.

Jeannette retreated to the big house and stayed there for the rest of the day and all the next. She ignored her surveillance videos and instead wandered in the garden where a crew of landscapers mowed the large lawn and pruned her plants and trees. She held her belly and thought about the baby, now known from a recent blood test to be a girl in the making. Jeannette let her imagination wander in the garden, through the hills and across the land under her feet and all she owned that someday would be given to the person now growing inside her.

Three days passed until on the morning of the fourth Jeannette sat back down in front of her surveillance monitors to look again into her winery. She accessed Virginia's office, which was empty. She opened her view of the tasting room and could see nothing but a black screen. She checked the cellar. That view also was black. She rewound the video to a point where an image appeared, that of a man wearing a Halloween mask whose hand for a moment filled the screen with something that shut out all light. She tried other cameras. All were dark.

Jeannette stood and trembled with fury. Who would do this? How? Clearly the cameras had been found. But she would fire the worker who tampered with them. She dressed and then stormed down the hill to the winery. She entered Virginia's office to see her clearing out her desk.

"What the hell is going on?" Jeannette shouted. "Who…I mean, what…what's happened to my cameras?"

Virginia shrugged.

"We didn't know you were watching," she said to Jeannette who had no response.

"Listen, Jeannette," said Virginia. "I have some good news and some bad news."

Jeannette stood silently and waited.

"The good news is that Tad and Lena are leaving. They gave me their letters of resignation last night. They're going to work for a big winery in Napa, the one with the gondola that takes visitors up the hill to their cellars. It's a big break for both of them and they're excited about it. And you don't need to worry about them, as if you ever would. Their mother left them a good deal of money, separate from the estate controlled by Jefferson. You probably didn't know that, which isn't an issue since you made out so well."

Jeannette heard Virginia's snide punctuation at the end.

"And the bad news?" asked Jeannette.

"I'm leaving, too. Taking the director's position for the county wine association. Pays twice what I make here. Also, your wine-maker Tomas is leaving. He's brilliant and Jefferson's vision held him close. But now he works for someone who doesn't know what she's doing. He's going to Leland Estates in Dry Creek. Yes, that Leland Estates. The one that makes $80 Pinot Noirs that are served at the White House."

Jeannette stood silent and so quiet she could feel the kicks of her baby.

"You know…" Virginia continued. "Even if Jefferson didn't

know that much about wine, he certainly knew a lot about people, and enough to care about them and to gain their loyalty. He might use security cameras, but he'd be certain everyone knew and that they didn't have to stop behaving badly, because suppressing bad behavior is impossible. And besides, an employee's secrets are important and, Jeannette, most are none of your business."

Jeannette said nothing and did not look away though it was all she could do to keep standing. Virginia picked up two bags and wandered past her to the door.

"Goodbye," said Virginia as she slipped away. "Goodbye and, I guess, good luck."

7

News of Virginia's departure, as well as that of Tad and Lena and the wine-maker Tomas, spread quickly among Jeannette's two-dozen employees. When she visited the winery she could feel their stares at her though few approached to speak or even to greet her. She now was suddenly more their object than they were hers. In an uncomfortable fury Jeannette fired her two domestics and her gardener. The intimate help, she realized, could not be trusted with any of her intimate secrets.

"Did you say something to someone?" Sam asked, as she tried to help Jeannette understand how her surveillance had been compromised and ruined.

Jeannette could not recall. She was six-months pregnant and her memory drifted into the shadows of every waking hour while she monitored the life growing within her.

"Anyway, someone found the cameras. It wouldn't be that hard if someone were looking. Shining a flashlight around a darkened room could produce a reflection from the camera lens. Infrared light does the same thing. You can find a surveillance camera using a TV remote."

Jeannette asked Sam to repair the cameras and to place them in new locations after everyone left for the day. She wanted to know everything that happened under her nose. She also had a score to settle with someone unknown and who probably still worked for her. Those who watched her would still be watched. Once the repairs were made, Jeannette returned to examining videos in the mornings and evenings, searching every recording for evidence of something suspicious though to say what was suspicious was a challenge. Knowing little about winemaking it was impossible for Jeannette to interpret much that happened in her winery. What was obvious? What was necessary? What was real? She could not confidently say.

"Have you made a wine blend before?" asked Jeannette.

The assistant winemaker Joseph said he had not.

"Tomas did it," he answered. "Tomas did everything."

For a substantial raise in salary, Joseph was willing to produce Burgundy Oak's fall vintages.

"But this *Gleaner*…I don't know," he said frankly. "Petite verdot? A blending grape and with what?"

It was agreed that Burgundy Oak would produce five reds, two whites and a sweet blush wine.

"Forget the *Gleaner*," said Jeannette. "Next year."

Fall arrived in the third trimester of Jeannette's pregnancy, though on the autumnal equinox it rained hard enough to threaten the grape harvest. Most white grapes were in the tanks but most reds, and particularly the precious cabernet, were still on the vines and dangerously exposed to rot.

And it was tourist season with every winery staging events to lure buyers into their tasting rooms. Jeannette gave Lena's job to a retail clerk named Judy who worked as a server. She could manage the cash register but had little knowledge of wine sales and promotion. Membership stalled in Burgundy Oak's fledgling wine club and there were no seasonal specials to promote.

"You need some help," said Ted.

"There are more than 400 wineries in this county and you're competing with all of them. But at least you have a reputation for quality. And you need to keep it."

Ted Bower was an old colleague of Jefferson who owned a consortium of wineries in three counties. Jeannette had asked him for a meeting at the winery.

"I don't know what to do," said Jeannette. "All I can think about is this baby."

She made a circle in the air around her protruding abdomen.

"We say the best way to make a small fortune in the wine business is to start with a large one," said Ted. "You're in good shape financially. Let's buy you some time. I'll send my accountant over to manage your payroll. Get your fall vintages into the tanks and barrels and sell out last year's wines. Remember, it's agriculture and some years are good and some bad. Don't sweat it. Go have your baby."

Jeannette thanked Ted and returned to the big house where she replayed their meeting on video and took notes.

And then she had her baby.

Jeannette did not think of her baby as an old woman though its wrinkled face and spindly frame suggested the body of one. The baby was early and had been born perilously close to dying, but she was alive. And now that it was apparent she would survive, all Jeannette thought about was how to sustain her fledgling presence. It was strange that a child born nine weeks before full term should look so decrepit and infirm. Jeannette expected something that would look like a baby doll or a mouse or even a frog. She did not expect a wizened face and fragile limbs that mimicked the features of a person advancing toward death. All that was left to Jeannette was her attendance now and forever to her child's precarious, fledgling presence as a living and survivable human.

"You need your privacy," said Joseph.

He and Judy were the only Burgundy Oak employees to visit Jeannette in the hospital. He offered to help her but there was no help he could give. In her new and unexpectedly premature role as a mother, Jeannette herself needed mothering.

She had stood one morning and her water had broken. She phoned

her doctor and in a half-hour was in the emergency room and prepared for a C-section delivery of her thirty-one week old fetus,
which emerged from Jeannette's unconscious body as Tania Louise,
weight three pounds and twelve ounces. Jeannette left the hospital
alone while little Tania spent her first three weeks in the intensive
care nursery. Every day Jeannette visited the ICN and sat next to
her daughter's incubator where she gathered in the rigorous surveillance of the newborn's vitals: heart, blood, breathing, brain function
and muscular response. All measures were in real time and Jeannette
watched the numbers rise and fall as her daughter lived her first days
as something like an appliance, all her life indicators monitored and
recorded.

Jeannette stared into the valley fog outside her kitchen window. It
blocked her view of the winery and the vineyards. Her baby lay in
a jolly jumper set on the breakfast table. It was Thanksgiving and
there was no family with which to share the day other than herself
and her nearly two-month old daughter. Someone might have invited her had they known she was alone. But her big house suggested
that as a rich woman Jeannette was popular and otherwise engaged.
And she was neither.

She gave her new domestic help the weekend off and stood alone
at the stove to prepare for herself a pasta dinner of fresh crab and
peppers, stopping only to nurse her daughter.

"You are my sweet little pepper," she whispered to the baby who
found a wet nipple and sucked vigorously as its open eyes fluttered
and reached deep into those of her reassuring mother.

"You are all I ever need."

That night Jeannette set up her new baby monitor. After dinner
she placed Tania in a crib in a nursery created out of the bedroom
across the hall. Her baby had her own room but Jeannette could see
and hear her every time she cried. It was surveillance of a fresh new
life Jeannette hoped her daughter would not be afraid to live nor
Jeannette hesitant to attend.

Though it was a life over which Jeannette had little control. She
was still wary of this new person's loud and frequently implacable

will. And while she monitored this precious new life Jeannette considered how she had hidden from her own.

In desperation she still sought some control though the monitoring of her baby was really just another kind of submission. Her baby was the new truth. Another life was taking its course and now had full control. Jeannette could not hide behind a camera to map or structure her daughter's living experience. She could not penetrate this new and formidable mask or remotely manage its future. She was at its mercy. She was now a monitor in waiting, a surveyor of all she could not possibly predict.

But all she could not know strangely comforted her. Ambiguity appeared suddenly as a virtue. Like the noisome night whispers of summer crickets, it aroused her and bothered her and kept her from sleeping. But it never abandoned her. And now it was the only truth she knew.

At that moment, the monitor burst with Tania's fearful scream.

"I'm coming," Jeannette shouted at the monitor.

"Mommy's coming."

———————————————

THE WAY HOME

Marjorie waited again to speak.

"I said Emily appears to be very happy. Didn't you hear me?"

Marjorie asked her question while her husband drove. Jake at last heard his wife, which confirmed that Jake was not paying attention. And he wasn't. He often wasn't. Jake was used to Marjorie's efforts to speak and to be heard despite what Jake considered her difficult thinking.

"You weren't listening," said Marjorie.

Jake denied her accusation until, as so often happened, he was subjected to Marjorie's festering archive of grievances. When he was at last beaten down, Jake admitted to not listening, not being thoughtful or even caring about Marjorie's observations or feelings or pain.

"I'm listening now," Jake said at last.

It was futile to argue though Jake was ready. He faced a long drive back from Thanksgiving at their daughter's new home in La Selva Beach. Emily lived in an artfully crafted rental near the ocean with her new, kind and competent husband who also was the new vice-principal of a local high school. Emily was very pregnant and had taken a leave from her job as a counselor at the region's community college.

It was a milestone for Emily's parents to attend Thanksgiving at their daughter's own home even if Marjorie and Jake needed to sleep on the living room sofa and through the night whisper quietly to each other the resentments and rage that had become the mutual understructure of their increasingly painful intimacy.

"Emily knows we're not getting along," said Marjorie.

"How do you know?" asked Jake, his eyes riveted on the road ahead. He would not argue with Marjorie's general assessment of their floundering life together.

"I just do," said Marjorie. "I'm psychic."

"Psychotic is more like it," responded Jake, knowing he should not have said it.

But his intemperate words had the desired effect.

"You fuck," sneered Marjorie. "You know I'm struggling."

She began to cry.

"I'm sorry, sweetheart," Jake responded without looking at her. "I shouldn't have said that."

But he did.

A grove of redwoods filled the view to Jake's left. It was early and also late. They had left after breakfast but were still four hours from their Humboldt County home. It would take an hour just to get through Petaluma and Santa Rosa before they could navigate the two-lane traffic in Willits and the weaving roads beyond.

A half-hour passed in silence as Marjorie dried her tears with a Kleenex and stared out the window while Jake attempted to ignore her. He had had enough of his wife's needs to last the rest of his life, which he assumed would not be long. They had spent more than forty years together and for much of that time had ignored the ways they grew away from one another until the morning after Emily left for college when Marjorie, after one of their harrowing and hurtful reckonings, walked out of the bedroom to find a bottle of pills and to swallow them, which she did with a wild brio that frightened Jake.

He phoned 911 and thereby opened to public scrutiny the miserable life he shared with Marjorie. Court-mandated therapy was embarrassing but it taught each a new vocabulary of neurosis that, in moments of resentful intimacy, could be used to finely and accurately describe their every hostility.

"You've never understood what I struggle with," Marjorie muttered through a low growl.

"Really?" asked Jake. "Marge, are we going back to the bad place again? And again? And again? That's in the past. When will you ever let go of it?"

To deny the past was to deny passing time and Marjorie was determined to keep the past in front of her. If the past succumbed to her she would likely not succumb to the past. So she cursed it, denied it, and blamed her husband for the formidable failure in her past. Which he denied, of course. He had his own past to protect and his own life to preserve

"I think he likes us," Marjorie said tentatively as she tried with all her will to convey a thought that might be agreeably approachable.

"Her husband is a good man. And he was kind to me," Marjorie emphasized in a way that suggested broadly Jake was not.
"I was a little tipsy," she admitted, as if to apologize for her lack of control during the Thanksgiving dinner.

"Tipsy?" said Jake. "You were shit-faced drunk. You remember going off on me? Do you recall you accused me of adultery and incest and staggered out onto their patio in a fury until your daughter—our daughter—came out to calm you? And what calmed you? I'd like to know so I can try it sometime."

Jake did not spare his words. He had spent his one marriage curbing resentments so as to make a path for his wife's. He was finished. Or so he thought.

"This is all so confusing," whimpered Marjorie in a familiar, if temporary, retreat.

And she again began to cry as if an expression of her heartfelt sorrow might be enough to earn Jake's forgiveness, which was the first step toward gaining his attention and, because he could not stand Marjorie's indulgent tantrums, an eventual apology.

And it worked. It always worked. Despite all their vigorously shared anger, Jake did love Marjorie. And she knew it. Jake, for all his resentment, thought himself man enough to bear the burden of all pasts everywhere. He could not think himself a man if he did not. It is what fed his self-regard and also denied his culpability in a relationship built on the endless repetition of increasingly embedded resentments. But invariably it left Marjorie with the very last word.

"I'm sorry," Jake said at last and, again, quickly drained of his resistance to his wife's theatrically repressed sobs. The front seat of their sedan was too small a stage to contain Marjorie's masterful drama. And she knew it.

"I'm sorry, dear, but…"

And the "but" was too much. Jake did not finish his sentence before Marjorie spoke an anger that leaped toward him with bared claws.

"What but?" she shouted. "There is always a goddamned 'but.' Your defenses are so perfect. Nothing is your fault, is it? Nothing. You make me crazy with your denial. That's what Morton says. He has no patience for your bullshit anymore and neither do I."

Morton was Marjorie's therapist and had been for nearly a decade. Jake suspected it was Morton who had armed his wife with defenses stronger than his, though he seriously doubted Morton had lost his patience. To remain Marjorie's therapist for any length of time must have required enormous fortitude.

Jake and Marjorie had reached a common point where the terrain of their spousal warfare pushed uselessly across a narrow front. Like the battles of the Marne, their squabbling produced only microscopic movements in and out of each other's territory and over many years. There were successful advances that also incurred inevitable retreats. And there were substantial casualties. Their daughter's early departure from their home and her refusal to return was perhaps the first they actually noted. And it was impossible to know when their struggle would enter some conclusive phase. The only security left was that their marriage, much like their battles, probably never would end. They were too old and too deeply enmeshed and to leave their marriage would be to leave their thoroughly blended lives.

Why did Jake have so little compassion for the severe anxiety that drove Marjorie's illness? And she was ill, her mind as much a mess as her weakening and increasingly fragile body.

"You know my heart can't take this," Marjorie muttered fiercely.

Yet she continued with her accusations, which Jake returned with his denials. Their fateful meeting, the problematic birth of their daughter, the stillbirth of a son, their real and imagined infidelities, and their mistaken, conflicting and fateful choices of where to work and to live and how. The world they inhabited was the world they made and anger was its nearly constant weather.

"I'm scared of death," Marjorie said after a last lingering silence.

She said it with a peculiar tenderness that revealed the paralyzing resentments driven by anticipated and expected loss. It was enough to move Jake, as it always did. He reached for her hand but she pulled it away to clutch her throat.

"I can't breathe!" Marjorie shouted.

She held her hands tight around her neck and thrashed forward in the seat.

"I'm going to stop," Jake said calmly. "Take some breaths, Marge. You'll be OK. Easy, now…"

A gas station's towering sign loomed at an exit in the distance. Jake activated his turn signal and eased into the highway's right lane. His mind converged at some location between mourning and loss. He responded to his urgency, one driven by a profound and familiar feeling of remorse. He no longer knew what was real. He no longer cared.

2

Their dead son was the hardest reckoning. As he stood in line at the Ignacio gas station's mini-mart, Jake relished the many accusations he could hurl at his wife and rejected them all. It was her pain as much as his. More so, since it was her body that choked up the unfinished and never completed fetus they tried so long to create.

A newspaper rack under the cash register shouted its headlines:
Three killed, nine wounded in Colorado Planned Parenthood attack.
Ninety-percent of world's glaciers retreating.
Three lives lost in Texas floods
Jake had spent nearly a week without checking the news and realized in a moment why he had not missed it. "Wounded, retreat, lost…" the nouns in headlines changed but never the verbs or modifiers. As syntax, news was never really new.

"Here," Jake said and handed Marjorie a plastic bottle of fizzy water while with the other hand he held her neck at the base and gently stroked her back.

Marjorie drank the water fast while also swallowing a fat, white pill intended to prevent a heart attack. Though Jake did not believe his wife would ever have a heart attack. In his experience, his wife was vulnerable to panic attacks and Jake's own doctor said it was impossible sometimes to distinguish the symptoms of one from the other, though it appeared that biologically Marge was prone to panic and not necessarily to heart disease. A brief period of heart arrhythmia following the stillbirth had drawn a doctor's interest. Marge was convinced she was dying though her doctor was certain she was not, at least not yet. And her history of mental illness suggested an obvious potential for any physical symptom to become the subject of a gross and destabilizing drama.

Jake was exhausted by drama. He sat twisted in the driver's seat as he helped Marge take long sips from the bottle, her hard breathing either a symptom or a ploy. Jake could not say which. And wouldn't.

"Feeling better?" he asked after a long, quiet minute.

Marjorie nodded.

"We need to get going," said Jake.

"You'd love it if I died," said Marjorie, her bitter recrimination a sign that her panic was subsiding.

Marjorie's most lucid and concise indictments were almost always those given from her most secret, hostile place. In this instance, she expected the answer she asked.

"Marge…" Jake's voice sank behind him as he stared at the ridge of mountains looming to the west and north.

"You know that's not true."

"I do?"

"Yes, you do," said Jake as he started the car.

Within an hour they were traveling the twisting, two-lane remnants of Highway 101 as it made its final pass through the steep hills north of Cloverdale. Anger still bristled, but silently. After more than four decades together, Jake and Marge were still not what each had once said they wanted to have and to hold. To marry Jake, Marge in her mind had turned down Cary Grant, Orson Welles and John F. Kennedy. What chance did Jake have?

To marry Marjorie, Jake had overcome his phobia of undergraduates to submit to seductions he could not resist since they fulfilled his long and suppressed fantasy as the commanding mentor. Marjorie's enjoyment of raunchy language and rough sex unraveled Jake's least spoken inhibitions for both to see. It was their secret now and Jake married Marjorie in large part to limit its access and to quiet its voice before it became a chorus.

"If nothing is ever wrong, why do you keep trying to find it out?" asked Marge at last, seemingly desperate to restart their fight.

"Can't we just be friends?" Jake requested as he stared forward. "Like right now. We're married, right? Let's pretend we're friends."

"And how do we do that?" asked Marjorie, suddenly and obviously curious.

"We could get beyond our anger," said Jake. "I won't deny you have a lot of reasons not to respect me. It's been a long time together. Why wouldn't we be sick and tired? We have exhausted every illusion."

"Are you suggesting we make a deal?" asked Marge.

Jake's lower lip curled as he pushed the accelerator and moved them into the fast lane.

"Didn't we make a deal by getting married?" Jake asked. "In sickness and in health, richer or poorer…"

"We never said those words, " snapped Marjorie. "We said we would love each other and say it to each other every day. Well, how long has it been, Jake? All couples break their marriage vows. We're no different."

Jake wondered if Marge were judging him, though judgment was a minimally satisfying substitute for any truthful reckoning. All expressed feelings were for Jake simply heralds of more trauma. No joy in his life was left unpunished. He was fated to love Marjorie. Love was the excuse he used to explain his repression, denial and suffering at the hands of others. He thought all his sacrifices were for his wife though he could not remember her ever asking for anything. Instead, each of his own emotions was a herald of trauma, even those feelings of joy and pleasure, for their evident presence only predicted their inevitable and constant departure. A lifetime of living with Marge had melded him into another version of her. He was a human being, a reality he did not control and for which the only cure was death.

"We could get beyond the blame," Jake said at last from a place of unfamiliar urgency. "We could forgive each other."

"Forgive?" Marjorie asked. "You sound like a priest."

Jake retreated from his wife's religious reference. Before they married they agreed not to invest any faith in the presumed benevolence of a god. Death was an inevitable consequence, one asserted perpetually by Nature. Therefore a god died every time a human died and good riddance. A god was no consolation for the suffering it inspired.

Mendocino County passed as a blur of rolling hills, vineyards and, toward the north, encroaching pine forests that blocked all views of the mountains. In Willits they slowed at each of the town's several congested intersections.

"Do you need to stop?" Jake asked his wife.

"No, oh hell no," she answered from a stupor.

Marjorie was sleeping and Jake had not noticed.

"We'll make a pit stop in Garberville," Jake said to no one but himself.

Jake waited for Marjorie's objection but she said nothing and he was relieved. He wanted to stop soon but also wanted to get home where he imagined pouring himself a generous glass of bourbon. The longer the trip the larger the glass he imagined. It was his secret and he could not tell Marge that what he wanted most was a big pour of whiskey. An hour ago he would have traded her for one. But he said nothing. Honesty was the pledge they had made to each other and one they honored until their lives bore more truth than either could tolerate.

Marjorie fell asleep, leaving Jake to drive without the commands of his verbally abusive co-pilot. She was awakened by a sturdy shove.

"Here," Jake said suddenly. "Let's stop here."

"What are you doing?" asked Marge.

"Remember this place?" said Jake.

At first Marjorie did not until a familiarity gelled behind her eyes, which opened wide with what Jake hoped was a happy surprise.

"Where are we? Cook's Valley?" Marjorie asked.

"It's the special place…remember?" said Jake as he found a gravel road off the highway and followed its sloping turns toward a fat, flat beach on the South Fork of the Eel River. It was a secret location and also a hallowed one, which was perhaps why they had never returned.

"Was it '69?" asked Marjorie.

She couldn't remember.

"It was 1971," said Jake.

He remembered the date on the contract he signed as an adjunct history instructor at the college.

"We didn't know if we'd last even a year. And…well…here we are."

"The larger question is what we are," said Marjorie after what Jake later recalled as a disquieting silence.

She was calm and lucid, which surprised Jake whose feelings ran wild between fond remembrance and unhinging anticipation.

"We did our best," Jake said, trying to recover some sliver of hope.

"Speak for yourself," said Marjorie.

She was having none of it.

Jake left her at the bank and walked down river past a copse of pines and toward a clearing. It was the place where they had the first picnic in their new county and where they also made love. Jake and Marjorie had chosen this place to declare their young, untested hopes and now Jake wandered alone and wondered what had become of them. His lowly adjunct job grew in a few years into a tenured faculty placement. He wrote a book. And another. Marge's teaching credential landed her a job as a math instructor at the high school. Seasons defined their experience though the small town life could be boring and, in the relentlessly wet winter, a trial.

In what they called their home, Jake and Marjorie seemed through the passing years to be the only people to get older. Arcata was a college town and, along with students, their friends came and went in the flow of a place that hid like a snug cubby behind a vast, redwood curtain. And as bored as Jake thought he was, it was nothing to Marge's festering ennui and, ultimately, neurosis. His serial affairs with young students were eventually no match for Marge's enduring affair with another teacher named Henry. Jake enjoyed the annual arrival of young undergraduate bodies while viciously envying the enduring poetry of his wife's long-term tryst with Henry. After more than a decade, and following the wrenching end of her affair, Marjorie consented to work with her husband and to solve their drift into separation by becoming pregnant and having a daughter. So successful was this ploy that they tried hard to have another, only to produce a stillborn son and with it the return of a spectrally larger despair.

There were troubles now. They lived in a place heavy with dope and unemployment and limits, always limits, and where they had chosen together to limit the reach of their own lives through harsh, colliding moods.

Jake heard Marjorie's footsteps grind the sand and then felt her hand in his. He turned to see her looking into his eyes, a look so bright and luminous he nearly turned away.

"It's been a life," Marjorie said briefly before lifting her arms to Jake's shoulders for a full and quiet embrace.

"I will give you that."

And there was a kiss, a kiss of solemn and unuttered grief that brought tears to both, tears they met again with their lips. It was a bittersweet problem: to feel intimate again with a partner that for too long had existed as a remote and unsearchable stranger.

3

"I'll wait," said Marjorie.

She was tired, still very tired.

"Coffee will help," said Jake. "I'll be right back."

Garberville basked in a fall sunshine the coast could not see. Fog peeked over the western ridges that created a watershed for the Mattole River while Jake ran into a coffee bar on Redwood Drive and ordered two lattes. It was noon but late for a fall day when the sun would set before five. And Marjorie wanted to take the long way home.

I want to see the Cape, she had said through a weak, withered voice. *I want the crazy, violent sea.* And Jake would not deny her. He would drive west through Briceland and out through Honeydew to Petrolia and toward the mouth of the river where they would climb the ridges of Cape Mendocino and descend back into Ferndale. Making good time they would drop into the view of Humboldt Bay under the black of a night sky and still be nearly an hour from home. But Marjorie would see the ocean's rough, white waves.

Coffee refreshed them and by the time they reached the Ettersburg turn-off, Marge was again unrepentantly garrulous.

"I lost the baby," she said plainly and without emotion.

"You weren't alone," Jake said instantly though he was startled by Marjorie's admission and also by her words that he was not complicit.

"I made him, too," Jake responded. "Why do you take it all on yourself?"

The truth was that Marge wasn't certain Jake was the father of her lost fetus. She had her reason to be grateful for its demise and in a way she would never share with her husband.

"Men don't carry fetuses," said Marjorie. "They barely carry babies."

Caffeine appeared to stimulate again Marjorie's hard feelings in ways Jake thought he could understand but wished not to enable.

"I'd have carried yours," said Jake. "Even if it weren't mine."

Several minutes passed in silence.

"How long have you thought that?" asked Marjorie.

"I don't think anything," answered Jake. "I don't know anything."

"But you said it," said Marjorie. "You must have a thought. What is it?"

"More than a thought," Jake answered. "It's never just a thought. It's a fear."

"A fear of what?" asked Marjorie.

"The truth," Jake answered.

He did not take his eyes off the road.

Marjorie was quieted by the thought of truth and settled back into the car's swings and surges through the mountains. To reach the ocean before dark they needed to cross two mountain ranges. At a half past one on a late fall afternoon they were just cresting the first.

"We're still an hour from Honeydew," Jake said to no answer from Marjorie.

Her silence filled Jake's mind with all the years he shared with Marjorie and he labored to recall each of them. Sometime in the early Seventies, among new friends and the first bloom of their careers, Jake and Marjorie confronted the claustrophobia of their marriage and, in the spirit of the time and their community, opened their relationship to others.

It was during this time that Marjorie stopped at home one afternoon at lunchtime to find Jake in bed with a younger neighbor. Jake remembered her flummoxed expression and quick departure. He tried unsuccessfully to phone Marjorie and waited anxiously until she returned. And when she did arrive, she was not angry. In fact, she had stopped first to visit the neighbor and to assure her they were still friends.

"So this is how it is to be," Marjorie said directly to Jake before he had any time to offer his quickly rehearsed and hopefully mitigating regrets.

"You are free now," she said firmly. "And so am I. There are no questions that need answers. Not ever again."

But how will we live together now? Jake thought to ask but did not and it did not matter. Marjorie saw the question in his eyes.

"We're doing well," she said. "We pay the rent. We are friends. We're survivors. And we're a family."

But there was no mention of love and even as Jake thought to say it, to say he loved his wife, he did not.

"Is that all? Will we just be friends now?" asked Jake.

"No more questions," Marjorie said. "No more ever."

And she left the kitchen to drop her bag and change her clothes. Jake made dinner and they ate together as they always had. They shared their workdays and discussed their plans for the weekend. And there were no questions.

As he drove the last switchback of the ridge, Jake's mind continued to clock the calendar of his and Marjorie's milestones and breeches and the legacies attached to each. They lived like roommates for many years. One year Jake took up residence in the spare bedroom while he stayed up late to write his books. Their only rule was that their time with lovers was always spent away from the home. Since Marjorie's teacher was a bachelor, that wasn't hard for her. But Jake's trysts usually involved young coeds who shared apartments or dorm rooms, which required him to find a motel or a cottage or wrestle with a lover like a goofy teenager in the backseat of his car or, during warm weather, on a blanket behind rocks on a secluded beach.

It was Marjorie's idea that Jake's lovers and her lover would re-lieve their boredom in marriage until the problematic limits of fuck-ing others also tested their own patience and capacities. If Jake's annual flings with students had the character of a fetish, Marge's obsession with Henry became ultimately a debilitating and neurot-ic dependency as she fought for years to love without commitment someone she worked with every day. In the end it was too much and she chose to fall deeply in love, or at least the most fragile and vul-nerable parts of her did, until—split utterly down the middle of her psyche—she succumbed to the pathologies that were her birthright and that grew comfortably among the psychic contradictions and re-pressions she had invoked as desire. When Henry left for a summer and did not return in the fall, Marjorie collapsed. Her attempted sui-cide was feckless and, as her therapist concluded later, an intentional and premeditated cry for help.

Jake pushed on the brakes as the car plunged abruptly down the west side of a ridge, his mind still on the words of his wife who, he acknowledged, had experienced some healing at the end of her affair and enough to rejoin him in bed and to make their baby Em-ily. But she was still not well. She was not well then and she was not well now. The diagnosis revolved around a vortex of symptoms that ranged between bipolar disorder and a possible borderline personality. In her more lucid moments, Marjorie acknowledged this. In her more and increasingly inchoate states however, she denied everything and returned to confidently loathing all within view, including and especially herself. It was at these times Marjorie resorted to selfish acts intended always to impress her husband with the truth of her unspoken needs.

"It was a difficult time," Jake said to himself quietly but with words intended for his wife.

"We were flush with parenting but tired of it, too. We thought we wanted another child, but we really didn't or we wouldn't have slept with others, wouldn't still have fed our habitual and polymorphous hungers. But we did. I've never asked about the loss of our Anthony. I was happy to assume he was mine, as you did when you told me. But there was so much we wanted to believe and, in order to sustain our belief, so much we would not, could not say."

Jake tried to draw a circle around his and Marjorie's most difficult time and to thereby delimit it. But it was useless since, whatever a circle's size, another could be drawn around it.

Jake dropped down to the bottom of a mountain as the road aligned with the rushing white waters of the Mattole River. He followed the river into the Honeydew junction and drove into the parking lot of a general store. Marjorie appeared exhausted and seemed again to be napping. As he tried to awaken her Jake felt a first flash of concern as Marjorie responded barely from within a tenaciously groggy fog.

"I'll get some water," Jake said nervously, not certain his wife could hear him.

Jake ran into the store.

When he returned, Marjorie was sitting up, her eyes wide open but in a way that appeared to Jake as a kind of trance.

"How are you feeling?" he asked.

"Fine…"

Marjorie's voice was tremulous but also calm. Jake released a sigh of relief.

"Fine? You're OK? Hungry or anything?" he asked.

Marjorie smiled warmly in a way that Jake found reassuring.

"I'd like some potato chips," Marjorie said directly. "I'd like a Coke."

Jake went back into the market and quickly returned, wishing he had not listened to her about driving to the ocean.

"We're 45 minutes from the beach," he said quickly and handed Marge a small grocery bag from which she pulled a small package of chips and a soda bottle.

"This is wonderful," Marjorie said as she held up a chip and then unscrewed the cap on her Coke. She handled her snack as if it were the Eucharist.

"Wonderful," she said again.

As he drove west, Jake remained quiet through Marjorie's labored chewing of her chips. Occasionally she lifted the soda bottle to her lips for a brief, weak sip. She drank again as Jake swung through a tight turn in the road, spilling a trail of coke drops across her blouse.

"Shit, I'm sorry," Jake said.

"It's OK, hon," Marjorie responded with uncharacteristic intimacy. "It's OK."

A long moment of silence passed while Jake navigated a bumpy grade.

"I love you, Jake," Marjorie said, surprising and frightening her husband who had no current context for her affectionate words.

"Well…I love you, too," Jake said, struggling quickly to offer from behind his well constructed defenses something of his true feeling.

"You know, we can argue forever over the truths of our experiences," said Marjorie. "But there is only one truth. It's what we've lived, Jake. It's who we have been and all the bargains we've made for better or for worse, for richer or for poorer."

Jake took his eyes off the road and looked directly at Marjorie.

"Yeah, I said it," she said. "Yeah…"

"Are you OK?" Jake asked again.

His wife's generosity and willingness to see through his prism was an unfamiliar experience.

"Oh yes, Jake," she said in a voice that seemed melodic, as if she were about to burst into song.

"We have our own ways of understanding our lives. But I want you to know now—it is important you understand this—that ours is the only life we've ever lived and the only one that has ever mattered to me. Surely there is an end to all of this and I am willing to be that ending. No more regrets or jealousies or trauma, dear. No more. We have had a daughter. We have had a marriage. We have had our lives. I have no more complaints. I'm finished. And now I'm tired. I need to rest."

Marjorie fell back into her seat and parked her Coke in the car door's drink holder. Jake drove over a bridge that crossed the Mattole, Marjorie's body bouncing limply as the car touched down on the road's rough asphalt. They would soon pass through Petrolia and cross the low hills along Singley Creek. Beyond was the ocean, the ocean Marjorie wanted once again to see.

"We're almost there," Jake said to his wife who appeared in her sleepy stupor nearly perishable. Was she waiting? For a moment Jake thought Marjorie had given up waiting and that perhaps she despaired of waiting and had no more demands.

At McNutt Gulch the road opened to the ocean, white surf swelling against a long stretch of sand that reached north toward Sugarloaf Island and the land's end. At Domingo Creek Jake pulled off the road and tried to awaken his wife who struggled to open here eyes to see the dark sands that reflected in a coruscating patch of wet fissures the last rays of a richly red and setting sun.

"You OK?" Jake asked. "You need something? A pill?"

Marjorie smiled weakly and closed her eyes. And then she began to shiver.

"Are you cold?" Jake asked.

There was no answer.

Jake no longer thought. He only acted. After starting the car Jake drove north, his foot heavy on the accelerator as he banked into sharp turns along the road's protracted rise and fall above the coastline. Crossing the median he sped suddenly and quickly through endless bends of the road.

He turned frequently to watch his wife and to check her condition. He spoke to her often and assured Marjorie they would be home soon. He reached to hold her wet, cool hand.

4

Emily phoned her parents Monday morning and got their answering machine.

"They should be home by now," she said to Marcus.

Emily was in no hurry to speak with her mother. It had been a hard holiday, harder even than Emily could have imagined. She knew her mother's threats and every one of her worst capacities; how she could simply clear her throat at a dinner table in a way that silenced everyone. And Marjorie had done it and more during a Thanksgiving that had become another one of Emily's futile attempts to demonstrate daughterly affection, offered to her parents as, likely unknown to them, a final effort to establish a basis for continued contact. Emily's parents did not appear to understand this, so that what Jake and Marjorie thought a happy and accepting reunion with their daughter was, in fact, a last audition for a very limited role in her expanding life.

That new life was to include even the newer life of a granddaughter and while Emily had hoped Thanksgiving with all its traditional family tropes might open a door to some new kind of intergenerational love, she was instead left with her mother's self-absorbed and undisciplined neurosis, made louder and more invasive by her alcohol-fueled tirade. It took more than two hours to peel Marjorie out of her brutal and punishing cocoon, and another hour to sober her up. Even before desert, Marjorie's solipsistic drunk had done enough of the talking to push everyone, even papa Jake, to the edges of their chairs.

"I'm sorry," Emily said later to her husband, a man who had never conveyed any need for an apology. "She's just really sick."

"She has a hard time," answered Marcus. "She's not well. That's not all her fault, honey."

Emily loved her husband and his reliable empathy. She needed it now. She needed some sense that being pregnant and having a baby weren't simply gestures that assured the continuation of a badly flawed and dangerous line.

"They had you," said Marcus. "And you're the best, sweetheart. Nothing wrong with you."

Her husband's kindness assuaged Emily's bitter feelings but did not relieve the incipient worry she felt.

"Are they home?" she asked Marcus. "Why don't they answer?"

"Phone them in the morning," said Marcus. "Early. Catch them before they get going."

"They're retired, honey," answered Emily. "They don't get going."

Emily phoned again on Tuesday and again was pushed into voice-mail on both her parents' phones. She phoned several times in the afternoon and one last time before going to bed.

On Wednesday Emily phoned and was told her mother's mailbox was full.

"This doesn't feel right," she said to Marcus.

"Maybe they're visiting friends," said her husband. "Maybe they took a vacation. Anyone along the way they might want to see?"

Emily couldn't think of anyone.

"Is there a neighbor you can phone?" asked Marcus.

"The Trotters," answered Emily. "Live down the street. Known my parents since I was a kid. But I don't have their number."

Marcus did a web search and found the Trotters address and phone number. It was a landline phone.

Thursday morning Emily phoned the Trotters.

"Good heavens, darlin'," said Mrs. Trotter to Emily. "I was getting ready to phone you. Where are your folks?"

The question alarmed Emily.

"They asked me to watch the house and said they'd be home Saturday," said Mrs. Trotter. "I've been picking up newspapers in the driveway for nearly a week. Is everything OK?"

"Is it?" asked Emily.

"They haven't called you?" asked Mrs. Trotter.

"No," said Emily, her voice shaky and hesitant.

"Well, that's not like them, is it, darlin'?"

"No…" Emily said.

The Trotters had known Emily since she was two years old. Emily had toddled with her mother down the block to say hello and to borrow butter. Alma Trotter and her husband Martin described themselves as old-timers, residents who remembered Arcata before its college became a university. Martin was a retired salmon fisherman and Alma a stay-at-home mom with three sons older than Emily and employed as loggers. Alma had thought one might marry Emily until she left for college and never returned.

"Are you worried?" asked Mrs. Trotter.

"Yes…do you think I should be worried?" asked Emily.

It was a meaningless question conceived in the collision of Emily's fierce judgment of her parents as flawed, foolish people with the urgent and stammering fear something bad had happened to them.

"Maybe they stopped to visit friends," said Mrs. Trotter.

Emily heard the neighbor's effort to reassure her.

"I don't know…why wouldn't they…it seems so…"Emily had no words and depended on her old neighbor to help her.

"Maybe you should call the police," said Mrs. Trotter."Can you take another look?" asked Emily.

"I was out in the yard a half-hour ago," said the neighbor.

"Nothing's changed. No car and I picked up another paper in the driveway."

"OK…" said Emily.

"You calling the police?" asked Mrs. Trotter. "If you won't, I will."

Mrs. Trotter's statement sounded like a threat. Was Emily a caring daughter? Was that the question suggested by Mrs. Trotter's statement? While Emily wasn't certain what she was in this strange and developing circumstance, it was not for Mrs. Trotter to decide.

"I'll phone the police," said Emily. "I'll keep you posted."

"I hope they're OK," said Mrs. Trotter.

Within an hour the Arcata police had arrived at the residence of Emily's parents, a three-bedroom bungalow on the south side of campus on a hill near the city's Redwood Park. Mrs. Trotter gave the reporting officers a spare house key so they could complete what they described as "a welfare check." No one was home and nothing in the home had been disturbed.

"Anyplace else they might have gone?" Officer Reilly said to Emily over the phone.

"The house hasn't been lived in. It's cold and the kitchen counters were covered in ants. Your neighbor is cleaning them out," he said.

"Any place else your parents might be?" asked the officer.

"No," said Emily. "That's why I phoned you."

"Do you know their route home?" he said.

"Straight up the highway. From Highway One to 101…and home Saturday night. They wanted to get home before dark."

"We'll put out a bulletin to all agencies," said the officer.

"Maybe someone saw something."

"It's been nearly a week," said Emily.

"Yeah," said Officer Reilly. "You have reason to be concerned."

"Should I come up?" asked Emily.

"Not unless you need to," said the officer. "A lot of people change their plans without telling anyone."

Officer Reilly asked if Emily could e-mail him a recent photo of her parents to be used in a bulletin.

Emily had a photo she had taken of her parents sitting together on her couch, made before the family's holiday dinner.

Alma called Saturday to tell Emily the picture of her parents was in the newspaper along with a story describing them as "reported missing."

Emily had heard from Officer Reilly that many of her parents' friends had phoned him with their concerns, but no one knew where they were.

By Sunday her parents had been missing for more than a week, leaving Emily fraught with worry and guilt as she counted all the times in her past she had wished them dead and gone. Now that such an outcome loomed as a grievous possibility she had no protection from its weird and potentially tragic implications.

She herself was soon to be a mother and, whatever her resentments, Emily had taken full if unacknowledged comfort in her role as a daughter making another daughter. It was a role that justified her difficult childhood; her painful adolescence and the hard work of making with Marcus some safe place that would protect a new child from any possibly errant parenting. But to make this happen she needed the witness of her parents and their reflection back to her of the success she was and they were not. It was selfish but it was true. She thought at one time she would be happier without them. Now she realized they were essential and irreplaceable. They would witness her good parenting and feel the failure of their own. They would have to witness a truth that Emily imagined might at last set her free.

Officer Reilly phoned on Monday. A clerk at the store in Honeydew saw her parents' photo in the paper and remembered selling chips and a Coke to Emily's father. He couldn't remember the date but thought it might have been a week ago.

"If he's right, your parents took a detour," said Reilly.

"Anyone out there they'd visit?" he asked again.

Jake had a university colleague that lived in Ferndale but it had been too long and Emily could not remember his name. Otherwise there was nothing.

"We'll search the roads," Reilly said. "There are a mess of them, but we'll check the highway first. The clerk remembered your dad saying they were driving to the coast."

Emily thanked the officer for his help and hung up the phone. There would be nothing else for a while, nothing else but waiting and without any clear picture of an outcome, other than the worst imaginable.

5

Emily gasped before handing her husband the phone.

Marcus watched his wife collapse into a chair and hold her abdomen tightly as she rocked through a surge of impulsive sobs.

"Oh God…Oh God, Oh God…" she cried.

"Who is this?" Marcus asked.

It was Officer Reilly.

"We found them," he said.

"Where?" asked Marcus.

"Over a ridge south of Capetown. The car went through a turn and dove a hundred feet to shore. Their bodies were still inside the vehicle. Coroner says it's been at least a week."

Marcus heard the word "bodies" and knew, just as Emily now knew, that her parents were dead.

"What happened?" Marcus asked as he reached with his free hand to touch his wife.

"We don't know yet," said Reilly. "The coroner will need to weigh in. We think her mother was dead before the car went off the road. But I can't say anything for sure. Right now, it's considered an accident but there will be an investigation."

"An accident?" asked Marcus. "What else could it be?

"We can't rule out anything yet."

The officer's comment produced an awkward silence.

"So what now?" Marcus asked finally.

Officer Reilly said the bodies were being transported to the county morgue in Eureka and that an autopsy would be needed to determine the causes of death. The bodies eventually would be released to the family.

"And…?" asked Marcus.

"It's probably time for someone to come up here," said Officer Reilly. "I'm sorry."

Marcus ended the call.

He pulled a chair from the kitchen and sat next to Emily whose sobs were beginning to subside.

"Why? Why? Why?" she cried through a barely stifled moan. "And now? Why now?"

Marcus was silent through his wife's agonizing purgation. Her questions had no knowable answer.

"I'm so sorry, sweetheart."

Marcus held Emily close, her wailing gradually shrunk into weakening sobs until words found their way across the river of her tears.

"I'm pregnant," Emily said directly. "Of course. That's why. She couldn't stand my being pregnant."

Marcus heard Emily's anger. It was not what he expected but he knew it had little to do with the facts of Marjorie's death.

"I don't think your mother wanted to die," said Marcus. "We don't know what happened."

But it did not matter to Emily. She thought, even as she hated herself for it, that her parents were not victims of an accident. They were escape artists intent on abandoning Emily at the one encroaching time in her life when she needed them.

"I always wondered when they would leave me," Emily said as she gasped for breath.

"They've left everyone," said Marcus. "They've left everything."

"Why?" cried Emily again.

Marcus did not know why. Whatever the eventual explanation, it would have to be used to interpret facts that might never be fully known.

Despite her husband's concerns, Emily decided immediately to drive home to Arcata. That she called the town "home" made the argument that won out over her husband's concerns.

"You're going to have a baby," he pleaded. "And they're dead. You don't have to go anywhere."

But she did.

She was about to give birth to a child, of course, but now in the shadow of her parents' death she also was a child and abruptly returned to some origin of what she understood as her daughterly duty. In fact, she was a child that, without her parents, existed as some kind of unfinished, adult orphan. If nothing else, there was work to be done that only she could do. And while nothing any longer mattered to her dead parents, everything about their lives and deaths mattered deeply to Emily.

Reluctantly, Marcus agreed to Emily's decision to drive north in the morning. She would stay at her parents' house and phone him when she arrived.

Marcus offered to take a leave from work but it was his first year as a vice-principal and Emily said he should stay.

"My parents," said Emily, as if to own for herself the authors of her life.

"This will take a few days. Maybe a week," she said in an effort to reassure both Marcus and herself.

What Marcus feared, and what Emily knew, was that something more than an accident was involved. His dear wife, however she sought to separate herself from the neuroses at the source of her existence, needed to grasp and understand her parents' last living act.

The drive north held Emily still enough to feel her baby twisting and presumably fussing inside her.

"Just a long drive," Emily said to her fetus, thinking it a rehearsal for the longer drives ahead when as a child the life inside would have something to say about it.

By mid-afternoon Emily arrived in front of her family house in Arcata and walked over to Alma's to retrieve her parents' house key.

"Oh, darlin'," cried Alma as she reached to embrace the woman she had known before she was a woman and even before she was a girl. Emily endured Alma's firm, enveloping hug, which she had known for the entire trip would be essential to her passage back into the life she years before had left with no expectation of return.

There were tears, but almost all of them were Alma's. In reality it was Alma's life and not Emily's that had been upended. Emily had lost the parents whom she saw rarely and reluctantly. Alma had lost lifelong neighbors she saw and spoke with every day.

Emily entered the old house, struck by its cleanliness and warmth before remembering that Alma also had entered to clear away an insect infestation. No doubt she stayed long enough to prepare the home for occupancy. It was loving and laudable and also an irritation in the way it suggested to Emily a further and unwelcome connection with Alma.

The home was silent in a way Emily had never known. She found her own room, her childhood bed pushed up against a wall while boxes and a dust-smeared desk were shoved into a corner, signs of some suspended work to convert the room to another use.

There was no landline phone in the house so there were no messages to retrieve. The sheriff, and presumably the coroner, had her parents' cellphones. And it would be another day before she could speak with the authorities.

Emily phoned Lena, a friend from high school and the only one with whom she remained close.

"I'm so sorry…" Lena said, and she was sorry because the death of Emily's parents was yet another break in the continuity of her own childhood. Emily heard her genuine sorrow and stifled a sob.

"Can I see you soon? Let's get dinner. There's a new grill at Jacoby's Storehouse. We can have a drink and catch up."

Emily said dinner sounded great but no drinks for her.

"I'm pregnant," she said before bursting into tears. Every emotion now seemed to herald trauma, even those feelings that should otherwise provide joy, happiness, or the comforting familiarity of a reunion.

Was Emily like her mother? After agreeing to meet Lena, Emily phoned Marcus to tell him she had arrived safely.

"Any surprises?" he asked directly.

"Can't talk to the sheriff's detective until tomorrow," she answered.

"Am I like my mother?" Emily blurted with a suddenness that surprised her.

"No, sweetheart," Marcus answered after an unsettling pause. "Your were their child and you had no choice. Now you are no longer their child."

"But did I care enough? Could I have…" Emily's voice trailed off.

"Your mother walled herself off from everyone," Marcus interrupted. "From everyone who might have offered her love or care."

"I'm sorry," Lena said again as she lifted her margarita to clink Emily's glass of soda water.

"How's work?" Emily tossed the question out as way to avoid immediately her own reckoning with the past.

Lena was fine. Her business classes at College of the Redwoods had brought her to the university as an administrative office assistant.

"So in a certain sense I'm at last enrolled at the university."

Lena laughed at her own joke until she saw that Emily wasn't laughing.

"What happened?" Lena asked, suddenly serious and attentive.

"It was an accident," said Emily.

Her tone was firm, serious and reverent, telegraphing a gravity that held Lena down.

"Would you ever think of moving back here?" asked Lena.

"Oh, no…Oh, hell no," said Emily without reflection.

As a child Emily had wandered in endless circles of despair. Home was the geography of trouble and a situation without a cure. Emily may have returned to bury her parents, but already she had buried her past.

6

The sheriff's coroner had told Emily her parents might have died together but probably did not. Tests suggested that Marjorie died first, and likely from an overdose of medications though the coroner was not ruling out a heart attack separate from the accident. Jake's death resulted from blunt force trauma though he was found with his arms around Marjorie, as if he had decided to die with her.

"Had he driven off the road accidentally, his hands would have been on the wheel and we'd have seen tread marks on the highway," said the sheriff's detective who phoned Emily with the coroner's report.

"It appears your mother was already dead. There was no sign of a struggle. For whatever reason, your father decided to end his life."

The sheriff said no crime was involved, which was the department's first concern. But even if a crime were committed there was no subject left alive to arrest.

It was no consolation to Emily who knew more about the dysfunctional lives of her parents than she would ever tell anyone. She thanked the detective and instructed him to send her parents' remains to the chapel for cremation. She then phoned Marcus.

"I'm scheduling a memorial service," she told him and asked him to come up to be with her.

"I want this over. Now."

Her parents' deaths were becoming for Emily a test of her capacity. After any loss what remained? For years she had imagined them dying, one after the other, quietly, and without a peep. She would answer a phone and give brief instructions and they would be gone. Death did not frighten her, especially if her presence wasn't required.

But here she was, presiding at a quickly arranged memorial service for Jake and Marjorie, their ashes sealed in urns and set on a slender table at the front of Paul's Chapel. Nearly thirty people sat among the rows of seats that surrounded the table, most friends and colleagues of Jake and Marjorie but few known to Emily. She saw Alma and her family. Lena was there. A few faculty members from the university appeared familiar but she did not know their names. A man she thought named Morton sat in the front row. Halfway through the service Emily remembered Morton was her mother's therapist.

Marcus sat in the front row and Emily looked at him from the pulpit, explored his warm, wet eyes for the strength she needed to continue. He had paid $320 to fly from Monterey to Arcata via San Francisco. He was here with her through the duration and he would drive her home.

"Thank you all for coming today," Emily said even though she was not thankful for anything, least of all the assembly of those drawn to this quickly arranged funeral. A tall, gaunt man who stood at the back of the room appeared to her like a vagrant who might have wandered in simply to use the grief of others as a passport to a free buffet.

"My parents loved you all," Emily announced disingenuously, knowing there were many present that, like her, could not possibly have loved Jake and Marjorie.

"We—Marcus and I—saw them shortly before they died," she announced as she struggled not to sob.

"They were happy," said Emily. "They were looking ahead to…"

Emily held her breath uselessly. It did nothing to suppress her trauma. She choked on her words and walked away.

"Emily meant to say that Jake and Marjorie were excited about their new grandchild…"

Marcus spoke quickly.

He had rushed forward to help Emily to her seat before taking his place at the front of the room.

"We were a family...a strong and growing family."

While he expressed what might have at one time been Emily's fondest wish, Marcus did not tell the truth. There was no strength and there was no family.

Marcus continued to speak and stared back into the quizzical, probing eyes of all in attendance. He noticed no one cried. Alma, whom he had met that morning, held a handkerchief to her mouth but not her eyes. Marcus also saw the tall, gaunt man standing at the back of the room. Marcus cued the chapel staff to start the play of recorded music, selected quickly by Emily from her parents' CD collection.

A version of "Natural Woman," sung live by Laura Nyro, poured through the chapel's speakers.

Emily and Marcus quickly found themselves at the head of a receiving line that flowed from the chapel room and into a space set aside for a buffet lunch. Wine was poured and guests grabbed glasses and pushed themselves together into separate social clusters. Regrets were expressed to Emily. There were hugs she accepted weakly until Lena held her tight and Emily shrunk into a convulsing moan.

The last to approach was the tall, gaunt man.

"I'm sorry," he said as he found Emily.

"I knew your mother. Taught with her. She was a brilliant woman."

The tall, gaunt man reached with shaking hands to give Emily a cordial and heartfelt hug.

"You taught at the high school? What's your name?" asked Emily.

"I'm Henry," he answered. "Your mother and I taught together at the high school."

"Were you there long?" Emily asked. "I don't remember my mother ever mentioning a Henry."

"Probably before your time," he said again. "We worked togeth-er for more than a decade. Math teachers, you know. Trying to get the best from our students. She was a genius at motivating kids. No one like her."

Emily invited Henry into the buffet but he declined.

"I wonder…and tell me if I'm out of place…but do you know where you might scatter Marjorie's ashes?"

Emily did not know. Or even if the ashes would be scattered.

"Where do you think she'd like to rest?" Emily asked Henry.

Henry's eyes brightened in surprise.

"There's a beach south of Wedding Rock up at Patrick's Point," Henry answered immediately.

"Palmer's, it's called. There's a sign. A trail goes to the beach below. She loved—that is, she told me often she loved that place." There was silence before Emily registered Henry's deeper feelings for his mother.

"You must have been a good friend," she said.

"Yes…" Henry answered pensively as he moved back a step. "We were very good friends. Would you let me know what you fi-nally do?"

He wrote his phone number on one of the memorial service pro-grams, handed it to Emily and then left before Emily could respond.

That night in bed with her husband, Emily stared through the shad-ows at the rearranged room that once was hers. Its spare furnishings and stacks of boxes held no obvious memories though it was impos-sible for Emily to lie prone in her old house and not succumb to old feelings.

She thought first about her fresh, interesting childhood that left her protected from the furtive, worrying lives of her mysteriously burdened parents. Then she remembered the year—she was thirteen—when she grew away from her mother and her mother from her.

Emily began her periods just as her mother was losing hers. Em-ily surged with fresh smells and hormones and also a new kind of arousal while her mother attempted to hold herself in place as she felt pushed along by patchy skin, irregular menstruation and hot flashes. Emily wanted to look older as her mother attempted to appear younger so it was inevitable they would clash, each trying to find her place as an adept and flourishing woman and for entirely different reasons.

One was entering the penumbra of her assertive womanliness while the other fought against her inevitable departure. Marjorie's late pregnancy and its failure in a still-birthed son was the bitter surrender that became a cool, confusing and, at last, abiding and resentful distance. Emily's mother did not welcome her daughter's loving attention to the loss of a fetus, hating that Emily was an intimate witness to failure.

"Should we sell the house?" Emily asked Marcus as he drifted off.

"What's it worth?" he asked sleepily.

Emily didn't know.

"This is Humboldt County. Probably not as much as we think."

"We could rent it," Emily said again.

"And come up every few months to clean it, make repairs, and find new tenants?" asked Marcus.

Emily was quiet, quiet enough and for long enough that her husband fell asleep.

She waited for a feeling of peace to comfort her though all she could summon was an irascible resentment that rendered her helpless and left her infected with shame.

"I'm better than them," she whispered furiously to herself. "I'm better than this."

She was still the prosecutor of her life that still included all the burdens of her past. Her parents had nothing more to say. What they could no longer say for themselves Emily would now say for them.

7

"I don't know what I can tell you," Morton said grimly as Emily sat on the couch in his office.

"Even in death your mother is entitled to her clinical privacy."

"It's just so sudden and strange," said Emily. "I can't say I understand at all what's real. Did she commit suicide? Did my father? Why?"

"Tell me more about your feelings," Morton asked.

He was an experienced therapist. He likely would not tell Emily anything about his work with Marjorie until he understood Emily's reasons for knowing. It wasn't enough that Marjorie was Emily's heir or even the executor of her estate. Morton could still have decided not to meet with Emily. It might not be worth the risk. Not worth revealing a prognosis developed over years and, while at the time likely helpful to Marjorie, could become something that Emily might use against him.

"I'm angry with her," Emily said directly. "I'm going to have a baby. Her grandchild. It was my chance to prove something to her, to prove I was a good daughter bringing her another daughter to love. So much of my life as a child was marked by her inattention or rejection. At least that's how I remember it. I had...I thought I had...at last shown my worth. Had nearly fulfilled the debt I bore for the life she gave me."

"You speak like a homeowner preparing to pay off a mortgage," Morton responded. "There was a debt? Tell me more about your debt to Marjorie."

Morton could see Emily's swift and self-conscious fall to the center of his targeting question. Emily's eyes were suddenly wet. Morton's analogy framed the terms of a deeper issue and Emily went immediately to its heart. She appeared shocked by Morton's candor but also curious about his suggestion. Emily was angry but also honest. There was much Morton would never tell Emily about her mother but he might say something that could provide her daughter with a solace sourced by truth.

"She was mean. She was cold," said Emily. "She would drink and for fifteen minutes be giddy and fun. And then she wasn't. It was as if she'd known happiness before I was born and then lost it. And nothing could bring it back. I couldn't. Daddy couldn't. There was no offering of love or caring that she ever would accept. I know Daddy felt he was never good enough. Neither did I."

Emily wept and Morton reached for a box of tissues to hand to her.

"I'm not surprised by your description," Morton said. "You must have had a very difficult time."

Emily heard his professional voice offer a prescribed empathy.

"Your mother suffered through persistent melancholy," said Morton. "And melancholy is a sadness that can exist without relief. Whatever judgment you felt from your mother, well, I assure you she was much harder on herself. She accused herself before anyone."

Emily stopped weeping.

"We know the world will end," Morton continued. "We know our life and the lives of everyone we love will end. But they won't end now, not in the here and now. All things end, but only in some 'after' that seems forever unlikely. The melancholic is born with the 'after' as their continuous and eternal present. They smell first the death in everything. *Who loves me?* they ask. *Who cares that I live?* These are questions that go unanswered because death is a strange comfort to them.

"It is those who love them that make the hard choices, must determine what they can or cannot do. You were forced against all your instincts to make a choice. And so was your father. That you could love, could continue to love, is a sign of your vitality and health. It is something you have chosen that you have always owned. And it, not your mother's, is the legacy you will pass to your child."

Emily was still and waited a full minute before responding.

"And you know this?" she asked Morton. "You know some truth?"

Morton also waited before answering.

"Only Marjorie and Jake know," he said. "The rest of us are left to wonder. What is real? Something is always growing behind the wallpaper. There is always something we can't, don't or never want to see."

Emily grimaced as if there were nothing words could convey. But she tried anyway.

"They hated each other or, at best, simply didn't care because their joys, their touches, were given to others."

She spoke as if rendering a summary judgment.

"They never touched each other."

"But they touched you," said Morton.

"Yes," answered Emily. "But never together."

"Your mother experienced deep pain," Morton said as he swept the air with his hand.

"It must have been very hard for you to have been subject to the control of a mother who herself was completely out of control. But certainly she loved you. Your father loved you. And what you must accept…."

Morton corrected himself.

"What would be helpful for you to accept is that the point of the lives of Emily's parents was not Emily. Certainly they both loved you. But their deep feelings, as yours, were drawn from their own childhoods to become the harbingers of inevitable and inescapable traumas. And their needs would almost always dislodge yours."

As Emily finished packing she thought it possible she was bringing a child into a world populated by ghosts and hallucinations. Living was beginning to feel like the charade created by a ruthless puppeteer.

"I'd like to dump the ashes first," Emily said to Marcus as he carted two cardboard boxes of family photos into the living room.

"No ceremony?" asked Marcus.

Emily shook her head.

"Of course, sweetheart. Where?"

"Patrick's Point," said Emily.

After locking the house, and without saying goodbye to Alma, Marcus and Emily first drove north. They pulled off at the Trinidad exit and found the park entrance. It took ten minutes for Emily to shake from two plastic bags the white, carbonic dust that had been her parents.

"Let's go," she said to Marcus when she returned to the car.

"So we'll sell the house?" Marcus asked as they passed through Eureka.

"After spring," said Emily. "After the baby. After we come back to see what we need to take and what we will leave."

Emily was silent until the Highway turned west at the town of Loleta.

"Take the road to Ferndale," said Emily. "I want to see the cape."

"Is that wise?" asked Marcus. "You want to retrace your parents' last trip? It's going to be dark before…"

"Yes," said Emily directly. "It's what I want. Don't worry. We'll be home before Christmas."

Marcus smiled. Christmas was three days away.

Emily remained quiet through Ferndale and as the Mattole Road rose into the hills of the cape, large storm clouds formed above them. Within an hour they passed through a verdant valley and rose again along the ridges above Singley Creek.

"Here!" Emily suddenly shouted. "Stop here."

Marcus found a pullout at the edge of a descending bluff where the road made a sharp and difficult turn south.

Emily got out of the car and walked to the edge where Marcus joined her.

"Here. It happened here," she said.

Marcus stared down a steep bank that ended nearly a hundred feet below on a jagged altar of boulders and sand where high waves smashed against the rocks and receded in streams of white, clotted foam.

Emily stood quietly and faced what felt to her like the last frontier of her grief.

"I see," she said vaguely. "Perhaps they rest in peace. But however they rest, they're dead. And while they no longer suffer, I am left here with my life and that of another. I am left as the one to care."

Marcus had no response and waited until, after several minutes, Emily turned and walked back toward the car.

"Let's stop in the next town," she said. "I have to pee."

Marcus shopped for a soda at the Petrolia store while Emily used the bathroom. As he stood at the cash register to pay he heard Emily call to him. He turned to see her peering from behind the restroom door.

"Honey, come here…I need you…now," she shouted.

Crowded inside the bathroom Emily showed Marcus a trickle of moisture running down her leg.

"It isn't pee," she said to him.

"I think I'm leaking."

"Any contractions?" Marcus asked.

"Not yet. But get me some pads, will you?"

The store clerk told Marcus there was a hospital in Garberville.

"I think I just had a contraction," Emily said as Marcus slowed to enter Honeydew.

"And the seat's all wet."

The cashier at the Honeydew store phoned the sheriff. A deputy met Marcus and Emily at Briceland and escorted them to Garberville.

A nurse in the hospital's small emergency room estimated the time of Emily's contractions and as a doctor performed a vaginal exam her water broke. Emily was admitted and given a room.

"We don't know when but it might not be long," said a nurse to Marcus.

Emily's contractions were more frequent until sometime just after midnight she was fully dilated and pushing hard. In another half-hour Marcus watched the wet and bloody birth of his small, screaming daughter.

"Quite a Christmas present," said the bedside nurse.

"And her name?" the nurse asked while Emily held her wailing, crying baby and Marcus took pictures with his phone.

There was no name. Not yet. There could not be a name before something else was named. One name never considered was Marjorie, the name given Emily's mother when she was born. And Emily's mother, as she did with most everything in her life, disparaged her name, even hated it since it was also the name given to her own mother's distant and disliked sister. But it was a name Emily knew before she knew her own. And now it was the only name Emily could imagine.

ABIGAIL, BRUCE AND OLLIE

It was her first apartment and Abigail loved it. For a woman who never before had her own room, a private bedroom was a sanctuary. It was the smaller of the two rooms in her also very small apartment. A kitchenette might have counted for a room but it opened from an encroaching wall and was detached from the apartment's living space only by a metallic strip that separated linoleum from carpet. She could stand at the sink and hand a drink to someone sitting at the dinner table. It didn't count nor did the apartment's one, small bathroom.

Small was the word though it meant nothing special to Abigail who simply loved the diminutive more than the large, the precious more than the grand. She awoke at noon every day and each time she did the bedroom's enclosing walls made perfect sense to her. They were bright with daylight from the long window high above her. She had furnished the bedroom with a plush double bed buried under a duvet, the cover and pillowslips of which were decorated with bright red bows and the loudly printed phrase *Paris, ville de l'Amour* printed so that the "A" in Paris erupted into a dominating Eiffel Tower that filled the duvet's full surface.

Abigail had not visited Paris but imagined a fabled city of love, a city where she visualized its residents smiling, kissing, hugging, even fucking for no special reason other than that the could. It was a fantasy that aroused her and that kept her longer in bed and longer still once she fell back asleep.

Bruce was gone. He had left without waking her. She wondered how he did that. He was a man of stealth though with her and in bed he was often restless, wild and assertive. Abigail enjoyed his enthusiasm even when it was too much at times, when she had to grab his wrist to keep him from reaming her vulva with his fingers or pushing violently into her. She still did not know how to manage him since he did not seem to hear her or grasp her requests.

"Slower," she would say. "Softer."

Though he was rough with her in ways that were sometimes pleasing. He commanded her, moved her body around with his strong arms and sometimes slapped her buttocks just enough to thrill her in a way that stung but did not hurt. And he indulged her rough play, her attempts to pin him to the bed, her fury that was more than gaming but something deeply urgent, even angry at times. It was puzzling and most always arousing. But it was never enough to make her come.

Invariably, sleeping with Bruce brought Abigail's mind back to Ollie. She might have described him as her other lover if he weren't also her fiancée. Ollie was the man she loved enough to marry, or at least to consider marrying, even as she played rough and hard with Bruce. She loved Ollie and wondered if Bruce loved her, especially on mornings like this when Bruce slipped quietly away.

Ollie was sweet and patient and reliable. He listened and gave Abigail all the love she might ever have wanted. But love was not always enough. And even if Ollie were reliably loyal, Abigail was not and knew she might never be. Bruce provided what Ollie could not give her including her new job as a bartender at the Café La Grande—a job that was just a few blocks from her Oakland apartment and which had nearly doubled her pay and tripled her tips. She no longer waited tables or waited for tables to turn enough times each night to pay her rent. Now she earned tips every time she poured or mixed a drink and Bruce watched her approvingly as the bar now filled with men interested in watching Abigail move, which she did with self-confident and also self-conscious grace.

But she was engaged to Ollie and wore his ring to prove it though Abigail often reminded herself, as she did this morning, she had not yet married Ollie. Had not married anyone. But there were benefits to wearing an engagement ring. The men at the bar might flirt with her, but they left her largely alone to mix drinks even as she served them with teasing panache. Left her alone in the presumed arms of another man who, for all they knew, was a brute that could crush them like bugs if Abigail complained.

Ollie was small and quiet and kind in ways that were pleasing to Abigail not unlike the qualities of a good and abiding girlfriend, perhaps a girlfriend who was also a boyfriend. She was not used to finding this in a man and certainly in any man who pushed himself to the front of the pack of her pursuers. She was attractive, of course, and knew it as measured by the persistent intensity of males that since her early puberty had watched, called, chased and impetuously pursued her. Ollie had not. He met her where she was. He was the sous-chef at the downtown Marriott hotel where Abigail last worked as a waitress and he was friendly and kind and, when Abigail decided one night to "reward" her new friend by sleeping with him, he rewarded her with what she only later could describe as an enveloping poetry of words and touches and lovely considerations. His attention was riveting and, after making her breakfast and sending her home, Ollie granted her the wide room other men did not. A naturalized Filipino, Ollie was a family man and the space he made for Abigail impressed her. If this was love, and love led to marriage, Abigail was ready for Ollie to ask the question. That he did not hesitate further encouraged Abigail to say yes, at least to an engagement ring.

"It might be awhile before we can marry," Ollie said.

He said he was saving money to buy a house and to open his own restaurant and bar. Ollie's family lived in Stockton where his father owned property.

That was fine with Abigail. She was ready to have a ring on her finger. She loved Ollie as she'd never before loved anyone. But she could wait to get married.

She could wait and wait and as she stood up Abigail faced the wide mirror at the end of her bed. She was naked and turned to reveal a new tattoo on her left thigh, a garnet red heart pierced from one side by an arrow and from the other by a dagger. No one would see it unless she wore a swimsuit or a short dress. She had seen the design on the forearm of a customer at the bar, a burly man with a weathered face and bad acne. He said he had served time in a Russian jail and that the tattoo was intended to represent "revenge for a desecrated love."

Abigail did not care about any love, desecrated or otherwise, but only that a red heart penetrated by a knife and an arrow looked cool, would make news with her friends and also allow her to appear strong. She wanted to be an outlaw though she could not imagine having the stomach to be punished as one. The tattoo arrived with an urge she could not explain. When asked she would answer only that *it's a Russian criminal tattoo* and she was proud in her self-absorbed and alert way to wear the badge of an outlaw even if she did not possess the urgency or courage to be one.

Ollie had a tattoo on his chest. It was the head of a large roaring tiger that spread below his nipples and reached nearly to his navel. He said he put it there so he could cover it for his work at the Marriott where tattoos were not welcomed.

"Easier for me, since I'm Filipino," he told Abigail. "I don't want no hassle."

It was beautiful, though, and while Ollie slept one morning she photographed it with her phone. Later she printed the image and slipped it into her top drawer where she viewed it every evening before leaving for work.

Abigail was the occupant of her life just as she was the occupant of her room. The room, the room, the room and now she wondered if at last she was only in love with her new and private room and the freedom it gave her to fuck, to love, to dream and to sleep away her blues. It might in any other time have been a holy place of personal consecration. All Abigail knew now was that she rarely wanted to leave it. Her room was her homeland and traveling out of it too often required her to cross a dangerous border.

"Can you come in early?"

Her phone rang and now Abigail was sorry she answered it.

It was Bruce.

"What happened to you last night?" she asked as if to change the subject. Abigail did not want to show up early for work.

"You were out cold," he answered. "And I had an early meeting.

So, can you come in? Luanne called in sick."

"Fuck," she said to Bruce. "I'm tired."

"Just tonight," Bruce pleaded. "I know it's a pain. I'm sorry."

Bruce was rarely contrite and his empathy moved Abigail enough to agree. Though she knew she had no choice. Bruce fucked her, of course, but he could also fire her.

"You were incredible last night," he said.

"Thanks," Abigail answered coolly.

"I mean it," Bruce said, aware he was pushing too hard.

"OK," said Abigail. "What time?"

"Three?"

Bruce asked it as a question though it was really an order.

"See you then," said Abigail. "You know, maybe I'm sick, too."

What she might have said was that she was sick and also tired but Bruce was her lover and also her boss.

2

Abigail showered and again stood before her mirror. She wore a short peacock blue dress and could see her tattoo peeking out from below the hem. She turned in a balletic twirl that swung the silk fabric out into a higher orbit that revealed the whole tattoo. She looked proudly into her face. She saw her blonde hair drop over her eyes and pushed it away, distracted by its dark part that stretched like a small cavern over the top of her head. Yeah, she colored her hair and she didn't care who knew. Everyone did it.

"You are still pretty," she whispered to herself. "For a woman nearly thirty you are the real thing."

Abigail loved herself though if she truly did she knew she might not have to say it so often.

Abigail was resigned to working early. More hours meant more tips, even if the work would wear her out and it was only Wednesday. Her workweek was Tuesday through Saturday. She had Sunday and Monday off and she guarded those days preciously. It would be a long week. And it was Ollie's night to visit. It was a challenge to schedule her life from its occupancy of the long, black night. So much of what she needed to make life work were activities that happened exclusively in daylight. Shopping. Laundry. Banking. Doctors. When to phone? When to schedule?

Ollie would not care if she were tired. But she worried about falling asleep, which seemed absurd since the whole world was usually asleep and had been for a while by three in the morning. But it was her dinner hour and Ollie, dream that he was, accommodated her. The Marriot's kitchen closed at 11 and Ollie waited in the hotel bar until two, nursing soda waters and talking with the bartender until the bar closed and he left to drive across town to Abigail's apartment on Walker Avenue. He usually brought kitchen leftovers and they would eat and drink until getting into bed where they would make love and fall asleep just as a grey and indirect daylight began to spill through her window and paint the opposite wall with the first evidence of a suddenly impinging new day. She loved Ollie's sex. He appeared proud to be her lover and was deeply considerate. Abigail had nothing she needed to do other than to recline and to open to him and to receive him. He offered sweet touches and pure intentions, all welcome to Abigail as the stuff of stunning delight.

Ollie often left early but not before waking Abigail who swam out of her dreams to kiss and embrace her betrothed before letting go of him and taking hold of herself. She would then reach under her bed for her vibrator, a fat tube the color of raspberries. Getting out her phone she captured videos of the vibrator inside her mouth before smothering the tip with lube and walking it sensually down her body to her vulva where she inserted it. Her other hand held the hovering phone over her crotch as she moved her vibrator gently in and out. Eventually she dropped the phone, wrapped herself up in the duvet and nurtured her sexual strength until all of it was used to give her a wild and sweetly relieving come.

Of her three sexual choices, this always gave Abigail her biggest, hardest pleasure, though it sometimes left her feeling lonely while she considered some incompleteness in her life and her failure to address it. She understood that her drives served specific needs. Bruce met her need for success and to merge with success. Ollie gave her the tender expression of vulnerability that opened her so easily to a feeling of genuine love.

But it was her command of her own desire and its pleasing, if lonely, pleasure that, like a recirculating loop of compulsion, kept her coming back for more. She liked her own sex the way she also liked alcohol and certain drugs. Whenever possible she let other people stone her or get her drunk or fuck her and, too often, in ways that sometimes felt incomplete. The one way that pleased and also frightened her most was the contact she made with herself.

In her room Abigail spoke directly.

"You are one hot bitch," she said to the mirror.

"You are one stupid bitch," Abigail also said when she overslept into the afternoon or forgot to pay her heating bill.

In her room she sang to herself, sang to the world, shouted into the air her fury or joy. It was an experience she had not known until now. Nothing of her life until now had been lived so perfectly alone. She treasured her two current men even as she held them at a distance and kept them separate from each other. Though Bruce knew she was engaged he did not know to whom and Ollie, he had no idea his fiancée's boss was also her lover.

"Ollie doesn't need to know and Bruce doesn't want to know," Abigail said confidently to the mirror. "It's perfect. At least for now."

And now was all Abigail ever had. She accepted her transient existence. She expected trouble. Her goal was to postpone it as long as possible.

"Two men are better than one," she told her mirror. "You'll see."

And it would. The mirror at the foot of her bed saw everything.

When she arrived home in the early morning, Ollie was waiting for her. As her fiancée he possessed both her intention to become his wife and also a key to her flat.

"How come you're late?" he asked.

"Do you have food? I'm famished," she said, ignoring Ollie's question.

Ollie had brought a full order of pork ribs and fried potatoes. He went back to Abigail's kitchenette to lift the order out of its box and onto a plate, which he then placed in the microwave.

"We'll eat in four minutes," Ollie announced.

"Bring it to bed," shouted Abigail as she entered her bedroom. "I'm beat."

Later after the meal and their good sex and after answering in a dull daze of exhaustion Ollie's questions about her tardy return home, Abigail drifted into a drowsy remembrance of her last and disquieting conversation with Bruce.

"You free after work?" Bruce had asked Abigail.

The bar was full and Abigail had told her boss to wait. She knew he wanted to spend the night again but it was Ollie's night, though whatever Bruce requested Abigail felt obliged to consider.

"Doesn't work tonight," she told Bruce during her 1 a.m. rest break.

"How about Friday?" she asked.

Abigail knew Ollie would be away all weekend visiting his parents in Stockton.

"Throw in Saturday and you've got a deal," Bruce responded through a tight, controlled grin.

It was the first hint Abigail had that Bruce wanted more of her time and not just a place in her space.

"Can I think about it?" Abigail asked.

"No," Bruce answered immediately.

Abigail heard in his burnished tone an alarming insistence, one she identified as a man's brewing infatuation with her. She knew the signs well and she had quietly cursed the ease with which she had admitted Bruce into her life and room and body. But he was her boss and he had been good to her.

"I need more time," said Abigail in the morning, her head on the pillow and one eye focused on the mirror where she could see Ollie's mouth talk backwards.

"I'm making money now, babe," Ollie said. "Really. It's time to get married."

He described his earnings and said he was looking with his father for a business to buy in Stockton. And he had a big family to back him up.

"And you'll be my wife," he said with earnest confidence and with a smile that reflected in the mirror his clear anticipation of Abigail's wifely obligations.

Which was what worried Abigail and had always worried her. To be married was something she could still not yet imagine. Bruce and Ollie were two men, each offering something while also threatening something. How long could she play one of these men against the other?

"I love you," Abigail said to change the subject. She wanted everything to slow down. She wanted to impose her own inertia without having to resort to discouraging words.

3

Abigail could care for others but never more than she cared for herself. She had learned this from a deciduous childhood that countered nearly every one of its promises with assured disappointment. Were it not for her libido she might have fallen into a deep depression before the age of twelve. But twelve was the magic age when, in the literal flow of her emergence into womanliness she encountered the terms of her body's greatest pleasure, though she was told by too many adults that to touch herself was at best a neurotic obsession and at worst a mortal sin.

As a nubile teen her nightly bath had been a private time when she could lock a door and run water and, during the several minutes the bath filled, lay on a towel on the floor, her head pushed against the hard porcelain of the tub as she spread her legs and rubbed herself with her hand open against her mons until the onset of that slashing, tingling, gorgeous release. It was hard to achieve at times and when her wrist was sore she needed the help of her other hand to rub out the richly satisfying feeling that had no words. For a while it was the source of all her good feeling, at least until she was at last uplifted from an unattended youth and given foster parents who liked her, protected her and also largely left her alone.

Bruce took her out to eat before driving her home. He knew an all-night drive-in in Emeryville and he had a car, a luxury Abigail could not yet afford.

"Good fries, " Abigail said agreeably. "I'm starved."

"It's always dinner time somewhere," said Bruce. "Like right now. It's dinner time in Bangkok."

"It's dinner time here, " said Abigail.

It was all she cared about. Bruce was feeding her and within an hour would be fucking her. It was also always Saturday somewhere and she had the day with Bruce and also the following night, the first time ever she agreed to give up any part of her Sunday for someone else. He had insisted and she did not resist.

"How are you feeling tonight?" Bruce asked cautiously.

For Abigail the question was too wide and large to fall into without risk. Bruce was fishing, which she knew was what men did.

"Fine," she said succinctly. "How is the Café doing?"

She returned a question to Bruce. At some point it would be necessary for one of them to answer. The Café was business and Abigail knew men loved to talk business.

After eating they rushed back to her apartment where Abigail fell with Bruce into bed and then watched the mirror while Bruce's ass bounced high and hard in the light of a single candle. He was making a statement of desire that might, if she multiplied it through the time in front of them, turn into love. But only for Bruce. He was a lover, of course, but not necessarily a friend. He had given her a good job but one he also could take away. Were love to grow in him, so an obligation would have to grow in her. It was not what she needed and this weekend would prove or disprove something. It would give her power or deprive her of freedom. Whatever the outcome, she said to herself that nothing would enslave her.

Abigail escaped early Sunday morning by telling Bruce she would have to meet her sister (she didn't have one) at Jack London Square.

"I'll drive you," said Bruce happily. "I'd like to meet her."

"It's better I take the bus," Abigail said nervously. "I don't know when she's going to arrive."

"Then what's the hurry?" asked Bruce. "Why not wait for her to call?"

It was a good question and Abigail had no answer for the motives of a non-existent relation.

"You don't know my sister," responded Abigail, rolling her eyes.

"Then when do I see you again?" Bruce asked presumptively. "Tomorrow? Tuesday?"

"Bruce…" Abigail answered, the truth on her sleeve even as a lie stuck in her throat.

"I'm engaged, dammit. I'm going to get married. What do you think?"

Bruce's eyes widened.

"I've been meaning to talk with you about that," he said.

Abigail anticipated the worst possible outcome.

"Thursday," said Abigail. "You can come over Thursday."

"You really want to marry this guy?" said Bruce. "What if I wanted to marry you?"

"I'd tell you I'm not available," she answered directly.

"Wrong answer," Bruce replied as he sauntered out of the bedroom. "We'll see."

And he was gone.

From that moment forward Abigail carefully lived one day after the other. Bruce gave his attention to her exclusively. He cultivated her at work by watching her, helping her, intervening for her. She accepted his protection guardedly, careful to express gratitude without appearing to offer anything more. She knew how to do this, or so she thought. The trick was to appear mysteriously distant but not in a way that would appear rejecting. She remained an attentive employee and when a grumpy diner or inebriated drinker hassled her it was an opportunity for Bruce to model his prowess and for Abigail to admire him.

She thought herself imprisoned by Bruce's invasive care until she remembered she had a criminal tattoo. She was a criminal, she thought. She would behave like an outlaw forced to live indoors and behind bars.

Though just as Ollie was too naïve, Bruce was too cynical and Abigail could not shake him off her trail. He was oddly devoted to her and also suspicious of her. It was apparent to Abigail that Bruce wanted her for himself but still had not devised an effective way to take her. Bossing her wasn't succeeding and, while Abigail lived in fear of her boss, she never showed it. And he was still wooing her. Offense and fear were the last feelings he wished to inspire in her. And Abigail knew this, knew she could in the early stages of Bruce's strange and illicit courtship assert her criminal will and hold him off. How long, however, was uncertain. She tried to think like a criminal. She tried to imagine how a prisoner would convince a guard to give her privileges and also to leave her alone.

Abigail was not above skimming money from customers who paid with cash nor was anyone else at the café. It was a hazard of short-term employees that Bruce resentfully absorbed until Abigail, as a way to limit her vulnerability to Bruce, stopped skimming and began reporting others who did. In a week she had saved the café a few hundred dollars while costing two fellow workers their jobs.

By earning Bruce's trust Abigail had gained a certain control over him and likely the most a prisoner might imagine possible. She had some authority now and could manage Bruce's attentions with some strength of her own.

That is, until the morning Bruce called her into his office.

"You're going to think this strange," Bruce said, his voice nearly a whisper.

"But there's a share for both of us in this business."

"What do you mean?" asked Abigail.

"Half the people who work in hospitality take their cut before closing," he said. "They need to."

Bruce said he and Abigail were no different. But as the café's manager, Bruce knew the rhythms and flow of its business. He knew the times the restaurant did well and when it didn't.

"Pockets appear from time to time," he said.

"One night the place is packed. The next night it's nearly empty. One week the owner drops in every night. Another week he's out of town. I see these rhythms and I chart them. The owner depends on us to make his money. It's fair for us to have a share."

"How?" asked Abigail

"Let's try something," answered Bruce. "For some of the cash orders over $50, void a drink before submitting the receipt. Make a note of the amount and keep it in your pocket. We'll use your total to determine how much more money we have in the till. Whatever it is, we'll split it."

"That's stealing," said Abigail.

"Not really," said Bruce. "Not if I say so. I'm your boss."

Abigail again became the docile, conniving prisoner.

Bruce said he would signal Abigail each night. He would hold up his fingers with the count of the number of checks from which Abigail could void a drink or a menu item.

"We won't speak about this," Bruce said. "Just watch for my signal. And it's important they pay cash."

Bruce described his plan.

"Some nights I'll signal a couple. Some nights I'll signal as many as five. Some nights I'll hold up two fists which means don't do it. You pick the customers. Big orders with lots of drinks and side dishes are best. You decide who's the best mark. You initial the void and I'll approve it. It's all cash. And we'll split the take before we leave."

Abigail got it. It was fool proof, but only because the manager was involved. And the manager was a man who fucked Abigail and was falling in love with her and wanted her enough to make her an accomplice in a profitable and criminal contrivance. She thought she should be grateful. Instead, she diagnosed Bruce's scheme as another application of his mulish desire.

4

Early fall was warmer than summer. Abigail loved waking to October mornings, the sun's rays pouring through her bedroom window and bending in ever sharper and warmer hues. The yellow and orange glow of fall days was enhanced by the sun's southerly journey and the tilted, steeper angle of its radiance.

Abigail did not need to know this to enjoy the light. October was the Bay Area's driest month. Oakland's worst fire had burned in October. Abigail loved the heat that let her roam naked in her room, windows open while a fan circulated the air. Her upstairs apartment heated up fast and her room became a sauna but she did not mind. She sweated happily like a visitor to a hot springs.

It was Tuesday afternoon and she was ready to return to work. She picked out a short cotton skirt and a bright green halter-top. Highs were predicted to be in the 90s and she wanted to appear sexy and cool. It had been two weeks since her meeting with Bruce and the agreement that had given her nearly $200 in extra weekly earnings. And since their meeting he had slept with her only twice, leaving more time for Ollie who added to his weekly schedule another night with her in her room. Abigail also had more time to be alone, the time she enjoyed most.

"We're killin'," Abigail said to her mirror, beads of translucent sweat visible at her temples.

"We're in the goddamned money and we're not getting screwed."

She laughed, which meant the mirror laughed back at her. Abigail loved the idea of a best friend so much like herself.

Ollie enjoyed his extra time with Abigail and made it clear to her he wanted more.

"Come on, babe," he said through his Filipino accent. "Come on and marry me. We been fooling around enough to know we're meant for each other. I can do this. I will take care of you. You won't have to work or nothin'."

More time with Abigail had given Ollie the idea they should always be together and as her fiancée he assumed that was also Abigail's desire. It wasn't.

"I need more time," Abigail said one night as Ollie snuggled up to her.

"I haven't met your family yet. There's a lot I don't know."

The next evening Ollie asked Abigail to join him for a visit with his parents.

"Couple a days," he said. "Whole family will be there. They really want to meet you."

Abigail fell into her own trap and blocked out the next Sunday and Monday for a trip to Stockton.

Abigail liked to work. Abigail could not imagine living without her own income. Ollie wanted to take care of her and why? Why take care of a woman who could so clearly take care of herself? Ollie's attention was beginning to feel to Abigail more like a power trip than a courtship. But at least she had a choice. The money at work was good now, better than ever and Bruce not only made it possible, he seemed also to have stepped away from what Abigail feared was a fatal attraction to her. And it could be fatal, she thought, as she imagined what might occur if Ollie and Bruce collided.

Abigail first met Ollie's grandparents, an elderly man and woman he called Lolo and Lola. They were the only family at home and they were old, Lolo teetering on a walker while Lola closed the front door with a push of her cane. An air conditioner mounted in a living room window blasted cool air, which was a welcome relief after stepping from Ollie's car and into the torrid valley heat.

"Where's my papa?" Ollie asked Lola.

"Working. Everyone they working."

"Everyone's always working," answered Ollie. "Where's mom?"

Lola shook her head.

"This is my fiancée," Ollie announced proudly.

His grandparents turned to look at Abigail.

Lola smiled while Lolo, his hands trembling as he held his walker, appeared confused.

"We're here to visit," Ollie shouted. "Where are we staying?"

Lola had no answer.

Ollie walked down a hallway, searching behind the doors of several rooms before walking into one.

"Here," he shouted to Abigail. "We're staying here."

Stockton was flat and hot. Ollie had awakened Abigail Sunday afternoon. He wanted to arrive at his family's home before supper. Abigail slept most of the way until arriving at the San Joaquin River when she was awakened by the stop and go of congested city traffic. Ollie navigated through a ravaged section of town before arriving in a modest residential area.

"Lakeview," said Ollie. "Not the best. Not the worst."

The home was a five-bedroom two-story with a small backyard that backed up to a row of recently constructed apartments.

"How many in your family?" Abigail had asked.

Ollie wasn't sure. Two cousins had arrived recently from Manila and two sisters still lived at home.

"They all work for dad," said Ollie.

His father owned two motels near an exit to Highway Five.

"They pay the mortgage," said Ollie. "He's going to buy another. He's also buying a restaurant. He told me Friday he wants me to come back to manage it."

Abigail carried her bag down the hall and entered a small room with high windows. She fell onto one of two twin beds and closed her eyes.

Abigail awakened to voices speaking dialects and words that sounded vaguely Spanish and which she could not understand. Her nose was filled with the stink of burning meat and boiling vegetables that incited pangs of both hunger and nausea. A black sky filled the windows. It was night but how deep into the night she did not know until the bedroom door cracked and Ollie entered. He turned on the overheard light and Abigail squinted.

"You awake," said Ollie. "Come out. Come out and meet my family."

Abigail was slow to move until Ollie took her hand and leveraged her upright on the bed. She sat for a moment.

"OK," she mumbled. "Let's go."

From down the hall she entered into a large living room where later she would recall that more than a dozen wide faces stared at her, all various shades of the golden brown that was Ollie's complexion. It was Ollie's family and she was introduced by name to each. Janella, Bituin, Maricar, Crisanto, Danilo, Rodrigo, Momma, Papa, Diwa, Tadhana, Banoy, Joriz, and, the easiest to remember: Lola and Lolo. Some were Ollie's brothers and sisters. Some were his cousins. Older men and women who were not Momma and Poppa were aunts and uncles. Of the 14 gathered for dinner, 10 lived in the house. Ollie and Abigail had taken the room of his younger brothers who for two nights would sleep in the living room.

Dinner began with prayers to Jesus as Abigail's attention was taken over by Ollie's platoon of a family. For several minutes she sought uselessly to see and identify everyone and to smile cordially.

"Ollie is a great guy," she recalled saying before accepting a platter of sliced pork and smelly greens smothered in an oozy brown sauce. The odor was of some once living thing now killed and cooked and it triggered in Abigail a gagging response. She jumped from the table and ran to the bathroom.

"I hope they understood," Abigail said as Ollie drove west across the river. "What a time to get sick."

"No problemo," said Ollie. "They understand. They like you."

"Really?" asked Abigail. "I spent almost the whole visit sleeping or throwing up in the bathroom."

"Like I said, they understand," said Ollie. "You're going to be my wife. If I love you they love you. It's family."

Abigail had no context for the experience of such a large tribe of interconnected relations or of people that, however kind, were so different from her. She tried to imagine herself in one of Ollie's family photos, her blonde hair and pale skin aloft in a sea of alluring mahogany surfaces. And the women in this family—did they do anything other than cook and clean? Ollie's cousin Diwa was an undergraduate at the University of the Pacific. She had her own apartment.

"Social work" Diwa had answered to Abigail's interest in her studies. Even if Diwa were an ally, and even if Ollie's family were a democracy, Abigail would always be outvoted.

The return drive to Oakland was quiet. Ollie let his fiancée rest and heal. Abigail let silence open to what within her was an enemy. She was grateful none of Ollie's family had seen her tattoo.

"Where you been?" Bruce asked Tuesday when Abigail returned to work. "I've been trying to reach you."

"Visiting with family," Abigail said.

She would not share the details.

"I have something I think you'd like to try," said Bruce. "I'll come over tonight after work."

"Not a good time," said Abigail. "I've been sick."

"Not so sick you couldn't come to work," responded Bruce.

"I need to rest," said Abigail.

"I'll take care of you," said Bruce.

"You know, I'm the one, darlin'" Bruce announced with an invasive wink. "I'm back in your life. You don't have a choice."

Abigail felt instantly the tug of thick strings tied to her by Bruce. He had generously drawn her into a profitable conspiracy but in a way that left her the only one exposed. Even though they split each night's illicit take from the cash register, it was only her initials that appeared on the bogus receipts. *Yes, Bruce was back,* thought Abigail. *Back to stay.*

5

"You snort it," Bruce insisted. "You'll want to sneeze but you need to get it up your nose."

A hand mirror floated on Abigail's bed, vulnerable to shifts in the covers as Bruce poured on to it a precious quantity of white powder and with a razor blade separated it into shriveled lines. He brought out a small aluminum straw.

"Here. I'll show you," he said.

Bruce held the straw over one of the lines and inhaled. As he dragged the straw forward the line of powder disappeared. When it was gone, Bruce took a breath and fell back on a pillow.

"Your turn," he mumbled.

Abigail followed, sucking up a line of powder that stung her nostrils. She held her breath and waited.

"Cocaine," Bruce spoke. "Cocaine all 'round my brain…"

It was early morning on a dark Thursday though the time and date meant nothing after a few moments. Abigail was lifted high, higher than ever before. She knew about cocaine though she never had tried it. It was expensive and no friend of hers, other than Bruce, could afford it.

"This is pretty amazing shit," she said from within what felt like a rocket to the moon.

"You'll be fine," said Bruce. "Now it's time to play."

He reached for her with an uncommon tenderness, which Abigail noted instantly and into which she ardently fell. It was a leap and in every leap there was more distance than she could cover though later she had no recollection of any of it. Only that every one of Bruce's touches burned away another of her criminal fears. She made believe she could both suffer and forget.

And then there was silence. And then Bruce was gone. She could not answer why it made any difference at all because there were no other witnesses to tell her what had happened and why. She was so high and the night so suddenly bright with its lights and stars. She tried to sleep and could not distinguish her thoughts from her dreams.

"I think I love you."

Thursday at work Bruce returned to Abigail what he told her were the words she said to him.

"And I love you," said Bruce, which left Abigail frozen and frightfully amazed.

Words of love were reserved for Ollie and she was stunned to think that, however high she was, she would have said those words to Bruce. She did not love him and while she wondered whether she could ever marry Ollie, she knew she loved Ollie. Was Bruce lying to her or was Abigail lying to herself?

"You said it," Bruce declared. "You act like you don't remember."

Abigail turned away.

"I'm holding you to it," said Bruce.

He sounded angry.

"I'm here for you and you're here for me. Is that clear?"

Nothing was clear anymore. As Abigail might try she could not explain why the more she feared Bruce the more she allowed him into her life, allowed him to direct her, manipulate her and now tell her lies for her. He was not a friend. He was a force, an energy that activated Abigail's urgencies and lust but increasingly ate more than it fed.

Abigail needed a girlfriend and she didn't have one. Angelina counted for someone, but she also worked for Bruce. She was brought in to wait tables after Abigail's promotion to bartender. Abigail showed her the ropes and they found some common ground in lives lived at the wild edges. But Abigail couldn't phone her, couldn't share her fears. Would Angelina tell Bruce? Did he have the same control over Angelina as he had over Abigail? It was uncanny but also very real. What Abigail had found thrilling in Bruce's piracy now returned to her as a threat. If Bruce wanted something, he took it. And now he wanted her.

Abigail decided to tell Ollie the truth. Ollie, her gentle and kind lover, he might be hurt but she could only hope he would understand. Yes, she had been sleeping with Bruce and Bruce knew Ollie was her fiancée. She needed her job and Bruce coerced her and frightened her. She was a prisoner and, as such, thought of ways to frame her ugly truth as a story of employee intimidation that would earn Ollie's sympathy. Abigail hoped and expected Ollie would be angrier with Bruce than with her. She would marry Ollie. She would quit the café. She would live in Stockton if he wanted her to. So much did she want her freedom from Bruce. So much did the criminal no longer wish to be a prisoner.

"I have something I need to tell you," she said to Ollie before dawn on Thursday as they again rolled their bodies together in an aligned, sleepy embrace under the dark windows over her bed.

"What?" he asked.

"You know I have this job…"

As Abigail began to speak there was a loud knock at her front door.

"Who's that?" Ollie asked sluggishly.

"I'll go see," said Abigail.

While she jumped up to wrap a robe around her, the knocking grew louder and more insistent. She knew who it was.

She cracked the door enough to slip into the hall and close the door again.

Bruce towered over her, fierce and agitated in the shadows.

"What the hell do you want?" she whispered.

"You," said Bruce. "You. Now."

"You're drunk," Abigail said. "You need to leave. Now."

Bruce wobbled slightly, enough to give Abigail the courage to push him toward the hall stairs.

"You need to get some sleep," she said to Bruce.

"C'mon…let's go, let's go. You need your sleep. Come back tomorrow. Go on…"

Bruce was high enough and tired enough to accept her directions.

"Tomorrow?" he asked.

"Yes, godammit," said Abigail. "But not tonight. Go. Get going…"

Bruce stumbled down the stairs.

When Abigail returned to bed Ollie was snoring though in the morning he asked who had knocked at the door.

"My boss," said Abigail. "He's always trying to see me. He harasses me at work, tells people he's having sex with me, which of course isn't true. I wish I didn't need this fucking job. Wish I didn't need to deal with this asshole. Maybe it is time to get married. And now he's coming to my house and trying to see me…He told me he's coming back after work tonight…"

Abigail let Ollie grab the bait.

"Oh yeah?"

Abigail was the good prisoner and smiled.

"Well, let him," Ollie said. "I'll be here instead of you. I'll answer the door and set him straight. I'll be waiting for him."

"Really?" said Abigail. "What do you want me to do?"

"Stay away," said Ollie. "This is a man thing. This fuck needs to be straightened out and I know how to do it. I'll call you."

"He talks a lot of shit," said Abigail, thinking how to inoculate her fiancée against the facts of her infidelity.

"And he's a big dude," she added. "And he'll say bad things about me."

"I'm not here to listen," said Ollie. "I'm here to tell him the fuckin' facts of life."

Ollie had a key to Abigail's apartment and gratefully Bruce did not. Ollie said he would arrive early and wait for Bruce to knock. He said he would answer the door.

"He might threaten you," said Abigail.

Ollie laughed.

"You don't know, babe. He doesn't know. Surprise is our friend."

Abigail was quiet. If there were things Ollie wished not to believe, then Abigail would not say them.

Though she worried that Ollie, so small and quiet would be no match for the hard, tall and muscular Bruce. She had fucked both and knew their bodies well and, were she to bet on an outcome, Bruce held the physical advantage. Yet there was something in Ollie's confidence that reassured her. How men settled scores was a mystery to Abigail who had never fought with her fists with anyone. And would it come to that? Would the men grapple and struggle? Oh shit, would they wreck her room? She would not know until Saturday morning. She would not know until it was done.

"Tonight. Right?" Bruce said to Abigail when she arrived for work.

"I'm surprised you remember," she said insolently. "You were completely shit-faced."

Abigail was fearless and didn't exactly know why.

"I'll make it up to you," Bruce said wickedly.

Abigail did not hear in Bruce's voice any penitent obligation. Rather, his words sounded more like a dare. He was intent on some kind of outcome and confident he would achieve it. Bruce sounded dangerous and Abigail thought to call Ollie and to warn him. But she did not. Men had their own ways of settling things. She refused to imagine what could happen because, even as the subject of a dispute, she had no vote in its outcome.

"Let yourself in," Abigail said to Bruce. "I lost my key and the door will be unlocked."

It was the day of an eventful year that ended Abigail's shift at the café and likely forever. She tried to think of some way out but her thoughts were all speculative and in their lack of clarity also unfriendly. She said goodnight to Angelina and walked two blocks to a Denny's to have a meal. Abigail thought she was hungry and ordered the club sandwich with sweet potato fries. She knew when it arrived it was too much food.

She tried again to imagine Ollie meeting Bruce and what they might do, and most likely already had done. Abigail worried about inducing Ollie into taking charge. He is a proud man, she thought, even though he is small. If provoked, she knew Bruce was strong enough to kill Ollie and as this thought swept her away she imagined other outcomes, the worst being that Bruce would phone to say he had beaten Ollie to a bloody pulp and would not leave her room until she came back to fuck him.

For a moment she raged at herself, imagining a succession of awful and increasingly worse scenarios by which something bad might—and would—happen. As the occupant of her dear and lovely room she wondered how she could so easily have surrendered her safety to Bruce. The entire conflict was about her and she seemed to have no voice at all in its outcome.

And she worried, too, that Ollie, and despite his denials and warnings, would grasp the truth: that Abigail had, indeed, fucked Bruce. And how much would that hurt the man she truly loved? Bruce might say things about Abigail's room, her body, even her sexual response, that Ollie also would know. *Why?* she thought. *Why wasn't I the one to arm Ollie with the truth? Why did I cover it up?*

She picked at her food for an hour, waving off the waitress when she stopped by to check on her.

"You OK, hon?" the waitress asked finally.

"Oh yeah," answered Abigail, embarrassed that her fear was so obvious to anyone.

"Just tired. I had a long shift tonight."

"Where do you work?" asked the waitress.

"Café LaGrande," said Abigail quickly. "I'm a bartender."

The waitress knew the place and had eaten there.

"Nice atmosphere," she said. "Want some more coffee?"

Abigail declined and the waitress went away.

Love had spent the night in her and Abigail waited for what the morning might claim. Would Ollie still want her? She would do anything now to make it better. She would marry him tonight. She would go anywhere he asked. She would do anything for his forgiveness. Why had she ever thought it possible to have two lovers when she was engaged to marry one of them? Abigail searched her thoughts for something truthful, only to realize that what answered her questions invariably saddened her.

Dawn arrived as the quickening of darkness into a grey illumination. Through the restaurant's window Abigail began to make out shadowed details of the Avenue. In the morning twilight Abigail watched people walking in the street, or now could at last see them. Perhaps they always were there. What was real wasn't clear until her phone rang.

"Ollie?" she asked anxiously.

"Sorry it's so late," Ollie said. "You OK?"

"What happened?" Abigail blurted. "Are you OK?

"Oh yeah, babe," Ollie answered. "It's fine. Everything's fine. Bruce isn't a bad dude. He understands the situation and realized he was out of bounds."

"Really?" asked Abigail. "He's been pretty tough on me."

Abigail could not resist an urge to again present herself as some-one victimized by a bullying boss.

"Well, that's over," said Ollie. "Bruce got it. I didn't have to spell it out. I'm your fiancée."

"And how are you feeling?" asked Abigail as she fell under a swelling wave of relief that opened a place to empathize with Ollie.

"I'm OK, babe," Ollie said reassuringly. "Listen, your weekend starts today. I'd like to take you back to Stockton with me. We could spend some time together with my family again. They'd love to see you. I can bring you back Tuesday in time for work."

"I don't know if I can work for Bruce anymore," Abigail said.

"I've been thinking I should quit."

"Yeah, that's funny," said Ollie. "I've been thinking I need to quit my job. Dad has a position for me in Stockton, but it would mean relocating. Could you do that? Let's talk about it while we're in Stockton. Where are you?"

Abigail told him and Ollie said he would send a cab to pick her up and pay for it when she arrived.

"Thank you, Ollie," said Abigail and then as much more than an afterthought, "I love you."

"Love you, too, babe," said Ollie. "See you soon."

Yes, thought Abigail, *I will marry this man.* He knows what love is and she had not known. For too long she had defined love as a strategy for hiking through a battlefield without stepping on flowers. It was perfect or it was nothing. Instead, love was exactly what she was seeing: perhaps a kiss at breakfast and none at dinner. Perhaps love was the confidence of a morning after making love and then an evening when no one knew what would happen. But through it all, love would serve love and, though Abigail had been unfair and unfaithful, Ollie stepped in to save her and to free her.

"He really loves me," Abigail said to herself. "And now I must love him."

When the cab arrived at her apartment, Ollie was waiting outside.

He helped Abigail out of the cab and handed a wad of cash to the driver.

As he turned, Abigail reached to embrace Ollie. Her movements surprised him and, after first flinching to defend himself, Ollie relaxed into her embrace.

"We gonna be fine," he whispered. "Everything's gonna be fine."

Inside her apartment, Ollie told Abigail to pack for a couple of days.

"And it really went OK with Bruce?" Abigail asked. "Can you tell me about it?"

"Sweetheart," Ollie said somberly. "It's OK. We're good. We're starting over now and it's good. Let's forget about Bruce."

"You look tired," Ollie said. "You pack and I'll make you some coffee."

Abigail submitted to another of Ollie's generous gestures.

"This man loves me," she said again to herself. "I'm so lucky."

Abigail went to her room. First she made her bed and then went to the dresser to pick out underwear. She opened the top drawer to see her secret photo of Ollie asleep, his lion tattoo on his chest. She found a pen and wrote on the back "Ollie, he's the best! " She drew a heart penetrated by an arrow and slipped the photo back into the drawer. As she zipped up her overnight bag, Ollie arrived with the coffee.

"Oh, and I forgot to tell you. My brothers are in town and we'll be giving them a ride back to Stockton. Is that OK?"

Abigail said it was fine. Everything was fine. She lived in an enlarging presence of what she thought was a deep and proven love and from which she never again would stray.

It was noon before Ollie's brothers arrived at the apartment. Abigail was tired, too tired, she thought but remembered she was usually asleep now and had not slept for nearly a full day. The brothers entered Abigail's apartment and Ollie said their names. Abigail tried to express her affection for them but they stared at her strangely, as if she were a ghost.

Ollie helped Abigail into the front seat of the car, which she noticed was a Toyota sedan and not the Honda Accord Ollie usually drove.

"A rental," he said to her. "Toyota's in the shop."

"And we're dropping Josh in Rio Vista so we're driving Highway Four to 160," Ollie told Abigail who did not care and nodded her approval.

The ride began and Abigail fell into a stupor of exhaustion. She watched as tall buildings and then houses and at last empty green fields passed her by. She never before had felt so tired.

"Was there something in that coffee?" Abigail asked Ollie.

He laughed as if revealed.

"Just beans, babe," Ollie said affectionately. "You've been through a lot. You can relax now."

At some point in this soporific journey, Abigail heard one of the brothers say he needed to pee. She looked up to see a wide, brown river nearly at the edge of the road. Ollie pulled over and the brothers leaped from the backseat. Ollie left to join them. Through the rearview mirror Abigail saw them all gathered at the car's open trunk. She struggled to push open the car door and climbed out to walk back. They saw her coming and Ollie stood back and away.

"What are you doing?" she asked as she stumbled forward to see something lumpy and wrapped in a plastic tarp in the trunk. It took a moment for Abigail to recognize two exposed and shoeless feet extending from under the plastic.

"And what's that?" she asked. "Is that…?"

Ollie approached Abigail from behind.

"That's Bruce," said Ollie as he spoke the last words Abigail would ever hear.

7

A little of everything remained somewhere. Stashed behind a bus seat, printed on a receipt or washed ashore, everything left a trace. Or so thought Detective Evaro as he walked into Abigail's cold bedroom. Cold was the operative word. It had been many days since anyone had seen or heard from Abigail Brewster or Bruce Rankin, her boss at the Café LeGrande.

"Think we'll find anything, Meryl?" he asked his colleague, another detective with the Oakland Police Department. She needed help reaching for a box on the top shelf of Abigail's closet.

"I think so Carl," said Detective Slater. "She must have left something helpful. This Abigail woman likely didn't know she wasn't coming back."

It was the detective's opinion there was a story in Abigail's room and she and her partner would be the ones to write it.

"I just hope it's not another homicide," said Evaro. "Eighty-one last year and we're on a pace this year for even more. I'm creaking under the case load."

"Maybe two homicides," said Meryl. "We have to consider everything."

Bruce was the first subject reported missing. The café owner used

168

a contact number to phone his manager's family on the second day Bruce failed to show up for work. Abigail also was missing but no one looked for her because on the day of her presumed disappearance she left a phone message for the café owner that announced she was quitting. Only when the new bartender discovered that Abigail had been embezzling cash from the register did the owner try unsuccessfully to contact her before at last phoning the police.

"It's a cold trail," said Evaro. "She had no close friends. A waitress at the café says Abigail was engaged, but she'd never met her fiancée. And we have to wonder why he hasn't come forward."

Evaro had contacted Abigail's last foster mother who was not surprised Abigail was missing. She said Abigail had walked out four years before and never returned or called.

"Didn't want to see us again," said the mom. "We were feeling the same way."

"Whatever happened, there are no witnesses," said Meryl.

"There are never any witnesses," said Evaro. "Only distracted or forgetful bystanders."

"We can hope they ran away together," said Meryl. "Lovers and partners in petty crime?"

"But what about the fiancée?" asked Evaro. "Where does he figure in this?"

"Maybe there isn't one," said Meryl as she opened Abigail's bedside table.

"And scratch the idea she ran away," Meryl said as she reached into the drawer to extract Abigail's raspberry colored vibrator and a bottle of lube.

"Surely, she would have taken these."

Evaro was a tough cop but could still blush.

"She left here intending to return," said Meryl. "It makes sense. There's food in the fridge and, while she must have taken her purse, she left a closet full of clothes. And the bed is made. Neither she nor the café manager has charged a dime on a credit card or phoned anyone since, what's the date? Almost two weeks…not looking good."

Evaro began a search of Abigail's dresser. He opened the top drawer and found her photo of Ollie asleep on the bed.

"Bingo. I think we have the fiancée," he said to Meryl.

He showed her a photo of a naked sleeping man spread out on Abigail's bed, his eyes closed and a vast, intricate tattoo spread across his chest.

"She's written on the back," said Evaro. "The dude's name is Ollie. Judging from the tattoo he belongs to an Asian gang. Filipino maybe? He looks Filipino."

"What do you think?" asked Meryl. "A love triangle? You know someone always gets killed."

"I was afraid you'd say that," said Evaro. "Let's run it and see what comes up. Maybe it will help us. We really don't know what we're looking for. The landlord wants the place back so he can rent it, but the embezzlement at the café makes this a criminal investigation. Though that's not the crime we're concerned about, is it?"

Meryl nodded and together they left Abigail's room.

Lovers always make the same errors. It was a trust issue as far as Detective Evaro was concerned, and based in his experience solving the crimes of so many loves gone bad, Abigail had misplaced her trust.

"So now we have at least one body," Evaro said as he and Meryl again stood in Abigail's lovely and cherished room.

The corpse found floating off Bethel Island in a tributary of the San Joaquin River was identified as that of the Café La Grande manager, Bruce Rankin.

"Didn't need DNA," said Evaro. "He still had his wallet in his pocket."

"Any signs of a struggle?" asked Meryl.

"Coroner will check the chemistry," said Evaro. "And no obvious signs of violence. But, come on, a body in a river for nearly two weeks? You know what that looks like…"

"Of course that puts Rankin's dead body a lot closer to Stockton than Oakland," said Meryl.

"And Ollie, we know now, lives in Stockton, grew up in Stockton, is the son of one of the founders of the Filipino Bahala Na gang and also a member in good standing. Oliver Magsino. And he has an arrest record for car theft and drug possession. His father runs a couple of slum motels on Highway 5. Heartbreak hotels for prostitutes and drug addicts and last resort residences for the homeless."

"I know what you're thinking," said Meryl.

"We'll want to talk with him," she said. "Though you know he won't have much to say. He'll tell us he broke up with Abigail, left for a new job before the weekend. And though his DNA is all over this room, and so likely is the manager's, it will prove nothing other than that Abigail fucked both of them. Hell, her mattress must be a goddamned Petri dish of mingled DNAs. It will prove nothing, though. Someone got pissed off and it was likely Ollie. But good luck proving it."

"Ironic," said Evaro. "Why?" asked Meryl.

"A Stockton detective translated Ollie's tattoo for me. It says *Come What May—Family First!* I wonder if by becoming engaged to Ollie, Abigail imagined herself at last joining a family. Though it seems Abigail wasn't entirely certain she wanted to be a wife. Otherwise, why fuck around with Rankin?"

Meryl went to Abigail's bed and pulled back the blankets and sheets to expose the bare mattress, stained and blotched with the evidence of numerous sexual spills.

"And we don't have Abigail's body so we really don't know if she's a victim. Who's to say she's not the perp? She appears to have loved both men. She also could have hated them. Some desires have no reasonable explanation."

Evaro knew that both he and Meryl suspected that Abigail's body was likely also somewhere near Bethel Island and just hadn't yet surfaced.

"When it does bob up, we might have something to go on," said Evaro. "But for now Rankin is dead and Abigail is missing and Ollie has an alibi. Actually several if you count his brothers who say they drove home with him the Thursday before Abigail is thought to have disappeared."

"And no witnesses," said Meryl. "No one has said anything."

"No one was watching," said Evaro. "No one is ever watching."

A month passed before police ended the active investigation of Bruce's death. It was described as suspicious though what was suspected was never said. Ollie's father hired a smart defense attorney who kept the cops at bay by challenging their search warrants and holding off their investigation until whatever slender trails existed had dried up completely. Ollie's family did come first. And because the San Joaquin County District Attorney had enough to worry about in Stockton, he did not make the Oakland case a priority.

And Abigail was never again seen. For her, there had been at first only the distractions that occupied both space—her lovely room, and time—or what remained of her bitterly incipient and still forming life. She might have imagined consequences but not at the peak of her pleasure and not from a room that at last served her as an originating and much needed homeland. Whatever happened was about her entirely. For the first and only time she had actually managed the dealings of her life, that is until there was left for her no deal at all.

So much Abigail admitted to the heart of her at last delicious existence and inside the room that she loved and lived in as an anchoress might inside a chapel. It was the room that held her dearly, grew her desires and relieved her exhaustion, entertained her hopes and heard her sometimes weary sobs. The room witnessed everything, the mirror saw everything, and yet neither could speak a word.

—————————————

WHO'S YOUR DADDY?

There was no light to find where her roots spread under the soil. Dorsey's family ancestors existed as ill-fitted templates one upon the other and heaped with muses, archetypes and unproven facts of a most likely fictional existence. Dorsey's mother bragged about a father but could not say where he lived or how he died. Her vague recollections of aunts and cousins were intended to reassure Dorsey that, in fact, her life was grown from a nameable source.

But there were few mementos and no documents nor anyone who wrote to her or honored her existence as a member of a family. Only her mother who was named Charlotte offered any evidence of a family. It was a single photograph made a hundred years before of a sleeping baby in a christening gown.

As a child Dorsey asked constantly to look at the image, a glowing relic of sublime innocence and evidence of some relation's familial and caring love. Her mother told Dorsey the sleeping baby was the daughter of a great, great aunt and also named Dorsey.

"She was determined and she was strong," Charlotte said of the aunt whose name was born by her daughter.

"She told me to leave a bad man who came into my life after your father died. She gave me money to go to school. She taught me how I could not, should not, depend on anyone but myself."

Dorsey knew less about her deceased father than she did about her namesake, until her fourteenth birthday when Charlotte decided it was time for Dorsey to at last know the truth or at least something resembling it.

Dorsey's father was certifiably insane. He had not died and remained institutionalized, committed after what Dorsey's mother described as "an incident" in which he ended up naked on a highway and injured. Typically, Dorsey was denied the facts and told only that "no one" (meaning only Charlotte) knew where he was now.

"We're Martins," said Dorsey. "Was daddy a Martin?"

Charlotte said no and would not say who else was a Martin.

"It's just who we are now," said her mother.

The other truth Charlotte told her daughter was that great great Aunt Dorsey's christened baby was, in fact, a corpse. The daughter born to her lived barely two days but the newborn's body was dressed and before its burial christened and photographed.

"Great Aunt Dorsey never had another baby," Charlotte told her daughter.

"Who was the father?" asked Dorsey.

"There was no father," said her mother. "No one she would say was the father."

After the birth and the baby's death, Aunt Dorsey moved to Iowa and taught in a country schoolhouse for 37 years. She lived alone the rest of her life.

"I didn't know she died until one year I stopped to visit her," said Charlotte.

"I was taken to her grave in a small churchyard. Everyone knew her but no one really liked her. They said she was a strict teacher and did not socialize and, once inside, rarely left her home."

Dorsey listened to her mother quietly and, when she was finished speaking, asked again to see the photograph of the dead, christened baby.

"Did the baby have a name?" Dorsey asked her mother.

"I don't know," said the mother, an answer that did not surprise her daughter who was accustomed to an impenetrable past that gave her no foothold as the member of any kind of family, or at best a family without fathers who left no patriarchal trails for Dorsey to find or to explore.

"Did she have a last name?" asked Dorsey.

"I can't remember," said Charlotte.

Dorsey did not believe her mother but knew better than to ask further. Each time Dorsey sought the source of her existence, she risked a sullen look and then a sudden burst of her mother's anger. Dorsey felt like an orphan though she knew she wasn't and wondered, instead, if her mother were an orphan and ashamed to admit it.

There were no knowable relatives or ancestors, no identifiable or credible surnames that might provide Dorsey with an origin of belonging or the branding of a tribe. She was alone, as her mother also was alone. And her one talisman, her only relic, and one she had cherished as evidence of a legacy, was the photograph of a dead baby.

Four years later Dorsey sat in a history class awaiting her graduation from high school. She liked history and enjoyed the story parts of the subject, people who lived and died among fretful links and painful loves and dangerous desires. She hated to remember dates. Dorsey barely remembered her own birthday since there was only her mother to recall and to honor it. Her teacher, Mr. Campbell, said the country faced a recession and war was brewing in the Middle East.

"The class of '90 might end up drafted or drawing unemployment," he said.

He urged everyone to go to college, something Dorsey could not imagine as a choice. She was a good student but her mother said school was simply a preparation for work and that while grades mattered, Dorsey's job as a student was to learn routines, complete assignments, arrive and depart punctually and to graduate. Her high school diploma would win her a job and an income, as it had for her mother.

Dorsey knew the truth was that her mother could not afford to send her to college, could barely afford to support Dorsey on the salary she earned through her years of erratic retail employment.

"I work hard," Charlotte often said.

Yes, she worked hard, thought Dorsey. But we move a lot. She's always getting a new job. Price Club was the latest and Charlotte had moved with her daughter from Sacramento to Sonoma County to help a warehouse crew manage its deliveries. She found an apartment in west Santa Rosa and now Dorsey was finishing her second and last year at Piner High School.

"You'll make new friends," said Dorsey's mother to a daughter who rarely stayed long enough anywhere to have even an old friend. In her senior year Dorsey was a witness to her life and not its agent. She wore her friends' prevailing minimal fashions including a loved and cleverly torn pair of beige Aeropostale jeans and scuffed Converse sneakers.

But friends? Most at her newest school already were taken though another reason she liked history was that she sat next to a kind and popular boy who spoke earnestly and was not afraid to argue history with Mr. Campbell. He spoke often with Dorsey who, at first shy, came at last to like the boy who said his name was Kirk. She enjoyed his sense of humor, his bright thoughts, and especially his ingenuous kindness toward her. Sometimes they spoke after class or Kirk would walk Dorsey to her next period and they chatted so comfortably and without guile. Kirk was attractive and possessed all the privileges of a well-regarded upper classman. That he chose to spend more than ten minutes every day with Dorsey was for her an exhilarating affirmation.

One day after class Kirk asked Dorsey to go with him to the senior prom. Dorsey staggered under the invitation, easily drawn to the conclusion she was unworthy and Kirk either was kidding her or delusional. But it was true. Kirk chose Dorsey and wanted her for his date for the class's big graduation dance. Charlotte helped Dorsey prepare and borrowed from her savings to buy her daughter a stunning cami-style midi dress in powder blue lace that highlighted what she thought were Dorsey's best features: her clear and very blue eyes, her long neck, her honey hair, her small but athletic build that joined a willowy upper torso to a pair of strong, tapering legs.

"You are so pretty," said Charlotte as she helped Dorsey dress the night of the prom. When Kirk arrived, Charlotte used an old Instamatic to photograph them together and laughed nervously in a way that embarrassed Dorsey.

"You have a good time," Charlotte shouted as her daughter and Kirk left the house and she watched them drive off.

He's a good boy, thought Charlotte who could not resist imagining Kirk as Dorsey's husband. *He is a kind boy,* she thought. *He has family. He would be good for her. His family would be good for her.*

As any parent might, Charlotte wished for her daughter a life better than her own, a life ample with the happy noise of an intimate and contented love.

Charlotte fell asleep and did not awaken until dawn.

"When did you get in?" she asked Dorsey at breakfast.

"Can't say," answered Dorsey. "We sat in his car and talked for a long time."

"Will you see him again?" asked her mother.

"Yeah. In class on Monday," answered Dorsey.

"Did you have fun?"

"Oh yeah," answered Dorsey whose reticence to share was notable.

"Will you date him again?" Charlotte asked directly.

"He's leaving for college in three weeks," answered Dorsey. "He said he'd stay in touch. We'll see."

"Do you wish you were going to college?" asked Charlotte.

Dorsey shook her head.

Life would be perfect if she could follow Kirk to college but perfection was unattainable. Until the previous evening fun with Kirk had been foolishness at a distance. But on the dance floor he had touched her in ways that had awakened her. She had wanted to think it all through but there was no time. As they sat in his car she tried to tell him something of love's idea until he expressed its desire.

None of this she could tell her mother.

"I have an interview at Mervyn's Tuesday," Dorsey said.

"Counter sales but it's a start. Pays $5.40 an hour. I could get my own place."

"You'd move out?" asked Charlotte. "Why?"

"It's time, mom," said Dorsey. "It's just time."

2

Dorsey wondered why so many people who must have contributed to her arrival in life existed as shades, their presence never acknowledged or seen.

They are no more, she thought, even as they surely had been real somewhere and in some life not her own.

"We are estranged..." were words spoken by her mother from time to time and that Dorsey barely heard but were enough to make the point that what family existed had either been banished or done the banishing. Dorsey had in her life no one who could see her well enough to give her back a picture of her authentic self.

"They are all dead," her mother said. "They are all dead or nearly so. The family is dead. Leave it alone. They are ghosts now and we don't want them, don't need them. They will just hurt us."

So Dorsey grew up with a unique fear, not of strangers but of relations. Dorsey's mother was proud to trust no one thereby leaving Dorsey afraid to trust anyone.

That is, until Dorsey sat in class next to Kirk who gifted her daily with a passel of intimate moments shared exclusively with him. He was more than a passing kindness. He became a friend and one who aroused in Dorsey deeper feelings that, while appropriate for her age, were unexplored and also complicated by the emergence of generative urges she could barely contain. These several moments a day became the central fire of Dorsey's experience, one fed with a powerful attraction for which there were few words. It was a deep desire that grew over many weeks into a feeling that addressed near-ly all the questions Dorsey had about herself: who she was and what was important and, as someone without a family, what she might ever become. She took thoughts of Kirk secretly into her room and into her bed. She took him with her into the shower and the bath. She took her experience of Kirk on long walks, her mind speaking as she stepped. Earnest declarations tumbled from her even though he wasn't there to hear them.

A few summer weeks passed quickly, the present being little more than a brief space between a then and a therefore while Dorsey marched forward with her carefully planned adulthood. By mid-July she had saved $300 from her retail pay and announced to her moth-er she was going to share an apartment with a new friend.

"Elma works with me," she said.

Dorsey found it easy to befriend fellow workers. Elma, too, was without entrapping origins and had quit high school in her junior year.

"Elma has a place not far from here. Two bedrooms. My share is $275 plus utilities. I can do it. I just got a raise to $6 an hour."

Charlotte listened quietly. Her daughter's news was not a fantasy, nor was it a punishing slap of resentment. It was some truth of disintegration that was expected as the smaller part of a larger legacy.

Yes, she's leaving home, thought Charlotte. They all leave and so does she. Loss is the thread that links all histories.

"Well, come visit me from time to time," said Charlotte in a timbre that signaled she was hurt and inconsolable.

"Mom…" said Dorsey. "I'm not leaving you. I'm just grown up now. I should be on my own."

Life with Elma was for Dorsey much like life alone. Her roommate and fellow worker had a lover across town that visited on weekends and usually brought some friends. Dorsey at first enjoyed the parties that resulted from the collisions of lovers and acquaintances. One night, drunk and swept up with thoughts of Kirk, Dorsey invited a partying male to spend the night. He passed out before they could get into bed and in the morning she regretted her refused invitation and wondered why she would have expected anything other than disappointment. She knew what love was. She knew what it felt like to care deeply. She also knew that something deeper and more complex was at work within her. She knew, too, that she was avoiding it until the morning she awoke and ran to the bathroom to throw-up.

"How long?" asked the doctor.

Dorsey could not recall the date of her last period.

"I'm guessing at least eight weeks," the doctor said.

Dorsey accepted the brewing truth she had for two months been unwilling to tell herself. It was not a surprise she was pregnant. It was simply something she could not believe possible. That she would be a mother. Of course she wasn't ready. But that was irrelevant. Had she longed for this? Had she asked for it? Yes, she thought to herself. Was it a mistake? What could possibly be wrong with something suddenly alive beyond the measures of her caution, something that she loved in a yet unmentionable way?

She left the doctor's office, worried but also unafraid. A pregnancy was a baby-in-waiting, something she herself had been and that all others alive had been. What waited would make the days of its life and also fill hers. It would be hard, she thought, to accommodate an attachment that slithered like a vine across her heart. It would be hard but it would be a truth. It would be her child and one grown from the ephemeral but now enshrined beauty that made it.

Charlotte phoned to say she had received a letter for Dorsey that appeared to be from Kirk.

"I'll come by tomorrow," said Dorsey. "After work."

"I'll fix you dinner," said Charlotte. "Mac and cheese. Your favorite."

Mac and cheese was not Dorsey's favorite but it was one of the few things her mother could reliably cook. If there were highpoints in Dorsey's childhood, dinner was not one of them. It was a time her mother, usually fortified by two or three glasses of wine, unraveled a nonspecific but indelible bitterness about all life and not just her own. It could be too much at times for Dorsey who as an audience of one had no recourse but to listen while she ate. And so she ate quickly, rarely tasting anything served. She learned to excuse herself early by offering to do the dishes. It silenced Charlotte more often than it did not. Dorsey would do anything tonight to see a letter from Kirk.

Dorsey did not expect what she was about to learn. Kirk's letter was open and cheerful at the beginning, the tidings of a friend away at school whose adventures were prosaic but exciting because they were his first. That is, until Dorsey found a paragraph that said he was "seeing someone," those words that suggested Kirk was doing more than seeing and that what he saw was so much more than Dorsey. He thanked Dorsey for being such a good friend in high school and in an obvious way to say that high school was over and therefore so was Dorsey. The letter was superfluous since Dorsey had never written to Kirk. And now, briefly, she wondered why she did not. But in its clarity, and under circumstances not known to Kirk, the letter provided Dorsey with a view beyond the measures of her caution and of the love she bore in some yet indescribable way.

After doing the dishes Dorsey told her mother to sit down. Dorsey had something to tell her.

"Well, how long? And who's the father?" her mother asked.

Charlotte stood to approach and hug her daughter who remembered how good her mother smelled when she was just a child. Though now the hug her mother gave her was without a smell. Dorsey's mother, instead, used her words and wanted Dorsey to say what she would not say.

"When did this happen?" asked Charlotte, her eyes narrowing as she confronted what she thought to be an emergency. "I will help you get an abortion."

"I should never have let you move out…" Charlotte muttered in almost the same breath.

Dorsey waited for her mother to stop talking but she would not stop until, as her mother took a breath, Dorsey said she would not name the father—not name him ever—and there would be no abortion.

"I'm having this baby," said Dorsey, imagining a baby not like the one birthed by a distant relation and that died, but one that would live and thrive.

"We'll figure it out," her mother at last said, tears filling her eyes. "And you won't say…?"

Dorsey would not. She knew the father and did not want him involved. Never. She could not say why. It was an undeniable fact her life was not, and never had been, free and buoyant but, instead, had always been confined by its poverty of attachments.

3

The child 's name was Sharlie and, to hear her say it, she was no longer a child.

Sharlie's new breasts were sensual appendices that advertised a relentless womanhood and all its potentially discomforting secrets. Her mother watched them sway under a frayed sweatshirt as Sharlie

181

worked braless and with blunt vigor to do the dishes. Crouched over the kitchen sink, she scrubbed with absent regard a variety of metal and porcelain surfaces before slipping them into the dish drainer.

Her mother was critical but said nothing out loud while she spoke silently to herself.

She doesn't really care. My daughter doesn't care the way I didn't care. Sharlie is certainly my daughter.

Sharlie was a name shortened from Charlotte, the name given by her mother when Charlotte was born. Dorsey had only two family names from which to choose: one was her mother's and the other was her own.

"I need to do my homework," Sharlie said as she wiped her hands on a dishtowel.

"Really?" asked Dorsey. "You have homework?"

"I always have homework," Sharlie said with a shrug. "It's just that tonight I'm going to do it."

"Well, that's nice," responded Dorsey weakly. "That's nice."

Sharlie fled the kitchen and in a way that suggested she was fleeing her mother. Later Dorsey could hear from behind the closed door of her room Sharlie's rapturous, punctuated sighs while she talked on the phone. An hour passed and Sharlie was still on the phone, her voice strained with passion and eagerness.

"Ohmygod…" was still offered like a mark of punctuation in ways Dorsey remembered from her own youth.

Well, she's popular, thought Dorsey who was never popular and now felt intimidated by Sharlie's arrival at a social status she herself never achieved.

Maybe that will toughen her, thought Dorsey. *Already she is tougher than I ever was or will be.*

Sharlie would be 17 in a month and had a year and some change left before graduating from the same high school Dorsey once attended. That is, if Sharlie could manage to graduate. Her grades were poor and her attendance sporadic. It was a bitter truth that Dorsey's daughter was a poor student. Deeper and more despairing for Dorsey was the truth that Sharlie could not be trusted.

Time passed quickly and though Sharlie lived without a father she at least was never uprooted and moved. She met her two best friends in preschool and Sharlie's 11th grade math instructor not only remembered Sharlie's mother, but also could point out the desk where she once sat.

In the time it took Sharlie to fill the dish drainer Dorsey's mind had drifted through the years and seasons and her remembrances of Sharlie the baby, Sharlie the toddler, Sharlie at school, Sharlie scoring a goal, Sharlie getting grades, Sharlie having sleepovers, Sharlie having a period, Sharlie going to a school dance, Sharlie crushed by infatuation and, finally, Sharlie in love. Sharlie was having sex and Dorsey knew it even if it wasn't spoken. Still legally a child, Sharlie likely and already had had more sex than her mother.

"Mom…just stop it!" Sharlie shouted when Dorsey tried in a cautionary way to bring up the subject of sex, always with the thought she might be helpful.

"It's my body," said Sharlie. "It's my body now. Please…"

Sharlie's many firsts made a trail through the life of Dorsey's many postponements and what ifs. Dorsey worked hard and for long hours that paid not very much even if it was enough, barely, to support them both. A career in retail was not one flush with advancement but Dorsey's large employer provided medical insurance and modest matches for a retirement savings. Two more years would give Dorsey the status of a 20-year employee and a handful of additional company benefits including a month's paid vacation.

But she would have to get there first and Dorsey was concerned. Rumors circulated that Mervyn's was in trouble. She had noticed fewer customers the previous Christmas along with fewer sales. Everyone she knew in retail reported a slowdown. It was seasonal, she said to herself. It's a cycle. She had seen it before, though in some deeper place she worried that someone or something might take away her livelihood and with it any hope of happiness.

Dorsey now watched her daughter more carefully. After all the goofy pleasures and anxious touch points of her childhood, all its tender advances through disappointment and transgression, joyful parties and mean antagonists, good and bad teachers and, at last within reach, her graduation from high school, Sharlie appeared anxious to leave home. And while some parents might cheer this as a threshold, Dorsey's own experience was that it was a precipice. Dorsey both loved and feared her daughter in a way she also cared for and feared for herself. Her life had been hard.

And she did not want a hard life for her child. From the age of 14 Sharlie had been prescribed a progestin pill to regulate her periods. It was also an impermeable wall against pregnancy. Dorsey thought herself a strong woman and thought Sharlie's generation would be stronger still. But everything she saw suggested Sharlie and her friends were simply rougher. The fashions were more grungy but not very different and the shoes, instead of green Converse tennis shoes, were now checkered Vans. Sharlie had green streaks in her otherwise soft, brown hair, which she moussed regularly to keep it straight and unfurled. Holes in the knees of her jeans were still required and blouse collars fell to expose a shoulder. Sexual interest was everywhere on display but more directly than Dorsey remembered.

Sharlie referred at times to what she called "hook-ups" that sounded to Dorsey like a teen version of playing doctor. Boys and girls would connect casually and just for sex and just for a night, which Sharlie said had no appeal because she had a boyfriend. It was the kind of revelation that riveted Dorsey with its shock value and that reminded her how limited her own sexual experience had been. She was a single mother who at first rarely and, as her daughter grew older, never dated. There was no room in her small life, very small family and even smaller apartment for anything or anyone else.

"Who's my daddy?" Sharlie asked frequently and for years until, at last bored by her mother's terse response and refusal to engage the details, Sharlie stopped asking.

"He's gone," said Dorsey, which she thought a better answer than the one given her by her own mother. The father might be dead but Dorsey could not say what she did not know. Dorsey had asked her mother ceaselessly if she were like her father, which Sharlie had not yet asked and, Dorsey hoped, never would.

Of course if her own mother were alive she would have loved

that a grandchild was named for her. But Dorsey's mother died before Sharlie's birth, died when a winery employee fell asleep at the wheel of his truck and plowed across two lanes of highway traffic to collide with Charlotte's tiny Civic. She died instantly. The remorseful worker was charged, tried and found guilty of involuntary manslaughter and sent to jail for 18 months. The court said the worker owed Dorsey $20,000 but it might as well have been $2 million. Upon his release, the driver fled across the border. He would never pay Dorsey any of it. Dorsey thought to pursue him but, more heartbroken than angry and too busy with her baby, she let it go.

The death of her mother nearly on the eve of Sharlie's arrival left Dorsey again in a family of just two. And while Dorsey was now the matriarch and not the daughter it was still the barest family minimum. Dorsey gave birth alone at the hospital though her roommate Elma came to visit.

"I don't need to know math," Sharlie said often. "I'm going to be an actress."

"But you need to graduate," responded Dorsey.

"I want my freedom," Sharlie often shouted, exasperated with her mother's urgings and laments. "I want out of here."

"Then you'll need a diploma," answered Dorsey.

Though she loved her daughter more than life itself, Dorsey could feel the earth moving underneath Sharlie, could sense what was truly flourishing at the core of her daughter's still unassembled ambition.

One day, thought Dorsey. One day soon. It will be time. It will just be time.

4

The electrifying moments of Sharlie's young life studded the quickly passing years of Dorsey's. How long could intentions remain unfinished? Dorsey worried about her daughter. Sharlie was popular and had a closet full of beautiful clothes, many purchased by Dorsey using her employee discount at Mervyn's. Others were what Sharlie described as "loaners" from a few of her rich school buddies accustomed to wearing an outfit for a week and then tiring of it.

At some point Sharlie's beautiful loaners, comprising skirts, blouses, expensive jackets, boots and shoes, even necklaces and bracelets, filled her closet and dresser to brimming and aroused Dorsey's suspicions.

"Don't your friends ever want any of their things back?" asked Dorsey.

"They don't care when I return them. It's cool."

It was not cool. On a slow post-Easter holiday afternoon Dorsey's supervisor called her into her office.

"Police on the phone asking for you," said her supervisor. "Everything OK?"

Dorsey, immediately frantic, ignored the question and took the receiver.

"Several weeks," said the police officer at the other end of the line. "We've been on their trail. Finally got them at Macy's. Sorry. You sound surprised."

Sharlie and two of her friends had been arrested for commercial burglary.

"We'd call it shoplifting, but they've been stealing a lot and for quite awhile," said the officer. "Two girls would try on clothes then get into a fight to distract the salesgirl. The other would sneak into the dressing room to clip off the security tags. The 18-year-old…Monique…she's not saying anything. She's in a cell. But your daughter is a minor and you can come pick her up. We'll release her to you pending a court appearance."

"What then?" asked Dorsey.

"Can't say," said the officer. "It's serious and obviously premeditated. Lots of clothes and merchandise."

Sharlie was sullen on the ride home.

"How long?" asked Dorsey. "How long have you been doing this?"

"A month. Maybe two. I dunno," answered Sharlie.

"You're going to have to pay for it!" Dorsey shouted, exasperated but without any idea what she really meant.

"With what?" said Sharlie. "I don't have any money. That's the point."

It was Sharlie's best defense to imply her mother was too poor to buy enough clothes and accessories for her miserable daughter.

"Damn, Sharlie," said Dorsey. "It's a crime. You're charged with a felony."

Sharlie shrugged as if she had no agency, as if nothing that happened was her responsibility. Even the arrival of her period felt like something imposed, just like the sex imposed by her boyfriend or the expectations imposed by the two accomplices she desperately wished to impress. Another imposition, that of her disappointed mother, was to be expected.

Monique's parents were rich and needed to be. Their daughter was charged as an adult and bore the brunt of the punishment, especially since she had a previous conviction. Sharlie and her other friend, Tasha, were minors without criminal records and given the benefit of the doubt by the district attorney. In return for guilty pleas, and an agreement by each to pay back some $1800 in damages, the girls were put on probation. Dorsey was grateful Sharlie did not steal from Mervyn's though she wasn't certain Sharlie hadn't. Trust, once only a fragile consideration, was now gone entirely. Dorsey would not believe Sharlie again, not believe anything she told her unless it could be corroborated. Dorsey cashed out part of her retirement savings account to cover the repayment and court costs.

A week passed and Sharlie stopped going to school.

"You can't make me," Sharlie said one morning before burying her head in a pillow and pulling up the covers. Two such mornings passed before Dorsey could extract the truth from her daughter.

The arrest of the girls was well known at school and Monique, the rich senior and shoplifting ringleader, told everyone Sharlie had betrayed her to the cops. Threatened by Monique, Tasha agreed to confirm her version of events, leaving Sharlie the odd girl out who, despite her ephemeral popularity, had no status without the support of the girlfriends that so quickly abandoned her.

Her boyfriend, intimidated by the ensuing gossip, stopped calling.

"I can't go back," cried Sharlie. "I can't. You can't make me."

It took a day for Dorsey to make an appointment with the principal and a week to meet with a counselor.

"She says she won't be coming back," Dorsey told the counselor. "What can we do?"

"She can get her GED at the JC," said the counselor named Gloria, an obviously tired woman with little personal interest in Dorsey or her daughter.

"Or she can get a job. She just turned 17. She won't be considered truant if she doesn't go to school."

Dorsey took two afternoons off work to first, arrange with the high school for a home study program that would finish the school year. If Sharlie completed her course work, Sharlie would receive full credit. Next, she enrolled Sharlie in the JC's GED program for the fall.

"You'll be a college student," Dorsey said boldly and in way intended to convince her daughter she was stepping forward and not back. It was not convincing. Her daughter missed her friends and feared a new school, not to mention one dauntingly described as a "college."

"They have a drama department," her mother continued strategically. "You could take an acting class."

Sharlie's eyes brightened for a moment.

"Really?" she asked her mother who nodded firmly.

"But you have to complete home study," said Dorsey. "Can you do that?"

Sharlie paused and long enough for Dorsey's suddenly cold eyes to prepare her next speech and one she had rehearsed a hundred times on her way to work, in the shower, and on her pillow before falling asleep. Sharlie would have to work. Would have to take a job and likely any job. After completing her studies, Sharlie would need to support herself and, at some time earlier than later, even move out and away from her mother. In her thoughts, Dorsey already had pushed Sharlie hard beyond a shrinking circle of caring. *There will soon be a time I can't support you anymore,* Dorsey thought to herself. *I can't. I can't. And I won't.*

"Yeah, mom," answered Sharlie. "Yeah. Don't worry."

Her thoughts, just enough to quiet Dorsey's turbulent mind, were not enough to relieve her rankling resentment. Who tells a parent not to worry? A child that herself is without worries or children. Dorsey grasped that the subject of her exasperation was the total sum of her known family. There was no one but Sharlie, now and forever.

Two of Sharlie's old school chums from junior high drifted back into her life long enough to celebrate the end of her school year. Sharlie completed her class assignments and they were delivered to the school each Monday through May. The month of June burst forth via a weeklong blast of valley heat tamed at last by a summer fog. The new season arrived with a promise of more than warmth as Dorsey anticipated both her daughter's next steps and her own. Dorsey began repaying her retirement savings with an extra deposit. It was all good or at least going to be good, until it wasn't.

"I'm sorry to report to you that all Mervyn's stores are closing at the end of this year," said the manager.

His name was Morris and as Dorsey stared in shock into the other shocked faces of her fellow employees he continued talking.

"You've been a great crew," he said, stifling his own tears, which for him were the cathartic consequence of knowing the truth before all others. Dorsey noticed and wished she, too, could cry and knew eventually she would.

"I wish…well…your supervisors have information for you related to your benefits, your date of termination…yes, some of you will be staying through the end of the year…please see your supervisors first. Any questions?"

A few arms shot up. Medical insurance? Benefits? Recommendations for employment elsewhere? And one question that simply began "What the fuck…?"

"That's all," said Morris, recognizing he had reached the end of his employees' capacity to absorb both fear and grief.

Dorsey looked again into the faces surrounding hers: at least fifty and nearly all women. She considered another ruinous outcome of a business model that used women almost exclusively as its prima-ry resource. Women worked at Mervyn's and women shopped at Mervyn's. Women came and went and were, whether customers or counter clerks, all expendable.

Dorsey's longevity and experience would keep her working through the summer, at least, though her hours were reduced. The company planned another staff cut in the fall, dependent on remaining inventory. And that was the end, or at least the beginning of an end Dorsey never saw coming.

"I haven't done this before," Dorsey said to the social worker reading her application.

"I've always supported myself and my daughter. I don't expect this to last. I'll get another job."

"And who's the father?" asked the social worker named Margaret.

"Father?" asked Dorsey. "What father?"

"The father of your daughter," said Margaret. "Is he paying child support?"

"Why…no…," said Dorsey. "He's…I mean…no one knows…I mean…"

"Who is the father?" Margaret asked again.

"I can't tell you," said Dorsey. "I've never told anyone."

"Whoever he is, he most likely owes child support," said Margaret. "We'll need to look into it. If he hasn't paid anything he certainly owes something. The Department of Health and Human Services needs to get that going in order to help you. What's his name and where does he live?"

Dorsey sat flummoxed as she absorbed the return of a vague and attractive ghost. It was Kirk and though she saw him clearly she could not speak his name.

"I need some time to think about this," she said to the social worker. "I haven't seen him since …I mean…and I don't know where he lives or anything about him."

Dorsey stumbled over words and thoughts too old to be the stuff of something new. She had long ago stopped thinking of Kirk as anyone with agency over her life. Now he rose up as the phantom agent fundamental to her survival.

"Suit yourself," said Margaret. "But don't be afraid. We can help you and your daughter. If he owes it, he needs to pay it."

Dorsey left the office, aware that to get help she would have to break a trust. But it might be the only way to at last know how deeply such a trust had broken her.

5

Voices of the past shouted at Dorsey like earnest ghosts. Voices formed like the shadows in a room. She ranged daily through a bittersweet reverie as she tried at last to understand why she fell into the sex with Kirk that gave her a daughter. The experience was not a blur. She recalled specifically how Kirk arrived at her and within her. She was willing.

Of course she was willing. This was never the issue throughout many years of remembrance. Her heart had opened quickly and her body even more quickly. There was nothing to rationalize or to reconstruct or to reframe in a way that would allow Dorsey to reassure herself she was blameless. She wasn't. The odd details of the experience still aroused her: the memorable scent of his Canoe aftershave flooding her nostrils, his hands rough and firm until he found her vulva and opened her with light, slow and delicate touches she wanted never to end. He was affectionate even if his words were awkward and sappy. His voice was resonant and vibrated from his chest and against her breasts. The aggregate of her memories was irresistible and better than any fantasy Dorsey might create and she had created many.

Kirk was sweet, even considerate, but also insistent. This was endearing in the way it let Dorsey feel herself thoroughly desired. She was lovely. She was beautiful. The remembrance of Kirk, pushed so vigorously away through the passing years of her subsequent motherhood, now flowered again like a dream. And she did dream, did bring back in sleep the aura of a single hour with Kirk that had formed her destiny.

191

Now Dorsey was being told to bother Kirk, as if she just had awakened the morning after sex in his car and decided to phone him. Only it was nearly twenty years later and what would happen? How would she explain that she gave birth to his daughter and never told him? Years had passed and each year had shouted this dilemma to Dorsey until eventually she stopped hearing. Kirk's voice was always there but, in ways that mattered more, Dorsey assumed she would never hear it again.

Perhaps the Health and Human Services department wouldn't find him. And what if Dorsey refused to help? She was sorry she had mentioned a father to the caseworker, a reality she now could not withdraw. Had she said the father was unknown she might not be in trouble. But she knew the father. And if she were caught in a lie there would be no help at all, not to mention the potential for more trouble. Perjury? She had taken the terms of her sorrowful poverty into public view. She was asking her government to care for her, however briefly. Her government spoke for the people. Now her private sorrow was potentially public information. And if she lied, she would be judged. Judged and most certainly convicted.

Dorsey sat quietly at dinner and hoped vaguely for a miracle, at last asking herself why. A miracle implied redemption and not relief and, besides, she had already experienced a miracle. The miracle was her daughter.

"What's wrong, mom?" the miracle asked, at last concerned about something other than herself and concerned enough to inquire.

"You haven't touched anything on your plate."

Dorsey considered the question and, suddenly relieved to be asked, immediately wished to answer. But before speaking she realized Sharlie's question arrived as scrutiny and not compassion. And what truth Dorsey might tell about Sharlie's father likely would leave both of them to struggle with too many inexplicable reckonings and regrets.

"There's a problem at work," Dorsey said finally. "My hours are being cut. The stores aren't doing well. I may need to find another job."

"Does that mean I can't go to the college?" Sharlie asked fearfully.

Dorsey was not surprised that Sharlie's first concern was for herself. A parent might resent what appeared to be a grown child's ingratitude. But children weren't born to graciously give or receive. They were born to survive.

"Oh no, hon," said Dorsey, her words punched through the troublesome awareness of her own pain and uncertainty.

"It's paid for," she lied. "You're fine. We're going to be fine."

Dorsey sat again in Margaret's office at the Department of Health and Human Services. A week had passed.

"He doesn't know he's the father," said Dorsey.

"Then it will be a surprise," said Margaret.

"What if he says he isn't the father?" asked Dorsey.

"We'll do a genetic test. Easy. Swabs of spit from his cheek, your cheek and your daughter's cheek. Painless. We'll know in a week."

"What if he refuses to take a test?" asked Dorsey.

"We can compel him. But maybe it won't come to that. Maybe he'll be OK with all this. You aren't the first mom in this situation."

"How much money does he owe?"

"Depends on his income," said Margaret. "There's likely a limit on how far back we can go from the date you file. We have a formula based on your income history and his. He won't have to pay it all at once."

"I…this is so hard…there's nothing I've ever needed from him. I've tried…"

Dorsey began to cry.

"We won't let anything bad happen," said Margaret. "If he's broke and bad we won't let him anywhere near you or your daughter. But it's the law. If you want help from our office we need to assess his ability to help you. It's not his fault he doesn't know. But you aren't to blame for needing help now. It's the right thing."

"What do you need from me?," said Dorsey.

"You know his name? You know where he went to high school?

To college? We know he once lived in Santa Rosa. We'll find him."

"And then?" asked Dorsey.

"When we locate him, we'll send a letter. If he's like most men in this situation he'll phone me right away. I'll be in touch."

Dorsey stood and left.

"I think I'd like to work this summer," Sharlie said to her mother as she peeled carrots for a stew.

"Doing what?" asked Dorsey.

"Dunno," answered Sharlie. "I've never worked."

"What would you like to do?" asked Dorsey.

"Act," Sharlie answered sharply. "Be an actress."

"Doesn't pay well," said Dorsey. "But there are some local theaters groups. Maybe they need some help. You could volunteer."

"I want to make money," answered Sharlie. "I'm tired of being poor."

Her words quietly shattered Dorsey whose love for her daughter did not depend on any capacity or strength and could not be assessed by what she could or could not spend. Now Dorsey heard from Sharlie an embryonic plea for independence and freedom from what she likely saw as an indigent existence with her mother. Sharlie longed for a life lived on the wings of a promise and one not constrained by the fears of a persistently invasive poverty. And from where did this urge grow? From within a life lived only with a mother; a mother that by her own assessment locked herself down, lived in panic, and seemed notably diminutive and feckless.

Sharlie wanted things others had and she did not. And, of course, to be much better than her mother, a goal that at first angered Dorsey who immediately wished her daughter a rough road of rugged and difficult obstacles that would teach her the limiting truths of life. Yet Dorsey was linked to her daughter by an umbilical flow of blood that was, like a constantly running river, the purest course of unmediated love. It was only Dorsey's idea that life was limiting and not her daughter's. And in this sense Dorsey had raised Sharlie well, raised her to want more than she had and to at least imagine how to have it.

"We found him," said Margaret when Dorsey answered her phone.

"Where?" asked Dorsey.

"Washington D.C.," answered Margaret. "He's an attorney. He's cooperative. But he wants a genetic test before going any farther. He was pretty blown away but he remembers you."

"What do I do now?" asked Dorsey.

"We'll do the test. We'll need a saliva swab from you and from your daughter. He'll register for a test in D.C. We'll have the results in a week."

"Then I have to tell my daughter," said Dorsey.

"You'll take her to the clinic and get her swabbed. Tell her what you like but the truth is probably best. That is, unless this guy is not her father."

Dorsey thought of Kirk's last touch, his arms around her at her doorstep, and his one last kiss, the kind of deep touch that can make either lovers or strangers. It was the memory that had frightened her in Margaret's office, her memory of bodies that had made more than love. Dorsey, for Sharlie's entire life, had kept the secret of Kirk's unknowable intent. Now Kirk was to know. It was an essential truth Dorsey never expected to tell and that she now wondered if she could bear.

6

The clinician spoke with a voice of sonorous snow, her words covered and cold.

"Open please," she said as Dorsey and Sharlie together opened their mouths and the clinician swept a cotton swab behind their gums.

"A germ going around at work," Dorsey had told her daughter.

Sharlie had no reason to suspect anything else largely because her mother had conspired with a clinic staff experienced in creating ruses for a paternity test. No child needed to know an unknown father existed if, in fact, he did not.

A tribal life was relational and did not involve people who simply came and went. Sharlie was entitled to a place in life from which she would not be abandoned. She had her mother. But her mother was currently a woman acutely aware of her history in ways Sharlie was not. Dorsey accepted the blame for a crush that had become a crash, a momentary fulfillment she had not expected. She had usually addressed the expectations of others before knowing her own and so was usually unprepared for all tempting interruptions. For so much of her childhood her libido was inaccessible.

Now Sharlie wanted to leap forward, wanted to seize the world. And how would Dorsey facilitate this? Her income had fallen, her capacity was diminished by fear and failure, her own mother died without leaving any legacy and Dorsey had no partner, despite the erratic presence of the few lovers she never allowed close enough to understand or to help.

A week passed before Margaret phoned and asked Dorsey to come into the office.

"Test is positive," said Margaret directly. "He is your daughter's father."

"Now what?" asked Dorsey.

"He wants to do the right thing," Margaret reported. "That's what he says. And he wants to speak with you. Are you OK with that? Could he phone you?"

"Yeah…" said Dorsey. "But what's the right thing?"

"That he pays support," said Margaret. "That he covers at least some past support. You are entitled to this. Beyond that, he may want to meet his daughter. If that's a problem, we might be able to help you. We could arrange a supervised visit. What have you told your daughter about her father?"

Dorsey's fingers trembled as she imagined Sharlie's reaction to a revelation devoid of either context or connection.

"Nothing," said Dorsey. "I've never said he was dead…or even alive. I've just not said anything. And Sharlie stopped asking a long time ago. Why would I want to tear up his life with my complications?"

"Wrong question," said Margaret. "Why have you made your own life so difficult? Why have you never until now sought out the father of your daughter?"

"I was afraid," Dorsey confessed, though these words only scratched at the surface of an ocean of family mystery. And the notion of family itself was a mystery for Dorsey, families of blood-fused links that spread in all directions: up and down, forward and back, big and small, never and forever, and that were populated by real people: living and dead, forgotten and remembered, loved and hated but always here and there, always present somewhere as members of an immortal tribe.

"Would you like to talk about this with someone?" asked Margaret. "I can recommend a therapist. Some people get a lot of support…"

Dorsey shook her head and held up her hand as if to wave off even the hint of Margaret's suggestion.

"No," Dorsey responded, at first quietly and then, surprised by the passion in her voice, she repeated "No. No. NO. NO. NO!"

"I know that voice," the man said at the other end. "Hello, Dorsey."

Dorsey knew the voice speaking to her. It was Kirk. She would know it wherever she heard it.

Dorsey also said hello and waited for a sudden silence to dissolve, which it did not. It would wait until it was filled.

"I hope this is a good time," said Kirk and then he waited.

"Yes," said Dorsey. "As good as any."

"Before we talk further, I want you to know I'm going to help you," said Kirk. "I'm going to help you and our daughter."

The words "our daughter" shook Dorsey from a depth of feeling she never imagined.

"I'm so sorry…I mean I never…" Dorsey sought immediately the protection of effacement. She held no one accountable.

"*I'm* sorry," said Kirk. "I must not have made it easy for you to talk with me about what was happening. I was off to college, you know. That's all I thought about."

"You were always kind to me," said Dorsey. "You were always

someone I thought of as a good friend. I think I wanted to spare you the consequences of a choice that was mine to make."

Kirk's voice choked perceptively.

"We're beyond that now," said Kirk. "We don't need to look back. Let's look ahead. Let's see what's possible. I'd like to meet our daughter. And help her. She's family. Can we do that?"

Who was Dorsey to argue? She had allowed years of complacent effort to become a hollow apparition of apparent living. Her life had clustered like a fungus into an aggregate of spores waiting to erupt. It was time. It was just time.

"Sure," she said.

"What's next?" she asked. "What do you need?"

"No, Dorsey," said Kirk. "What do you need?"

Who had ever before asked Dorsey that question? A need existed only as something drawn from her and never as something she might express or fulfill.

"Some help with Sharlie," she answered in a way that surprised her. "She has hopes and we have plans."

"Of course," answered Kirk. "I'd like to meet her. Would that be OK?"

"When?" asked Dorsey.

"Next week," answered Kirk. "I'm coming out to see my folks."

"OK," said Dorsey after a wary pause.

Things were moving quickly. Dorsey and Kirk agreed to meet a week from Saturday in the afternoon at a nearby park. Dorsey would bring Sharlie. If the visit went well they would all go to dinner together. It would give Dorsey time to tell her daughter about her father and to prepare her for the meeting.

"She's a lovely young woman," Dorsey said. "She has your bright blue eyes."

"They're still blue," said Kirk.

"We do have some business to do, Dorsey," Kirk said finally. "I need to send you some money."

If Dorsey gave him her bank account number he would make a deposit. "It will cover some of what I owe you," said Kirk. "It will get us started."

Started with what? wondered Dorsey. Was her life now to be somehow conjoined with Kirk's? He seemed to offer a sovereign assurance that aroused in Dorsey an anxious notion that nothing was assured. It felt to her like a bittersweet opportunity and not a reunion. Kirk dated her only once. Yet their lives continued to work under all the surfaces of passing time. And it was a real life—Sharlie's—that now moved surfaces into place and altered all destinies. She gave him her account number.

It was a Tuesday morning that a notification from Dorsey's bank reported a recent deposit to her checking account. She entered her password to see the new balance and, after checking and checking again, phoned her bank to affirm what she saw.

"It's a bit more than what he's on the hook for," said Margaret when Dorsey at last got her on the phone.

"About a hundred thousand sounds right. He rounded it up, which is nice since he's also going to pay $3600 a month through your daughter's 18th birthday. Listen, he's a very successful attorney. And he was straight with us. Didn't hide a thing. So don't worry. He can afford it. He knows the law. In any event, you don't need us anymore. So good luck!"

Dorsey was left to accept things as they were. And for a moment she disregarded the single instant in time and space that had so preoccupied her for years and, instead, looked ahead and beyond. There was no big picture and no view clear enough to offer praise or assign blame. There was neither good nor bad, only what at one time had been necessary.

7

"My father?" asked Sharlie, directing the question to no one in particular though her mother sat before her.

"Of course I have a father," Sharlie said, repeating her mother's first words to her. "Everyone has a father. But why haven't...I mean...why now?"

Dorsey told her daughter the truth as far as she knew it and as much as she thought she could tell. But Sharlie wasn't satisfied. It made no sense that the natural state of her mother's mind was amnesia, particularly around the subject of Sharlie's paternity.

"Why haven't I known?" Sharlie asked apprehensively.

The question was only the first and Dorsey had only one answer.

"Because he hasn't known," she said. "Neither of you have known. It has been my secret."

Dorsey felt undone and also relieved. It was a mess and only Dorsey knew the facts of her own life. But as she spoke them to her daughter, Dorsey had no explanation of her motives, either for their living or telling. And while her daughter was entitled, in fact very much needed, to know the truth of her life, the moment of Sharlie's creation was none of her business. Dorsey's daughter was born from an act of attraction and affection and not from an act of language or logic or any careful sifting of ingredients. She was alive. Her life was a work in progress and one already far beyond the grasp of Dorsey and, more likely, her father.

"And his name is… Kirk?" Sharlie asked. "Kirk what?"

"It's just so fucked up," Sharlie suddenly shouted. "I'm a goddamned bastard. Why? Why? Wouldn't he marry you?"

"He didn't know," said Dorsey. "I didn't know until he was gone Why do you think I put you on the pill?"

She said it crisply to hide her exasperation

And it was a spontaneous comment but one that hit its mark. Sharlie had been free to manage without consequence the same sexual impulse that had drawn her mother ineluctably into pregnancy.

"He wants to help us," added Dorsey, ignoring her daughter's sudden anger. "Sweetheart, I know this is a shock and I know I haven't been truthful with you. I can't say why, just that we are here and he's turned up."

"And I'm going to meet him?" Sharlie asked.

"He'll be here next week," said Dorsey. "It's been arranged. He wants very much to meet you. This is as big a surprise for him as it is for you."

"Yeah, but will he like me?" asked Sharlie.

"Of course he'll like you," said Dorsey with a mother's assured and presumably reassuring pride.

"Will you like him?"

She is his daughter. He knows it.

It was Dorsey's thought as she asked Rick and Sharlie to stand together while she took their picture. Fifteen minutes into their first meeting together and Dorsey was left to marvel at the resemblance of her daughter to Kirk. Sharlie was not tall but she was taller than Dorsey and standing next to Kirk she could see why. Sharlie had the same strong torso and long legs of her father. More evident were Sharlie's radiant blue eyes that were exactly those of Kirk. Father and daughter also shared an obviously high forehead and widow's peak of sandy, brown hair. The resemblance was an irresistible ice-breaker and a wordless affirmation that like a tribal talisman held them all suddenly and quietly together. Sharlie grasped immediately this was not a fiction. In fact, it was the best of one world without the worst of another. It was the pleasure of a new parent without a history, a parent with whom love might be learned rather than earned.

"I have something for you," Kirk said to Sharlie who now listened quietly to the words of the new man in her life.

He handed her an envelope.

Sharlie opened it to unfold two sheets of construction paper covered in pencil and crayon drawings of a house and a dog and a cat and featuring the ovoid, smiling faces of two young girls.

*For our new sister…*words printed by one and scripted by the other.

Sister? The word poured its attribution deep into Sharlie. I am a sister? The word was confounding but also riveting by what it said about what was both ahead and also behind. Like her mother Sharlie so far had lived a life with the barest of roots or tendrils. Now she held tangible evidence of a larger and wider family.

"Lila and Jasmine," said Kirk. "Lila is seven and Jasmine is eleven. They want to meet you. Maybe you'd come visit us this summer?"

He asked the question easily as if knew his place in the world and knew it so well and held it with such confidence he could share himself without giving anything away.

Kirk looked to Dorsey.

"My parents don't live far from you," he said directly. "Same big house off Piner. I've spoken with them. They'd love to meet another granddaughter."

Dorsey regarded the way Kirk continued to engage Sharlie with the markers of relationship though the thought brought Dorsey nearly to tears.

He likes Sharlie, thought Dorsey. *He wants her.* It was as far as she could go and far enough. To go any farther would be to fall back again and to wonder if, at another point of arrival Kirk might have wanted Dorsey. But she knew the answer. Knew it well enough to never again consider the question.

Grown and regrown from an uprooted past, Dorsey accepted that she never much believed in the prospect of happiness. Certainly not the kind she saw in movies or on television or read about in books. These were joys that never happened in real life, and certainly not in hers.

And yet here she was, putting her daughter on a plane to go visit an apparently willing and loving father hatched into existence by a frightening emergency. Dorsey's despair and panic were the parents of the moment that forced her into acknowledging and then identifying him. And that moment was like the birth of a star: a big bang that set into motion a vast new creation.

"I'll phone you when I get in," said Sharlie as she waited to enter the line for boarding.

"Kirk will meet you," said Dorsey. "Don't worry about phoning. You get settled and when it feels right…well…"

"OK," said Sharlie as she turned to leave. "OK. I'll see you in three weeks. I love you."

"Love you too, darling," answered Dorsey as she embraced her anxious daughter. "You have a good time."

Dorsey's words were both a blessing and a release. There was something lurking in the past that the future would make clear. But that there was a past, one rooted in the present, was both disturbing and a relief. As she left the airport Dorsey thanked misfortune for all its gifts, especially the ones made possible by a once frightening necessity.

Kirk's largess had purchased for Dorsey a new panorama of choices. She could take a year away from work; even go back to school to learn a new skill. Accounting interested her. She always had been good with numbers. And she could put money down on a small home and pay off a mortgage instead of paying rent though Kirk's father, a prominent realtor, told her to wait because a hard time was coming and home prices likely would fall. And she could see Sharlie through school and pay for her classes.

What Dorsey held inside was an inheritance, along with the ghosts that forged it. And what she now gave to Sharlie was a continued haunting. The dead baby that was Dorsey's first significant ancestor might have been the founder of this new feast. It was the glowing relic of relationship that held Dorsey in the flow of blood through time and space and that found at last for her own daughter a safe and welcoming destination. There was no blame to assess or praise to offer and nothing that was either good or bad. There was only what was real and now simply necessary.

YOUR BEST SHOT

"You may find yourselves confusing photography with life," Miles said to the students sprawled several seats apart from one another in the cavernous Santa Rosa Junior College art studio.

"I can help you with that," Miles added. "We can help each other."

There was little Miles confused with life. And photography was the least of it. He had been a photographer as long as he could remember. For more than twenty years photography paid Miles at least enough of a living to support his place within two marriages, both similar in their failures though for different reasons. Now he was at a crossroads: too old to change his profession but too young to abandon it.

Teaching income was a critical component of his survival but the college was closing down its photography program at the end of the year, the art department unwilling to pay for the replacement of a wet darkroom with the computers needed for a digital one. Over the years enrollment had dropped steadily and, though a minimum of ten students was required for any class, the dean had given Miles a break by letting him hold his last class with only seven.

"A little about myself," Miles said to the students, four women and three men widely varied in their ages and dress. All watched him closely for clues to what might be in store. Miles thought they were staring at his balding head or the unruly salt and pepper beard he had grown to square his otherwise moony face. Without a beard Miles' head would appear as spherical as a billiard ball. Miles sat on a stool to rise above the class though the bowled incline of his legs thrust forward a budding belly.

"Photojournalist for 15 years," said Miles. "Before that I had a studio that supported me with commercial assignments while I created my own fine art prints. I've brought some of my work."

An important element of Miles' class was the sharing and critique of a student's photographs. His students knew this from reading the syllabus but Miles offered his images first as if to say if I can expose myself, so can you.

He did not tell them this was the last class he would ever teach, that his studio business barely broke even and finally failed altogether during the Great Recession of 2008, or that his career as a photojournalist was a stint as a part-time photographer for a weekly newspaper and that it lasted only 18 months and not 15 years and ended when he showed up drunk to an ad shoot for one of the paper's biggest advertisers.

Nor did he tell them he was alone now and that no one missed him and that at the end of the semester he would mail in his class grades and fly to a Mexican village where for three days he would drink Tequila before at last plunging his hopelessly inebriated self into the warm, welcoming Sea of Cortez like a condemned prisoner dropped from a scaffold. It would not be suicide but, rather, a homicide. He wasn't killing himself. He was killing someone who had run out of reasons to live. Without any more life there would be no more confusion.

Miles opened a black portfolio box that rested on his desk and lifted from it a small stack of mounted prints. He set them in the chalk tray of the studio's wall-length blackboard and spread them out for the students to view. Four were black and white images and two were color. They offered varying views of sky, trees, people strolling streets in a public market, and an image of the legs and lower torso of a nude woman stepping through a dark forest. The last image was a double exposure that portrayed the woman's rapid, almost furious steps against a still, dark background.

"Souped the print myself. Enlarger was an old Besseler…three trays…the works." said Miles. His voice trailed off for a moment until he realized no one seemed to understand him.

"Took two hours to make a good print. You could do this on a computer in five minutes."

"Can we use the darkroom?" said one of the students, a young man who raised his hand but spoke before he was called.

"You'd want to?" Miles asked incredulous.

"Who else here is shooting with film?" asked Miles.

Another hand shot up from the back of the studio.

"You guys know Jeremy?" Miles asked.

Both nodded.

"Jeremy has the photo store in old town," Miles explained to the other students. "Makes these stunning portraits in tintype. Sold him all my film cameras five years ago. Loves those old processes. So are you guys going to be working in…?"

Miles made a gesture with his thumb as if he were cranking the film advance lever of an old camera.

The man and woman nodded.

"Well, that's a surprise. But I guess it shouldn't be. It's art. And we're all about art."

Miles' state of mind was perpetually informed by the history of the photograph. He was drawn particularly and irresistibly to the several and sequentially stark images made by Alexander Gardner and his assistant Tim O'Sullivan of the hanging of the Lincoln assassination conspirators. A large, slow camera caught the execution in excruciating detail that still shook Miles with its definitive revelations of context, expression and reality. Photography in 1865 was barely a quarter-century old and the stories it could tell were in that year just beginning to emerge as the only true ones. It was why Miles included in his class a brief history of photography and its many processes, including the fabled tintype, which Jeremy had mastered as a medium for fashionable high-end portraits.

Miles always wondered how Jeremy made any money selling film, paper and chemicals out of a retail store and in a time when digital thoroughly ruled. So profoundly ubiquitous was the digital image that it was possible if not likely that more photographs were made during the past year than had ever been previously produced.

It was the tintype business that kept Jeremy afloat. That's what

Miles concluded. Tintypes were beautiful, richly sepia in color and the essence of an old process that could reveal much more detail and warmth than most modern photographs. A tintype was a work of art. And if Miles believed anything, it was that a photograph, whatever it portrayed, was evidence of an interpretive and artful act.

Miles wasn't drunk yet. He had downed two drinks before class but not enough alcohol to be obvious to people who did not yet know him. Tired of talking, Miles asked his students to introduce themselves.

"I'm trying to get back to making art," said Sarah, a woman Miles judged to be about his age, somewhere around fifty. "My husband died last year. He left me his camera."

Miles lowered his eyes and nodded in a way to appear empathic.

"I'm into unburying the buried," said a young man named Mack. "I want to make my images into artifacts." He was at least twenty and wore a leather jacket, his outstretched forearms mapped with colorful tattoos. He was the one who raised his hand and said he shot with film.

"We'll see what we can do," said Miles wearily.

He had heard this before.

"Leslie," said the next student. "I'm a poet."

Everyone is a poet, thought Miles.

"Do you write poetry with a camera?" he asked.

"I make poetry and then I make photos," said Leslie. "You'll see."

Gerald was an older man who wore a bow tie. *At last, someone older than I,* thought Miles.

"I collect photos," said Gerald. "I have a Weston and a couple of prints by Duane Michaels."

Miles awoke from his incipient headache.

"Where'd you get those?" Miles asked.

"I collect photos," Gerald firmly repeated.

"Do you make photos?" Miles asked again.

"Of course," said Gerald, sounding impatient. "I'm an authority on photography. My work is inspired by f64."

"Know the group well," responded Miles. "One of the great, old schools."

Miles did not look forward to teaching Gerald, whose attitude suggested he had nothing to learn.

Marcie Rivers was a teenage girl who wore blue jeans and an olive green sweatshirt. She was ebullient and attractive and Miles had been watching her.

"I photograph myself," she said boldly, even as the rest of the students laughed.

"Hey…" said Miles quieting the class.

"You mean like Francesca Woodman?" he asked.

"Who?" asked Marcie.

Miles waited a moment and smiled.

"Welcome to the class, Marcie," he said.

Another young man named Fernando said he was the son of an immigrant and had begun photographing his family and friends but also laborers working in the vineyards. He recently photographed a confrontation between cops and strikers and was beaten by the cops.

"Didn't get my camera," he said. "They're bastards. I want to bust their asses with my pictures. The daily ran one of my photos."

Miles raised his fist in a faux gesture of solidarity.

The last student sat at the back of the room and Miles, who first thought it was a woman, quickly realized he could not easily ascertain a gender. The student was dressed in overalls and a red checkered shirt and said "Mort" when Miles asked for a name. Mort had also raised a hand when Miles asked about film.

"I use an old Yashica," said Mort in a voice husky and assertive. "Shoot 120 square. I photograph my world, from the bathroom to the commute. It ain't easy. I want it to be easier."

"What's hard about it?" Miles asked, hoping to learn more about Mort.

"Focus," said Mort. "It's a fucking bitch."

Miles asked everyone to bring their favorite photo to next week's class. He then gave a short lecture on the history of photography, passing in a half-hour through more than a hundred slides that flowed like a flattening curve over a century and a half of camera work. When the lights went up Miles noticed his two younger students had left.

"Last class, Johnny," said Miles as he lifted his double bourbon on the rocks and toasted the bartender at Louie's.

"Cheers," said Johnny offering the kindness inspired by sales and the affirming toast of a reliable tipper.

In a half-hour Miles downed three more doubles and before midnight could not stand to leave.

"Call me a cab," Miles mumbled to Johnny who was already on the phone. "And what do I owe? Hell, who cares? Keep the change."

Miles pushed three twenty-dollar bills across the bar.

"You're covered," said Johnny. "Need help on the way out?"

Miles shook his head as he tried not to fall off his stool. He could barely see in front of him, which was a familiar situation. He too frequently took the shriveled limits of his own field of vision to be the true limits of the world.

2

Miles thought he was clever and jabbered thoughtlessly. It was too early in the morning to make any sense and Fred listened at his end of the phone, listened and waited.

"It's probably the booze talking…" Miles at last confessed. "But I'm really not up for this now."

Miles chuckled but Fred did not.

"Sounds like you've fallen off the wagon," Fred said.

He did not sound sympathetic.

"Will you be there tonight?" he asked.

"Do I have a choice?" asked Miles.

"There's always a choice," said Fred. "Always a choice between living and dying."

Fred could not know it was a choice Miles already had made.

The meeting was the weekly gathering of a chapter of Alcoholics Anonymous and Fred Corn was Miles' sponsor. Fred had been sober for eleven years, six months and 17 days. Miles still wasn't sober.

"I'll be there," said Miles.

He promised.

"OK," said Fred. "There's no shame. We'll just get started again. Take care of yourself, buddy."

Miles Galbreath had a Scottish name and an uncertain history. He was curious about his origins but had only someone else's word about what they were. And that person, an uncle that was keeper of the family flame, was long dead, his photo albums, old family letters and press clippings scattered along with his ashes into the wind of an angry ex-spouse's denial of time.

Like Miles, Uncle Martin had been alienated from his wife and children. At his death he was not missed by anyone but Miles. The artifacts that might have told the story of Miles' family no longer existed. Miles was barely a teenager when he lost his parents in a mysterious accident. No one spoke of it but Miles later learned his father was drunk and driving. Uncle Martin cared for Miles while enduring the antagonisms grown from his own painful divorce. It was for Miles a rehearsal of an agony he also would experience and not once, but twice. Love's loss lingered and in the life of Miles it was a painful anchor so deep no amount of drink could float or free it.

Later after a breakfast of eggs and ginger ale at a downtown café, Miles sat on a bench in a nearby park.

"I no longer need to care," Miles said to himself.

The freedom to plan his death was exhilarating. And the time after his death likely would be identical to the time before he was born and also just as long. He would not be missed. An estranged son disappeared a decade before and had never returned. If he could find his son, Miles thought he might leave him his photographs. He would leave his savings, or what was left of it, to Fred.

But that morning, while rolling out of his headache and into a shower, it had occurred to Miles he could spend the last days of his life sober. If he could decide to end his life certainly he could decide how to live what was left of it. He did not remember the last time he had been without a drink for even a day. His alcohol addiction was way older than his photography. Yet he had had many drinks every day and had not made a single photograph in more than two years. It was one thing to wonder how long he might go without a drink. It was another to know actually how long he could. It was a challenge that, under the influence of a dizzying vertigo and a hollow, aching gut, he wanted immediately to assume. There was pain in life but there was pain in drink. And the pain Miles saw in the faces of others he too often recognized as his own.

"I'm afraid to ask you," said Fred as he waited with Miles for the meeting to begin. "But I'm your sponsor, so here goes. In fact, I'm not going to ask you. I'm going to tell you."

"Tell me what?" asked Miles.

"You need to do a hundred in a hundred," said Fred. "A hundred meetings in a hundred days. I'll help you. You can do two a day for a while. But you need to make these meetings, man. Hell, there's a goddamn meeting practically every waking hour within a 20-mile radius. But you've got to go, pal. It just isn't going to work if you don't lean in, if you don't make sobriety your constant and primary goal."

For a man whose current goal was to die, Miles was surprised to feel himself drawn to Fred's challenge. He would need to attend a meeting or meetings every day for more than three months. It was a long time but not as long as the time Miles expected to live before he died. Miles thought he could do that even if he had no idea what it would prove. Condemned prisoners did it all the time, waited sober for months, even years, before they were executed. Though Miles knew from his obsessive research of Gardner's execution photos that Mary Surratt, the only woman on the gallows, began sobbing before her execution and was reputedly fitted with a hood soaked in brandy.

Miles thought he could do it. If sobriety were a choice, he might find the challenge exhilarating in a way that itself could make him high. He had heard Fred talking at times about being "high" on sobriety. The hundred meeting commitment would keep Miles sober and that was enough. There were reasons why meetings were essential to sobriety and he was curious to know why.

"You're not a surprise to anyone," said Fred. "You're just another dude trying to make his way all by himself. But you aren't alone. That's what meetings are about."

Miles looked far into the shadows forming at the doorway of the small room where others gathered for the evening's meeting. *An hour a day,* he thought. *Sure. I've done it. I can do it again. It won't matter. It won't hurt. I'm a walking ghost. What do I have to lose?*

For a moment Miles beheld a bare glimmer of truth, until he looked again and saw only himself and a host of anxious uncertainties.

"Hello, everyone," he said when his turn came around. "I'm Miles. And I'm an alcoholic."

"Hello Miles," answered everyone.

Miles stared at the photos aligned and supported by the chalkboard tray of his classroom. He would have to think of something positive to say about each of them. And it would be hard. The photos were shit, he thought. He was irritated and, despite attending seven AA meetings in four days, felt close to exploding. He had not had a drink in nearly a week, enough by itself to provoke his suicide. Someone had told him at a meeting that he would never kill himself while intoxicated because once dead Miles would not be able to drink anymore. It was a test, of course. And Miles might be able to manage it. He took a deep breath.

"Interesting use of light," he said of the widow's underexposed photo of a cluster of orange poppies spread through a wide field.

"It's where we scattered Tim's ashes," said Sarah.

Miles swallowed and moved on.

"And what's this?" Miles asked, looking at a large black and white print with its human subjects thrown completely out of focus and swallowed in a pattern of scratch marks that seemed deliberately etched into the photograph's emulsion.

"It's the truth," said Mack. "It's the verity of our life experience. Memory is a blur and the markings signify an effort to obliterate it."

"But I'm drawn to your subjects," said Miles. "What if I want to know more about them?"

"You can't," snapped Mack. "That's the point."

Another photo featured a burst of flowers framed against an azure sky and printed on a standard sheet of photo paper with enough room left below the image for two hand-scribbled verses of a poem entitled "Natural causes."

"The poet," said Miles. "That's right. You're the poet and photos make your poetry."

"They're a part of it," answered Leslie. "But not the whole part. I make the picture first. Then I write the poem."

Gerald had brought the largest photo, a 13x19 inch color print that was technically perfect though the subject, a rocky seascape, might have come out of a travel brochure. Even in its technical perfection it was a notably unoriginal treatment and something Miles had seen a thousand times.

"Have you done commercial work?" Miles asked politely.

"Never," answered Gerald. "I'm an artist."

It was Miles' experience that no one was an artist until someone else said they were.

Next was an exuberant and vertical image in black and white featuring the nude blur of a young woman as she moved swiftly down a long hallway. The photo was taken from behind, the subject's legs and butt highlighted as they rose up in a wild leap.

"It's me," said Marcie. "It's my life. I'm always in a hurry."

"Photography can tell us important things about ourselves," said Miles.

It was bullshit and he knew it.

Fernando produced the most comprehensible image; an 11x17 color print of a phalanx of cops rushing a Mexican farm laborer carrying a protest sign during a rally at a local vineyard. Fernando had used a telephoto to frame a cop's angry face while in the foreground the protester, struggling to regain his balance, thrust the sign into the air.

"This is photojournalism," said Miles. "It's another kind of art and it's profoundly important."

He reminded his students they would all participate in an assignment in May when they would photograph the local Cinco de Mayo celebration.

The last photo was Mort's. It was a cigar box. Mort stood and opened the box to reveal a photograph pasted inside. The photo was a photo of another photo inside a cigar box. The photo featured an interior view taken from outside a window and that showed details of a bedroom: a rug, clothes thrown over a chair, and an unmade bed.

"What's this?" asked Miles, stunned by the assemblage.

"It's my life," said Mort. "My life inside the box."

<h1 style="text-align:center">3</h1>

Being aroused was another way for Miles to think about being high. Without alcohol he was also without sleep. He ranged around his one bedroom flat in the evenings, often talking to himself in a loud voice, giving instructions and admonitions until very late when, with no will to sleep, he threw on a jacket and walked outside where he wandered, sometimes for blocks, in the tempting, threatening darkness of his distressed neighborhood.

Miles once lived on a hill, roaming once through a warm, spacious cavern of a home with wide, ethereal views of distant cities. It lasted a few years until his second divorce. Along with losing another wife and a big house he also lost an adolescent son in a subsequent war of parental loyalties. The son, no longer a child, was a casualty of the final ruined marriage of Miles' inattentive life. From within his delicate and provisional sobriety, Miles relived the facts of his many daunting losses and took personal responsibility for them all.

"You have quite a camera there," Miles told the widow. "You can do just about anything with it."

"That's the point," said Sarah. "I don't know how to do anything. And I just want to understand how to do something."

Miles' student had sent him an e-mail asking to meet for coffee. She wanted help understanding how to use her late husband's digital camera, an iteration of one of Canon's advanced models. Sarah was waiting for Miles when he arrived. She was a handsome woman, near Miles' age, and slightly corporeal in appearance but not in any way fat. She dressed casually for class but today wore a pleated wool skirt and long-sleeved aqua blue blouse that strengthened her upper body with its flourish of color. She had highlighted her eyebrows and applied to her lips a light, rouge gloss.

Was she saying something? Miles wondered. *Saying something to me?*

It was easy for Miles to draw conclusions. He was without alcohol and also suddenly without worry. His typically melancholy stupors were now replaced by surges of feeling that could grow completely out of his control. He liked Sarah, though he was more pressingly attracted to Marcie, the young student whom he had seen photographed naked running down a hall. Miles indulged the comforting thought that he might be attractive to Sarah.

"There are only three essential settings on any camera," said Miles. "They are focus, aperture and shutter speed. Each is critical to your image and if you can't decide what to do…well, this camera will decide for you. There's nothing wrong with that. But I think you want to go farther. You want to control the image. So I must ask, what do you want to do?"

"It was Geoffrey's camera," said Sarah. "I get some comfort from holding it and using it. But I want to make it mine."

The camera was a fetish of her late husband but also a foil for moving beyond him and for linking Sarah with a life after death. Miles tried to imagine how the widow might wish to live when all Miles wanted was to die.

"Photography is a way to document our way of seeing," said Miles. "Can you tell me what you like to look at? What you hope to see? What you want to show others?"

Sarah sat for a moment as if the question rested as an object on the table.

"Patterns…like the structures of leaves and stones," Sarah ruminated. "Or colors. I saw a clothesline on the way over here, brightly colored clothing blowing in the wind. Looked like a prism of fabrics. I like to look at people. But not if they are looking at me."

"You can let the camera work for you," said Miles. He took her camera and set the function dial to Program.

"You point and look. For now, you can let the camera just catch what you see. Program will do a lot of the thinking for you but also allow you to change some settings."

As Miles showed Sarah how to control the camera's basic functions he heard in the conversation his effort to be soothing and soliciting and to offer her some acknowledgment on which she might build. He was surprised to feel choking surges of sympathy for her loss while also feeling attracted to her. And he was attracted to everyone now, so sexually aroused without the comfortably numbing effects of drink. He felt pushed nearly out of control by his highly visual assessment of all things.

"Photographic art is a kind of handing off to others," said Miles. "You hand off the expression of feelings you've experienced with a hope they might become infectious."

Miles left the café and the widow, fighting hard to suppress any prompt of allure and knowing how useless any attachments were on the way to dying. *I'm like some fucking teenager,* Miles said to himself. *I'm horny all the time and utterly without discrimination.* Though something did matter and as the idea emerged he began to visualize a legacy. Miles could leave something of value with all his students. He could bestow encouragement and insight. He could disappear but they would grow.

As a dying drinker, Miles now imagined himself a cosmic phenomenon. He moved through space and could see for light years the uselessness of consolation. But while consolation was no longer crucial to his already ruined life, it might have important value to others.

There was no God. But there was alcohol that for so long had transported him into the supremacy he maintained with some living out of his own depressing destiny. Drinking had replaced art and now that he did not drink, he was perturbed and irritated by the challenges presented by creation, both his own and what he had at one time hoped to take from the world.

One Sunday after an early and red-eyed AA meeting, Miles drove to the coast with his Canon Rebel and a long zoom lens. He congratulated himself for remembering to charge both his camera and its back-up battery. The weather was predicted to be clear but windy, typical for mid-March. The sun would set after five.

Miles patrolled the bluffs, at first photographing surges of surf and the shadowed patterns formed among large rocks. He framed a plein air painter in front of his easel at the edge of a gulch. He shuffled through dunes to capture streaks in the sand made by the wind. He found the outstretched body of a young dead seal, its black empty eye-sockets forming an expression of ghostly surprise. Before sunset he came upon a man and woman dancing naked on a distant, empty shore. They did not see him and he snapped several frames at full telephoto as the grand, orange sun fell behind a slithering stream of fog and into the sea.

At home he went immediately to his computer and loaded his images into Adobe. He brought them up on the screen only to find that the camera's white balance was set for fluorescent light and not daylight, giving all his images a profound purple cast. As well, the images of the dancing couple were made in low daylight and at a slow shutter speed. Many were blurred. He jumped to his feet to find his camera. He wanted to throw it out the window. He would. He would throw the camera and jump after it. Either that or he would go buy a drink. Two drinks. A bottle. He staggered around his apartment in an apoplectic and self-degrading agony.

"You're a photographer?" he shouted at himself. "You're a fucking fraud. Good fucking riddance to you."

He went for his coat. He put it on but stopped at the door. Were he drinking he would have walked right through it. But he wasn't drunk and therefore no longer uselessly impulsive. It was too soon to die. In his enforced sobriety he found the discipline to stick with his plan: to finish his class, to book his passage, to find his way to Mexico where he could decide when and how his life would end. And it would, but just not now.

After making a cup of coffee Miles returned to the computer and searched the Adobe program carefully. He found controls for colorcast and color correction. He applied them and the purple in his images disappeared. He applied a sharpening tool and salvaged several photos of the dancing couple. He felt immediate relief, even if he refused to admit he was happy. He had most days of his drinking life never gone farther than the beginning of any happiness. He still wanted to die. But this one moment, and the few more he needed to fix his photos, held him still and in thrall. In a cynical way that made him grin, he thought of it all oddly as something to live for.

4

April began with rainstorms and wind. It was drinking weather and to resist the sirens of his besotted soul Miles locked himself inside his apartment with sandwiches from the mini-mart and a jar of instant espresso. He depended on Fred to keep him sober and Fred certainly would phone as Miles had missed an AA meeting at the county fairgrounds.

One meeting today is enough, Miles said to himself. Today he would attend a meeting at a church down the street from where he lived. He could walk from his apartment and not even pass a bar. In 40 days Miles had attended more than fifty meetings. He thought he might now know every recovering alcoholic in the county. Miles was on track to get his hundred meetings well ahead of schedule. Fred would be proud, Miles thought, though there would be no reward other than Fred's urging that he continue with his meetings.

"It's how it's done," Fred said. "One day at a time."

Miles attended a meeting where an older man kept all in attendance laughing as he described his typical progress through a drunk.

"When I woke up I'd decide I would not drink, that I wanted to be able to know if I were having a good time," he said. "But then I'd realize I wasn't having a good time anyway and that if I didn't have a drink, well, how I felt when I woke that morning was about the best I would feel all day. So I'd have the first drink…a relief to at last see things as I wished they were. Then I'd have the second drink and see things that weren't. A third would show me how things really were. And then I'd remember that I was in control. I would drink exactly as much as I wanted. And, of course, one drink more. And when I thought about it later, I realized I really needed only one drink to get me drunk. I just couldn't remember if it was the ninth or tenth."

Fred called in the early afternoon.

"You OK?" asked Fred.

He knew the perils of the dry drunk and quizzed Miles about his mood. Was he anxious? Did he think he might relapse?

"No," Miles said directly. "None of those things. They don't matter now."

Miles could not tell Fred why they didn't matter.

"But I'm having a bitch of a time with my class," said Miles. "They all think they're genius artists and most of their work is crap. They fight all the time. It got so bad I walked out this week. We'll see how many return."

"Sounds like you're having trouble," said Fred. "I suppose it's not easy teaching artists."

Fred was reaching out but Miles wasn't biting. He had nothing more to say.

"See you tonight at the church?" he asked Fred.

"Sure," answered Fred. "Seven-thirty."

Fred knew that living with alcohol was living with death close at hand. Miles knew that living without alcohol had no useful bearing on death's proximity.

"It's been three weeks since we've had an assignment," whined Mack. "What the hell are we supposed to do for this class? Half-way through and no one has a grade."

Miles heard his student's complaint as the first grumble of a class mutiny.

"I'm sorry," Miles replied remorsefully. AA had given Miles many opportunities to rehearse his remorse. Now he found it helpful as a way to fend off his students.

"Let's look ahead," he said at last and firmly. "You've all been shooting, right?" he asked.

Everyone nodded.

"Mack, you've been in the darkroom. Anyone else need time to work on their prints?"

Four hands shot up. Gerald and Leslie sat still with their arms folded across their chests.

Formidable opponents, thought Miles. These are the artists who won't give an inch. The class had six weeks left and Miles improvised a plan.

"I've been saving this, but it's time now to tell you," said Miles as if his words were something more than an afterthought.

"Each of you will be given the opportunity to submit up to three of your best prints to a student photo show set for the campus art gallery at the end of next month. These need to be prints you offer for sale. It's a popular show and also a fundraiser. Several pieces always sell."

Miles didn't tell his students that the show was actually the entire art department's year-end exhibition and that photography would appear in only one of the gallery's several rooms.

"You'll be listed in the catalog," said Miles, knowing that what he described as a catalog was simply a typed and Xeroxed sheet of paper with every artist listed alphabetically.

But his vaguely described outcome was enough to quiet his artists and draw their bobbing heads forward as they listened for details.

"So our work from here on out will be to develop the best prints we can make," said Miles. "I'm shooting and I'll be working along with you. I'll submit my prints, too. Maybe I can sell something this year. Any questions?"

There were no questions, at least none that had yet come to anyone's mind. Miles watched the faces of his fledgling artists twist thoughtfully as he imagined them imagining what photos to submit for a show. It was an artist's desire to be seen and any venue was better than none.

"And don't forget, we have the Cinco de Mayo assignment coming up. I want everyone to participate. It counts toward your grade."

Miles was anxious when he spoke, as if he were a small mammal burrowing a large enough hole in which to shelter and survive. It was a lacuna that Miles visualized as his life and that existed at varying times and in many spaces and for varying durations. His species sustained numerous grifters and Miles was one of them. He had at last found his way on the teacher's path and today his students received his words as a defining truth. He now stood above the world. He was unreachable and also not intoxicated.

Miles believed life was an exception to the rules of the universe and because his life had been such a failure he accepted in his depressed sobriety that it must come to an end. Sustaining a discontinuous state of existence had been profoundly exhausting and seemingly without reward. His epiphany now freed him to be sober, since he no longer felt the need to live with pain. Miles knew Fred waited for him to drink and then, like all drunks, return remorsefully to his meetings to try again to stop. Fred did not know that sobriety served Miles as a temporary hold. Miles wanted to believe in a higher power, even as he fought with his presumed failure at living. What kept him sober might have been described as a durable and insistent shred of hope. What he knew, or thought he knew, was that hope inevitably was an illusion masking the inevitability of death.

"Photos don't usually reproduce the visible," Miles said to his students. "Rather, they make something visible you may not have been aware of."

Miles described for his students what he thought of as the "grammar" of photography, particularly in ways that photos could express motion.

"And it *is* much like grammar—you have a subject and even if it is a still subject, the motion of a photo appears almost like a stated sentence. The camera acts on the subject like a verb and pushes its subject against objects in bursts of interactivity."

Miles projected a slide of several young women posing together. The setting was a Victorian garden in the 1860s and the photographer was Juliet Margaret Cameron.

"What is this?" asked Miles.

"A portrait," answered Leslie. "They seem to be posing."

"Good guess," said Miles. The photo was entitled *The Rosebud Garden of Girls.*

"But what are they doing?"

"Nothing I can see," said Mack. "It's pretty static."

"Slow shutter speed, of course," said Miles. "Exposures at this time took awhile, sometimes as long as minutes."

"Two women are looking out," said Marcie. "Others seem to be looking within. Not much action."

"Maybe not in the bodies," said Fernando. "But their eyes… something's going on. Are they acting?"

"Another good guess," said Miles again.

Miles showed another slide. It was a painting by Pre-Raphaelite artist Dante Gabriel Rossetti. The painting featured a similar if more diverse group of women costumed and crowded close as if gathered for a ritual. It was titled *The Beloved.*

"Its similarity should be no surprise," said Miles. "The painting and photograph were made within two years of each other. The photograph portrays a scene from a Tennyson poem."

Miles read a few lines:

> *"Queen rose of the rosebud garden of girls,*
> *Come hither, the dances are done.*
> *In gloss of satin and glimmer of pearls*
> *Queen lily and rose in one;*
> *Shine out, little head, sunning over with curls,*
> *To the flowers, and be their sun."*

Miles described Cameron's life, the trappings of her wealthy family and how Tennyson, her neighbor, commissioned her for photographs portraying his poem, *Idylls of the King.*

"They were neighbors," said Miles. "She made 1200 photographs during an active decade and then gave up photography to move to her family's coffee plantation on the island of Ceylon. She died there ten years later."

Miles wanted his students to see how making something visible had been a feature of photography from its beginnings. It was not a distinction between what was real and not real but rather how this mesmerizing photographic process that could reproduce something graphically visible might itself be manipulated to create a novel, new vision.

"Painting with film," said Miles. "Or, rather, writing with film. It doesn't matter."

He gave his class an assignment.

"Photograph a subject. Make something about it truly visible in a way you've never before seen. Bring it next week. We'll talk about it."

After class Miles went to Louie's and asked Johnny to pour him a drink.

"A double Bulleit," said Miles. "No ice."

"Where you been?" asked Johnny. "Haven't seen you here in more than a month."

"Busy," said Miles curtly. "Too damn busy. Teaching is stressful and I need a break."

Miles knew teaching wasn't stressful. Nothing about his life was actually difficult unless Miles made it so. He was an artist and artists were drinkers. Who didn't know that? Maybe Johnny didn't know that but then Johnny probably didn't care. Johnny was happy to see the return of a reliable customer.

The drink arrived and Miles studied it for several minutes. Had he lost his way? He had heard artists could lose their way as easily as some people lose their loose change or car keys. Miles had been sober for two months, two weeks and two days. Three days if he waited until midnight to sip his drink. He knew though, he wouldn't sip it. He would toss it back and order another. And another. For a man facing the adventure offered by his determination to die, the idea of drinking again felt perversely predictable and even boring. Miles stood and took out his wallet. He waved to Johnny, left his drink untouched and a twenty on the bar before turning to walk away.

Miles entered his apartment and prepared himself for another sleepless night. With a cup of instant espresso in hand, he sat down to do his books. Several thousand dollars remained from his divorce settlement. His second ex did not want to sell their house so she offered Miles a $150,000 buy-out and refinanced the mortgage. Miles planned to use the money as a down payment on another home. But months passed into years and, now, after more than a decade, most of the balance had been squandered on rent, two divorce attorneys, three very expensive cameras, two memorable if fatally flawed relationships, and lots of booze. Still, with some thrifty planning Miles calculated that if he kept teaching his money might last into his sixties. But teaching was ending and, buried alive in his own irrefutable sorrows, so was Miles.

Fred woke Miles after sunrise to remind him of an 8 a.m. meeting at the St. Vincent Mission on Fifth Street.

"That place is so fucking depressing," Miles responded, hoarse and sluggish. "And the smells…and the crowd. A bunch of lost souls weighed down by the shadows of their miserable failures. Something out of hell…"

"We're all humbled by our addictions," Fred said as if to generalize suffering in such a way that Miles might recognize his own smells, his own shadows, his own poor, lost soul, and his own hell.

"OK," answered Miles who, like many dry drunks, sometimes thought he was addicted to nothing but his own propensity for failure. That was enough though, enough to motivate Miles to end all contributing addictions including those to breathing, to eating, to loving and to dreaming. It might not be as easy as he imagined. But any accompanying fear or pain would be his last.

Miles' students returned to class from their various photographic forays, each with new evidence of a personal and presumably artfully interpreted topography. That was the assignment, anyway, and Miles tried to interpret how each had fulfilled it. Gerald's print of an evening sunset did not surprise. What Gerald saw was what everyone saw and Miles tried to acknowledge his vision.

"You were looking for…what?" asked Miles.

"What do you mean?" answered Gerald. "It's there. What you see is what you get."

Miles moved on.

Mack presented an 11x17 print of a grouping of four naked young men, their faces and genitals scratched out of the print.

"Vision isn't what we see," said Mack, sounding contemptuous. "It's what we don't see."

Leslie presented three small photos of entwined hands framed among the calligraphic stanzas of a poem. One photo rested above a line that Miles read.

"*…you would not share your unauthorized fantasies…*"

He read more.

"...we sang our simple stories into abiding histories of delectable danger though we were rarely at risk..."

He was drawn into Leslie's writing, presented in artful hand-wrought calligraphy.

Young Marcie's color photograph was matted and framed and featured three young women, likely friends, whose faces were covered with white pancake make-up and whose toothy smiles and alert, penetrating eyes gave the impression of three weird and conjuring sisters.

"I call it *Fair is Foul 2017*," said Marcie.

"Macbeth?" asked Miles.

Marcie nodded, startling Miles with her erudition.

Fernando presented a triptych highlighting a confrontation between a police officer and a group of young Latino males. Made at night with flash, the stark black and white photos portrayed an arc of potential violence that began with a photo of the shaggy, tattooed boys shaking their fists as the officer passed them and ended with an image of the cop, his Billy club thrust forward, pushing the boys back into the shadows of a dark street.

Sarah held up three photos that captured the corrugated and colorful surfaces of unrecognizable household objects. The large prints impressed Miles with their comfortably disorienting detail made so large it was like looking at atoms blown up to the size of planets.

But it was Mort who presented the most intriguing work. She (or he) offered a box again but this time one that had doors, which were pieces of the box cover sliced in half and hinged at the sides, each door bearing the glued-on color photograph of the portal of a Greek temple. Inside the box was a flourish of white and lilac lace, stuffed like the foamy popcorn of a packing crate around a photograph adhered inside that featured a young girl spreading her skirt as if to show it off. The photo was a photograph of a photo—a snapshot dated in pencil with the numerals 1942 and made blurry from its several iterations of printing.

Miles was drawn inside the box and seemed to grasp the memories suggested by the snapshot of the child. What Miles admired about any photo was its capacity to transport a heart and mind into the imaginative landscape of a real experience long in the past but still invigorated by the immediacy of a photographic reality. It was what thrilled and frightened him about the Gardner-Sullivan photos of the executions of the Lincoln conspirators. And here it was again, cleverly asserted by Mort's lovingly constructed assemblage.

"It's called Grandma," said Mort.

"Yours?" asked Miles

"Yeah," Mort answered cautiously. "My photo and my grandma. She's a child here. Now she's dead, as dead as the ancient Greeks. Dead like all history, dead like everyone's history is dead. More dead after being photographed a dozen times."

That night Miles returned to Louie's and repeated his ritual. He again ordered a double and after considering the small glass of bourbon for several minutes he again stood, pulled a twenty from his wallet, and waved goodbye to Johnny.

"You OK?" the bartender asked as Miles turned to leave.

"I know what I'm doing, if that's what you mean," answered Miles.

"Thanks for the tip," said Johnny.

"De nada," said Miles, rehearsing his Spanish for the next time he again entered a bar.

In so intimately refuting his addiction to alcohol Miles practiced an essential defiance. He left the bar more confident he could assassinate the person he was and with whom he could no longer live. After all, wasn't every suicide really a homicide? To kill oneself was to kill a hated other the self had helplessly become. Miles would at last bury all the failures that described his life. It would be a great refusal, an *Il Gran Refuito*. He had not read Marcuse but was old enough to remember the Marxist call to action. Though instead of quitting his job, he would quit his existence. The person he was he loathed as a prisoner might a jailer. Miles was a worn down consumer of experience. He was a dissatisfied customer and no longer buying.

"I'm fucking spent," Miles shouted at Fred when he phoned at 7 a.m. to remind Miles of yet another early AA meeting.

"You're so close," Fred responded. "Like ten more meetings…I know it's hard…but you'll…"

"What? Get a merit badge?" snorted Miles.

Fred was silent for a moment before speaking.

"I guess if there's only one way of seeing the world, there's only one way of behaving in it. You're a photographer. You must see a lot."

Fred's words quieted Miles with an irritating suggestion of some larger mystery, one Miles—if he gave it enough time and thought—might come to recognize in his art.

"See you there," Miles said and abruptly ended the call.

6

Miles thought himself a conscious creature with tools. He was too far along in the evolution of his species to be thought of as a tool-maker. But he was a tool user and it was in this capacity he confidently addressed the work of his students.

"It's been my experience that a lot happens and you can't always know where or when," said Miles. "You film folks, be certain you have several rolls. The rest of you, take an extra battery and your charger. And shoot. God, just shoot, shoot, shoot."

Miles heard the urgency in his voice as if he were making a final appeal for the creation of something wondrous and brilliant.

Cinco de Mayo this year occurred on a Friday, which created the entrée into a weekend of festivities, parades and gatherings. Miles had a schedule of events to pass out to his class. He knew more happened than what was on the schedule. Much more. The nation's new president, decisively defeated in the popular vote but elected by the states, had threatened to deport Mexican immigrants. A massive protest was expected and a march was set for Friday morning that would end with a rally in the city's downtown park. Festivities would follow and where and for how long was anyone's guess though most activities were scheduled for an abandoned shopping center adjacent to the Roseland community's main street, Sebastopol Road.

"I'll be there," said Miles. "I'll be shooting. Phone me if you have a problem. Bring your prints to the next class."

He scribbled his cell phone number on the blackboard.

It was easy for Miles to live without a plan to survive. As he milled with others gathered Friday morning for a march from Roseland to the city square he thought of his years of accumulated photographs, all memento mori that revealed first to his lens and then to his eye how life and death existed as intimate lovers. He carried his old Canon Rebel mounted with a 100-400mm zoom. In a bag slung over his shoulder were two smaller lenses for close-up work but Miles rarely ventured close anymore. Like Sarah, he also found people interesting but only at a distance.

Miles walked with hundreds of Latino men and women, wide banners and Mexican flags held high as they sang and shouted. *"Viva La Raza…Viva La Causa…!"* The procession ended at the city's courthouse square where music and speeches observed and honored the immigrant struggle and the perpetual fight for cultural justice that for today was on enthusiastic display. Along the march Miles saw Mack running behind a truck that carried the suited and smiling members of a Mariachi band. Mack stopped and pointed his camera. Then ran and stopped and pointed again. Later at the square Miles found Fernando standing on the stage next to a row of waiting speakers. He was shooting out into the crowd, also with a long lens. After the rally Miles hitched a ride back to Roseland where an abandoned shopping center served as the staging ground for a community's devoted observance. It was a good day for photographs and for the first time in awhile, Miles thought he might have made photographs that were good.

The Lincoln conspirators were hanged on a Friday, an event attended by a thousand people that needed tickets to get into the arsenal where they stood before a quickly constructed gallows to watch three men and a woman fall to their deaths. And what about the crowd?

Was it festive? It included some family and friends of the condemned. And why were they there? Miles heard the music of Cinco de Mayo flow from two stages and collide in an unsettling cacophony. There was no music at an execution, Miles was certain of that. Meanwhile, children danced, men wearing sombreros drank beers and strolled what was now a makeshift public market with toys for sale, food for sale, and balloons and souvenirs on offer everywhere. A heavy man passed by, made heavier by all that he bore that was for sale. Miles photographed voraciously, thinking this might be the last time ever he would hold a camera.

"Hi, it's Sarah," said the voice at the other end of Miles' phone. He had stopped at a food truck to buy a taco.

"Where are you?" asked Miles. "Are you shooting?"

"Nearby," said Sarah. "I can see you."

"The children dancing," said Sarah. "They're so eager and also funny. They try to be grown-ups because they're dressed like them."

Miles had asked Sarah what she was shooting. While he waited at the truck he ordered her a taco and together they sat at a picnic table to eat and to talk.

"There is so much," she said. "The color. The people. The place. I wish I could photograph the music and the taste of the food."

"In a certain way you can," said Miles. "Think about framing your image in a way that makes a view into sound or taste. You might see the flavor of food in someone's eyes or the heartfelt sound of music pouring from the sweaty cheeks of a singer or the vibrant limbs of a dancer."

After their quick meal Miles accompanied Sarah while together they roamed the Cinco fiesta that, as the evening approached, grew noisier and more crowded. Sarah found subjects to photograph and, when he wasn't making his own images, Miles watched Sarah, smiled and said nothing. She knows something, thought Miles. Perhaps she wants something.

"Would you like to get together later?" asked Sarah. "We could get a coffee. My treat…"

Miles knew he appeared flummoxed when what he actually felt

was melancholy. He was a man too long without a woman and here in the intimate presence of one he was not certain how to feel. The male Lincoln conspirators were hanged with a woman. And what was that like? Redeeming or softening or nothing at all? Were her tears before dying a comfort or just horribly alarming?

There was no way to live easily with death. Death was always there. Miles never needed to look for it. It was the eternal continuity and, from within the course of his own discontinuous life, he was alive and married to death.

"Sure," said Miles finally. "Where?"

Miles' next class was a cinema of stills. His students' photographs lined the room, all presenting visions larger than what was seen. It was the triumph of an idea and it left Miles thinking that in some way he had moved all these photographers toward a common urge to discover and not just simply to see. Miles knew that artistic views grew from a hidden place and while he could not know where each student hid his or her imagination and mastery he could point a way toward discovery. He also knew he was curating the college's art show.

Miles wandered among the images.

"How did you get that?" he asked Fernando who had stayed late into Friday night to photograph an illicit car sideshow held in an alley behind the shopping center's vacant retail storefronts. His photo featured a spinning car caught in a blur as a strobe froze the frantic motion of young men and women leaping out of its way.

"Flash," said Fernando. "Rear sync…"

Miles nodded knowingly.

Marcie presented a color portrait of several dancing adolescent girls, their long dresses held at the corners to make them into wide concentric rainbows of blues, reds and yellows. Leslie offered a photo of a young mother nursing her baby and isolated in the front row of a cheering audience. Of course, a poem accompanied the image but for once the image stood high and alone as a strong photograph.

Mack's three photos presented group shots of a youth gang, a Mariachi band, and three old men sitting on hay bales while they drank beers. For once, his images weren't marked up or defaced. Even Gerald found something to move him farther along. His long view of the parade captured a line of marchers, their faces angry and urgent as they moved toward him. Again, Mort brought a cigar box, this one festooned with strips of crepe in the colors of the Mexican flag. Opening the box revealed a crisp black and white photo, a close-up of a male wearing sunglasses that reflected clearly the crowd before him. Mort titled it *Without and Within*.

Miles at last visited Sarah's three images, photos he had already previewed in her camera while they shared coffee Friday night at an old town café. The photos conveyed the successive and gentle gestures of an elderly woman helping an even older one to cross the road. Sarah's telephoto had compressed the depth of field so that waiting cars appeared to lurch like monsters over the women, as if each vehicle surged with an irrepressible desire to race forward while the slow, old women held all time in check.

"Our world conveys an infinite variety of idiosyncratic views and experiences," Miles said as he stood before Sarah's photos.

"You all have in your hands a rich art and a unique capacity to pluck a moment of present reality for infinite future consideration."

These are frozen moments, thought Miles.

At a thousandth of a second his students captured one of a thousand possibilities that existed in a single second of experience, the others flown away and unacknowledged. But this one, the possession of each of his students, now existed as an artifact that could outlast lifetimes.

7

Class ended and Miles, recognizing a lack of feeling as his basic defense against anxiety, pushed himself toward Sarah.

"I never thanked you properly for Friday," he said. "Would you let me buy you a coffee? I'd like to hear more about your photographs."

So many dangers that Miles was powerless to overcome, so many that his final line of defense was at last to avoid even the feeling of danger.

"Where are the photos you made?" Sarah asked as they sat at a table in a downtown café.

"Will they be in the show?"

Miles' photos were still in his camera. Four hundred images from Cinco de Mayo popped up irrepressibly every time he scanned his camera's memory chip. They were good and not at all good. They were rich in detail and also over and underexposed. They were brilliantly captured and also out of focus. They were sharp as a tack and also badly framed. In all he counted only twenty he would save, and only half of those would he print.

"But there's one…" he said to Sarah. "Damn, there's one—it must be the best photo I've ever made. An old man surrounded by very young children, all shaded under his expansive sombrero that fills the frame as if this very old patriarch is helplessly and effortlessly protecting all of them. Exposure is amazingly accurate and the detail…well…"

"I hope you put it in the show," said Sarah. "I want to see it. I've learned so much from you."

Her words were both appreciative and, if Miles might allow anything in, also and very likely affectionate.

"You're too kind," said Miles with perfunctory grace.

"Not kind enough," answered Sarah. "I'm serious. If you can make the best photo you've ever made once, you can do it again."

It was an obvious conclusion but for whatever reason one that Miles grabbed greedily as an insight that might lovingly hold him or at least let him lovingly hold himself.

Miles stood high on a ladder in the back room of the college gallery when Fred phoned.

"What you doin'?" Fred asked ingenuously but in a way that demanded an answer Miles had for a week put off providing.

"Hanging my students' photos in the school gallery," answered Miles. "A big show starts next week. You should come and buy something."

"That's what I'm calling about," said Fred. "We haven't seen you at an AA meeting for more than a week."

"Been busy," Miles answered crisply and sorry for himself that he had nothing to say that would actually sound like an answer.

"Been drinking?" asked Fred.

"No," said Miles, embarrassed to be quizzed by his sponsor. "No drinking. No meetings. I must be cured."

"No alcoholic is ever cured," Fred stated solemnly. "And you're so close…by my count you're four meetings short of a hundred. Believe me, you should go for it. It would be an important achievement."

"And what's my reward?" responded Miles. "More meetings?"

"Well, yeah…" Fred answered. "A lifetime of meetings and a lifetime of sobriety."

Miles was quiet. How could he tell his sponsor he wasn't tired of sobriety or tired of meetings? He was tired of living.

"Gotta go," said Miles abruptly. He heard Fred sigh.

"I'm always here," said Fred.

"Yeah," said Miles. "You're a good man, Fred. A better man than I am."

"You're a good man, Miles," Fred gently mimicked. "You don't have to be better."

Miles ended the call.

It must be a trick of nature that a child can never fully grasp a parent's love. Love is nature's camouflage intended to hide, through the precious first perils of a life, the source of all experience. So much a child cannot know or grasp while it struggles to make its way. These are the remains unknown among the shades of a child's origins and the roots of its lifelong sorrow. And I know—I know—that while you likely think yourself free of me you are not free from sorrow.

Miles wished to write a last letter to his son, but did not know what he wanted to say. He waited for the words to come but listened carefully for only the best and most important few. He wanted his letter to be short, clear and forgiving. He imagined his son not at all caring what his father thought after more than a decade without contact. He knew, also, that his son might not think himself the one to be forgiven.

It is still a mystery, thought Miles. *Still a mystery who to blame and what was lost.*

I hope you've had a good life. I'm sorry I could not share it. I have nothing to explain. I'm at this point likely little more than a ghost. And though I am your ghost there is nothing left of me for you to touch.

Miles imagined his son as an attendant at his execution, waiting with his ticket to watch his father drop from the gallows. He wondered if his son would cry or cheer or have no feeling at all.

It was going to be a good show. Miles knew that. The photos were strong and together hung like a tapestry. But Miles could not have known for certain that the student art show, and the photography section especially, would be a profound and unprecedented success. Every one of his students sold a photograph, even Gerald whose wide, detailed image of a street full of earnest Cinco de Mayo marchers was purchased by Miles. Red adhesive dots, indicating a sold work that would be picked up when the exhibit ended, within an hour adorned the frames or labels of nearly every photograph. Miles was confounded, as were two deans who, observing the intense viewer interest in the photos of Miles' students, huddled at a corner of the gallery before approaching the instructor.

The deans told Miles they wanted to grow the art department and realized it needed an infusion of technology. Three computers were being purchased along with a full Adobe Photoshop suite and would Miles teach, not one, but two sections of photography in the fall?

"Obviously, you're doing great work," said a dean. "Rich stuff here tonight. And it's selling!"

The photos of Miles and his students had attracted new investors in art, an experience of the evening not lost on the deans. Eyes were like grazing animals and the deans, sensing the arrival of a newly attracted herd, saw an opportunity suddenly aligned with the facts on the ground. Photography was a hit. And they thought, at least for now, they might need Miles to make more of it.

Later Jeremy from the film photo shop arrived and searched for Miles.

"You do photography justice," he said. "You have two of my best customers working under your wing. They appreciate your strong eye and good heart. I bought their photos. I couldn't resist."

Miles approached his one photo, the image of the old man in the sombrero, children all around him. The framed photograph also had a red dot affixed. Miles for a year had masked his deepest love under the guise of a life-denying apathy. His art was his love and it was no longer unrequited. He learned later from Sarah that she had purchased his photo. She shouted to him in the gallery's noisy foyer that she had wanted the photo from the moment he first described it.

"What would you say to another coffee?" she asked Miles.

"I'd say let's go," he answered. "Now."

The next class was the last, held on the day after the art show when Miles anticipated for himself and his students what the next week, the next month, the next year might become for them all. He praised each of them even as he discouraged their regard for him. Sarah understood and did not intervene. She would see him later. She knew now how to tell Miles what Miles could not tell himself.

Winter, thought Miles. Maybe spring. It would still be warm in Guaymas. The ocean, too, would still be warm, which was the most important thing. But for now, well, now was enough. He was still inexplicably busy with an urge to make something visible that was not yet seen.

A BUMP IN THE ROAD

I f each person were many people, as his ex-wife claimed, then Aaron Fisk wondered which among his many should he blame for his divorce. His ex-wife's consistent argument was that a personality comprised a multitude, what she described as an "egoistic corporation."

"Your psyche is a collaborative process," she would say in the heat of their arguments. "You don't know who you really are. So how am I to know who I'm listening to?"

Aaron knew now that her semantics were a diversion. Without Madeline in his life Aaron's mind had found again its center and, he thought, now sat like a beacon on the rock of his survival.

"She was a liar," Aaron said to himself. "She was a fraud. And she never loved me."

It wasn't an accurate assessment but Aaron didn't care. He had borne a year of despair to end a nineteen-year marriage to a woman eleven years younger than he. He had endured his wife's opprobrium, sighs, chilly silences and deceits for countless months until, before he could say it first, Madeline asked him for a divorce.

Aaron moved out of their overpriced home in Petaluma, purchased before the Great Recession and still not worth what they paid for it. His part-time job provided a modest salary. Aaron worked as an IT for an environmental conservancy in Marin County with the name *Many Rivers* and Madeline, a loan representative for a regional bank, earned much more than he did, which relieved Aaron of any obligation to pay alimony. And when his attorney suggested he seek payments from Madeline Aaron said no.

"Just get me out of that loser house loan," said Aaron. "We'll call it even."

He might have rented an apartment but instead Aaron accepted his mother's offer to live in the family's empty vacation home at Salmon Creek. Built by his architect father when Aaron was a small child, the small two-bedroom cottage stood at the crest of sandy bluffs facing the prolonged expanse of the Sonoma Coast's longest beach. It had been abandoned for a couple of seasons and needed some work that Aaron was willing to do. Aaron spent every childhood summer there. Now it was his to live in as long as he needed. It was a lengthy drive from work and a foggy coastal chill more often than not made it necessary to build a fire in the cabin's wood stove. Other than a heavy comforter it was the home's single source of heat.

In late spring evenings after his hour-plus drive back from Fairfax, Aaron walked along the beach, smoked a cigarette or two, and kindled his memories of loss.

"I need time alone," he said to himself. "This divorce is a bump in the road. But I'm still standing. Still working. No visitors, of course. Not now. And no dates. Not yet. Thank god we didn't have children. Here you are, Aaron mah man. Alone again."

His widowed mother was 83 and had recently moved to an assisted living condo in San Francisco where she could remain independent but call for resident help when she needed it. His one sibling, a younger sister, lived in Idaho and was married to a retired high school gym teacher. They had forty acres and a home on Lake Coeur d'Alene where Marthe had raised their two sons and worked summers as a beach lifeguard. Marthe rarely visited their mother and Aaron didn't care. However close he had been to anyone, Aaron thought himself fundamentally alone.

Though it was still troubling that Madeline had left Aaron for someone else. She said she was lonely living with him and that their relationship, while functional, financially secure and friendly, lacked intimacy she did not realize she missed until someone else offered it.

Without the multiplying factor of parenting Aaron was left only with the family he had known since childhood, a family already minus his father, a successful architect who died suddenly from a heart attack suffered in his early seventies. He had been gone nearly a decade but remained a stranger to Aaron for much longer than that.

Divorce left Aaron with the familiar and repressive isolation he pretended always to welcome. It had come to him before and he wondered if any life were anything more than the oscillating urge to merge and also to separate. It was a perpetual and scientifically proven metamorphosis.

"Proven," he said after a second shot of Mezcal, asserting through a satisfying inebriation his righteous belief in the truth of science. And it was a helpful, if brief, comfort against loss, which was more acceptable if it were inevitable. It was also selfish and as he sat on the porch to smoke his last evening cigarette, Aaron realized that, while the process of divorce was finally finished, his vigilance was eternal.

"She smoked, too…when we married," Aaron said to himself. Then she stopped and he did not and she became a terror, complaining about his smoking, about burn holes in the chairs and couches, the smoky smell of the house and his clothes. He still coughed and she did not.

"I'm thinking about you," Madeline said with her Argus-eyed conviction. "It's not just that you smell bad. It's not just that it makes me wheeze and cough. You suck that shit up all day and that can't be good, Aaron."

Her arguments were strong but Aaron's attachment to tobacco was stronger. And while he would never portray his smoking as the ultimate deal-breaker of their marriage, he knew it was enough, and probably more than enough, to tip the scales.

"Nearly a third of my life stolen by a bitch who didn't love me," Aaron shouted at the ocean.

It would be all Aaron all the time now. No one would argue with his righteous truth. There was no one else who cared enough to hear it.

Aaron's little home was named The Sand Box. It was the name given by his father who had a sign made and mounted above the front door. The sign was faded but still readable, which made the home identifiable to anyone invited to visit.

"Found it," said Joseph when Aaron heard the knock and walked downstairs to answer the door.

"I see why it's the Sand Box," said Joseph. "Look at the size of those dunes."

He pointed from the upstairs porch toward the rippling waves of sand that stood like a range of shifting peaks and valleys between the house and the shore.

Joseph worked with Aaron at *Many Rivers* and also lived in Sonoma County though his home was a condo in southwest Santa Rosa.

"This is beautiful," Joseph said. "Your dad built this?"

The comment seduced Aaron into reminiscence and he let alcohol open him up to his childhood, his father, his family, his young summers running along the beach and climbing in the dunes. He was thoughtlessly garrulous but Joseph didn't seem to care.

"And what about the commute?" Joseph asked.

"Out along the highway to just outside Petaluma where I turn back toward Nicasio and catch the Nicasio road to Sir Francis Drake. Then it's a straight shot to Fairfax. Seventy minutes through pure countryside and only three traffic lights."

"Damn, that's what it takes me coming down the freeway," said Joseph. "Far fucking out."

"I'm putting burgers on the grill," said Aaron. "Dinner in thirty minutes."

"Enough time for a toke?" said Joseph who pulled a joint from his shirt pocket and lit it.

It was good shit, though it made Aaron cough hard in a way that at first alarmed Joseph until Aaron urgently sucked down a tall glass of water while his watery eyes blinked and the coughing stopped. Joseph had brought his guitar to play for Aaron. It was the reason for his visit though both men knew no reason was necessary. They were friends at work and now resided together in the same county.

After dinner Joseph began strumming and singing, locking on the Guess Who song No Time that froze Aaron in place as he listened to the familiar lyrics. *No time left for you...on my way to better things*...Aaron fell back into a reverie of gruff, turbulent rejection. He felt strengthened in the home that held him with its memories, that aroused his love for himself and for a life lived well despite two failed marriages and no children and a professional career spent managing computer programs for a struggling non-profit. He was a good employee and thought he had been a good husband in the way he lived by values of loyalty, diligence and perfection, though nothing was ever perfect or could be. What he thought his virtues Madeline at last admitted she found maddening, especially when his righteousness entered their conversations about how best to live and what chores to do. It was, as she said on the way out the door for the last time, a bump in the road.

2

Welcome or not, the abolition of a family was for Aaron the return of liberty. Three times in his life he had abandoned a family or been abandoned by one. His latest was a family of two, the minimum number to comprise a family, leaving Aaron to wonder who left whom? He had abandoned the family home but Madeline had abandoned him. Either way, he was at liberty again. Free from anyone and everything save his job and his guilt.

The solitude Aaron nursed was a quiet, if barren, relief from the noise of engagement. He was determined to retain his liberty, to push away all disturbing reminders of family and to live thoroughly and devotedly alone. At an age most people give up employment, Aaron resented a need to work at least five more years to assure his security in retirement. He blamed his bad choices, and eventually himself. He would be seventy years old before he could stop working.

"I'll be back," said Joseph in the morning as he scrambled to get himself together. "You're a lucky man."

Aaron cooked a breakfast of eggs, toast and coffee and sent Joseph off through a seasonal morning fog to arrive at the same office where five minutes later Aaron also would arrive.

"Been fun," said Aaron. "Let's do it again. I love your guitar music. You know a lot of songs."

He looked forward to another visit.

Before leaving for work, Aaron watered a large, sturdy ficus living in a fat clay pot at the sunniest corner of the cottage's living room. The plant was several years old and an anniversary gift from one of Madeline's many friends. Madeline didn't want it and Aaron, who had cared for it and nurtured it perhaps better than he did their marriage, took immediate custody.

Aaron lit a cigarette from the lighter in his old Toyota and started the car. After two quick drags he phoned his mother.

"On the way to work, Mom," he reported. "How are you doing?"

He had forgotten it was the wrong question.

"Awful, son. I live in a prison here. I miss the Kensington hills. I have a nice view but the halls smell like pee half the time."

"Only half the time?" asked Aaron. "That's cool."

He knew the sarcasm would irritate his mother.

"Damn, there you go again, Aaron. This isn't funny. It's my life, goddammit. I'm not happy."

Aaron's mother was rarely happy anymore and Aaron, after listening for a quarter of an hour, was about to say so when a tickle in his throat collided with a deep drag of smoke to ignite a spasm of loud, furious coughing.

"Aaron?" his mother asked. "You there?"

"Gotta go…"

Aaron choked through his words and threw his phone into the passenger seat. He pulled tight on the steering wheel and slowed to stop in front of a hayfield outside the small town of Valley Ford. He sat through several minutes of hacking, choking convulsions that produced gooey, green phlegm he collected in a rag taken from under his seat. Aaron searched the stained rag for a patch of clean fabric. This had happened before and more times than he could count. He extinguished his cigarette, looked to see if anyone were watching, and then dropped the butt out the car window.

"I'm feeling better already," Aaron told the doctor.

It had been three weeks since Aaron had quit smoking but only a week since his boss had noticed how his periodic coughing fits sent him running to the restroom.

"Quite a hack," his boss had said ingenuously. "How long have you had it?"

His boss also noticed, but did not say, that Aaron was tiring easily, appeared short of breath, and had difficulty finishing his projects.

"Why don't you take some time off and go see a doctor?" said his boss. "We'll be fine."

Those weren't the words Aaron wished to hear. No place where he worked, no business that paid him a salary, would ever be fine without him. But his boss, a congenial philanthropist named Gordon who made a point of showing his humane concern for everyone in his employ, would not be denied.

"Let's check out your symptoms," said Dr. Lopez. "I think we might want to run some tests. Routine stuff. Just need to get some baselines."

Looking back later, Aaron understood that the doctor's avuncular reassurances were simply elements of a bedside manner intended to seduce his patient into a battery of invasive procedures. It allowed Aaron to presume the best possible outcome while, he realized now, his doctor had already assumed the worst.

Aaron spent a full day at the hospital for tests, leaving him the better part of a week before he needed to return to work. He phoned Joseph and invited him out for dinner. He spent afternoons walking the beach and sunbathing in the dunes. He had the ocean at his feet and evenings in the hot tub. One night he drove to town for a drink. Aaron met a woman at the bar of a popular wharf-side restaurant and felt relaxed enough to chat her up until, seized by a familiar surge in his throat and chest, he gracelessly excused himself and rushed to a restroom where he sweated, choked and threw-up his dinner.

On the day Aaron was to return to work, he received an early phone call from Dr. Lopez.

"We have a problem," said the doctor. "You have a mass in the right lung that needs a look. Surgery, I'm afraid."

"What?" Aaron heard himself say. "When?"

"Could you come in tomorrow?" said the doctor. "Time is urgent. We may be looking at a stage three or four."

"Stage of what?" asked Aaron.

"Cancer," answered the doctor, his otherwise affable and engendering bedside charm now offered as a terse, clarion alarm.

"No other way to find out what we're dealing with," said the doctor. "It will lay you up for a couple of weeks, at least. I'll give you a letter for work if you need it."

Aaron stared at himself naked in the bathroom mirror, the serious red line of a surgical gash appearing as if pasted to his chest, its stitches removed even as the evidence of stitching stood out like a bolt of garnet lightning.

"It's a gate," Aaron said to himself. "It opened me."

But what of Aaron did it open?

"We'll have to be aggressive," the doctor had said to Aaron, prone and groggy post-surgery.

"A lot depends on how you want to go," he added. "We'll discuss that when you're feeling better."

The choice for Aaron was that there was no choice. It was a bump in the road, of course. It was a bump that might be the end of the road.

From among his limited choices, Aaron chose drugs and radiation. He would be on a regimen for several weeks to see what could be done. Dr. Lopez, who at first was Aaron's accommodating medical servant, was now a messenger of difficult news. Mercurial and experienced, the good doctor offered confidently his best counsel with the sobering caveat it might not be enough.

"There's a lot chemo can do," said the doctor. "I've seen a few remarkable outcomes."

"Few" was the operative word and Aaron didn't let it get by.

"Yes," said the doctor. "It doesn't always work."

Aaron asked for the truth and the doctor was obliging.

"Someone with your advanced cancer has a 25 percent chance of living a year. An eight percent chance of living five."

Liberty for Aaron began with his adolescent rebellion against his parents who thought he should be for them and not for himself. What he wanted most was unconditional love, which he found in the deep loyalty shared among a rowdy crowd of young high school classmates he loved and chose and who loved and chose him. All, like him, were sons who felt expelled from their families. But then Aaron's body was another body broken by a fraternity of adolescent mates who smoked and wanted Aaron to smoke, and whose fellowship meant more than anything else in the world.

Who leads and who is led? When he thought of his life of smoking several times a day he recalled the first gratifying moment he fully inhaled to the cheers of his brothers. The deep absorption of nicotine calmed him, strengthened him and held him closer to the earth. Were he to die, it would be a fratricide.

3

Aaron felt like the meal inside an animal's belly. In his dreams and fears he rolled around and around with only one path out. At dawn he welcomed the daylight and at night cursed its disappearance. A week of chemo had weakened him considerably. He phoned Gordon to tell him the truth, asking that he tell no one else.

"As long as you need, Fisk," said Gordon, still in the habit of referring to his male workers by their last names. Gordon offered to help Aaron secure unemployment and disability pay. Both Gordon and Aaron knew he was not returning to *Many Rivers*. Aaron asked Gordon to keep his illness a secret and Gordon said he would. But within days a card arrived signed by most of Aaron's work colleagues with expressions of hope and sympathy. The conspicuous absence of any written wish to "get well soon" suggested to Aaron his boss had ignored his plea for privacy and had told everyone the details of his condition. As a wealthy philanthropist Gordon was accustomed to deciding what was best for others.

Joseph phoned several times and left messages Aaron could not decide to return. After another week of chemo Aaron awoke on a Saturday morning to at last address his new confusion, a prominent feature of his incrementally evident mortality. He had not been prepared for the way he would react to radiation and meds nor had he sought help from anyone. The prospect of death embarrassed him and, even if he were dying, it was not his wish ever to appear weak and unprepared.

Yet he was both. He was physically exhausted from a severe treatment regimen and incapable of managing countless new vulnerabilities. On Wednesday he had needed to ask a nurse to order a cab for his return trip to Salmon Creek, a ride that cost him more than $50. This morning he was nearly too tired to lift himself from bed and fell over trying to get dressed. He lived in a new world in which his daily routines shared a cramped and messy closet with death.

"You should have called me, man," Joseph said when Aaron phoned him.

"I'm calling you now," said Aaron weakly. "Can you come out? I need some help."

Aaron's was a shaming sickness, a fall from some impracticable grace he assumed would at last arrive through the final dissolution of his long and discomposing second marriage. The threats imposed by a serious illness were still thoroughly ungraspable. Pain and exhaustion were the more immediate torments and the therapies prescribed by his doctor hurt and weakened him in ways that made Aaron's daily life nearly unbearable. He wondered if all his new and sudden suffering was his doctor's way of casting death as a useful and welcome alternative.

"Shit," said Joseph when Aaron answered the door of his cottage. "You've lost a lot of weight, man."

Joseph appeared helpful and also helpless. Aaron's condition had slipped well beyond anything that might be changed with a drive to the store. More was needed and Joseph tried desperately to guess quickly what was possible.

"Let's get you some breakfast," Joseph said anxiously. "You sit down and I'll fix something. What you got?"

Aaron allowed himself to be guided to the large chair near the ficus where he sat to watch Joseph rummage through the kitchen's small cupboards.

"Coffee?"

Aaron nodded.

"Cream and sugar?"

Aaron nodded again.

"Some cereal?"

Joseph opened the refrigerator. "Milk's still good. Found an apple. Toast?"

Aaron nodded again and closed his eyes.

Joseph stayed the weekend, applying energy Aaron no longer had to all the tasks at hand. By Sunday night when he left, Joseph had filled the refrigerator with food, cleaned the house, done Aaron's laundry including the bedding, and attentively guided his friend to the top of a nearby dune where together they watched Saturday's fluorescent sunset.

Aaron had two more treatments the following week before the doctor would pause to assess the situation. Joseph drove Aaron to both.

"News," said the doctor as he spoke to Aaron by phone. "Too early to say it's good news but the tumor is shrinking."

Those people Aaron no longer saw or heard did not exist. To the degree he could act, he had banned everyone but Joseph from his existence. His sorrow was his dishonor and it was not to be shared with anyone. Though now the doctor offered a sliver of hope that, combined with a week of respite from radiation, restored at least some of Aaron's interest in living. He immediately imagined himself triumphant and well. He visualized his confident stroll back into Many Rivers and longer walks on the beach. He would never have to share deep pain with his mother or sister or anyone else. He would never again smoke, of course. He was grateful, obsequiously grateful to whatever—even a god, if necessary—for another chance to live.

Aaron recovered enough to become wildly angry. For so long his choice had been no choice. He wanted nothing. The world was an illusion and through an inventory of his memories, his marriages, and his most recent struggles, Aaron arrived at the infuriating conclusion he had been duped by life, its presumed pleasures someone else's entertainment at his expense. He could no longer imagine the life in his midst without his presence. It was all a mistake, this tumor, and this cancer.

He hated everything and everyone culpable in the creation of his troubled life. He would cut off everyone: his mother, his sister, his… Aaron realized there were a very few he knew well enough to cut off, and fewer still who would care. He considered pulling the old ficus plant up by its roots and burying it in the sand so it would have no chance to outlive him.

"Aaron…are you OK?"

The voice was Madeline's and she spoke over the phone with the caring regard she had at one time expressed as Aaron's wife. Aaron was surprised to hear her and wished instantly he hadn't picked up the call.

"Yeah…why do you care?" asked Aaron.

He was defensive and also unprotected

"Well…I heard you've been sick," said Madeline.

"I'm OK. Doing as well as expected."

Madeline ignored the hostile tone. The marriage was over and divorce had freed her from the anger her ex-husband was only now expressing.

"I heard you had cancer," said Madeline.

"Who told you that?" asked Aaron.

"Word gets around," she answered.

Aaron searched his mental Rolodex for the names of anyone who might have told her, realizing that together they had befriended a married couple employed at *Many Rivers.*

"So are you OK?"

"Fit as a fiddle," Aaron choked hoarsely and then was quiet.

"OK…I won't bother you again," said Madeline. "It was just I…"

"Thanks, Maddy," said Aaron as he cut her off and ended the call.

Wonder if she's pissed she divorced me? thought Aaron.

If Madeline had waited a year she would have inherited everything they owned and not needed a divorce. Aaron indulged the sweetly embittering idea that Madeline was counting up her losses and would feel irrevocably and interminably resentful.

The world was angry and so was Aaron. He fit right in. He

was pissed enough to live forever.

Perhaps it was a coincidence that the night before his sister phoned, Aaron dreamt he swallowed his father. His father was the patriarchal bond between them, the bearer and giver of their shared surname that sustained the sibling love and loyalty comprising Aaron's closest and longest bond. What have I inherited? Aaron thought upon awakening. What do I leave?

"We're coming out in August to check on mom," said Marthe. "We're bringing the boys and hope to see you."

Marthe had reserved a site at a campground near the cottage.

"I don't know if I'll be here," said Aaron weakly. He was determined not to tell his sister about his cancer. But, alerted by her brother's obvious agitation, Marthe pushed back.

"Are you OK?" she asked earnestly. "Something wrong? Is mama OK?"

"Mama's fine," said Aaron. "I'm not."

He began to cry and held the phone away while he first sobbed and then, again, choked hard until he was flush and breathless while he heard his sister shouting from the phone.

"Aaron! Aaron! God…Aaron…"

He was caught by the only person in his life that knew him well enough to find him. His mask had grown into his body, had become one with his eviscerated flesh, and what anger remained was useless and inapplicable to the truth.

"I think I'm dying…" Aaron said haltingly. "It's not good."

Aaron did not believe that God was his creator. There was no God who loved him. And if there were a God, Aaron would dare that God to appear before him, knowing a God feared death as much or more than Aaron did and would never make an appearance. Worse than dead, God did not exist and knowing this eased Aaron's suffering enough to speak again into the phone. He told Marthe the truth and she listened and also cried.

"I'm coming to see you," she said.

Aaron made a habitual and self-abnegating attempt to dissuade and to not trouble Marthe with the consequences of his poor life and its poorer choices. But she cut him off.

"I'm coming to see you," she said again. "I'm getting the next available flight. I'll rent a car and drive up to the beach house."

Aaron ended the conversation, sorry to have troubled anyone and especially his sister. What lived under the surface of his suffering frightened him. He thought death a specter, a meaningless passage into nothingness. Anything that reduced him to rubble could never be presumed to offer the radiance of a fetching truth.

4

Aaron began to think of himself as a performed character. Aaron's sickness was an act. Someone else was playing the part of a dying man. Not him. His sister sat next to him at the cottage's kitchen table while his mother strolled restlessly near the sliding door to the deck. Both were terrified by Aaron's slim frame and gaunt, grey face. And both were compelled to assure him he would be fine, would live. They were here now and he needed to live, if for no reason other than that Marthe and his mom were unable to imagine him dead.

Aaron, weak and weary, felt another wave of anger. He had an unexplainable urge to throw his mother and sister out of the cottage, to kick them down the stairs and to ban everyone—even Joseph—from what was left of his existence.

"The doctors tried everything," Aaron said weakly.

Marthe had made him a cup of tea and brought pastries. Aaron poked at an apple turnover and sliced off a small piece.

"Then we'll get other doctors," said his mother, her tremulous voice rising. "We'll find someone…"

"Mom, stop," said Aaron.

He turned to look directly at her. She was a small, thin woman and the creases of her face's many wrinkles caught the shadows of the afternoon sun in a way that made her cheeks appear as a pale, fissured moonscape.

"Just stop. Please…"

Aaron hated his mother's useless grief. He hated that her desire he heal was truly her desire her child not die before her. That would be unbearable and it was inconsiderate of Aaron even to contemplate dying until every last effort was made to live.

"We've done everything," Aaron said, shaking as he spoke to his mother. "That's all. If you need me to do more, I can't."

Marthe stood and moved behind Aaron. She placed her hands on his hunched shoulders and gently rubbed them before wrapping her arms fully around him in a gawky embrace.

"I love you," Marthe said to her brother. "Mom loves you."

Aaron did not speak. Nor did his mother.

Aaron wished for a quiet place where his family would never find him. As Marthe spoke, Aaron caught in his view the ficus plant near the window. It now would certainly outlive him. It would only die if Aaron murdered it and he would not, of course. He had saved the ficus from a vindictive spouse that, who knows, might have already disposed of it. He wondered for a moment if the ficus might be listed as a survivor in his obituary. It was humorous at first, a tease he recognized as his first attempt to accept his imminent death. He was several steps ahead of his family and now wanted them gone.

"Time for you guys to leave," Aaron said to Marthe. "I need to be alone."

Marthe looked at Aaron, the shock of rejection mirrored in her wet eyes.

"It's not what you think," said Aaron again. "I love you both. But you are no help to me now. You have no idea…"

"But Aaron," said Marthe. "All we want…"

"It's not what you want," answered Aaron. "Nothing of my life now meets any of your needs. You must leave me alone. Everyone needs to leave me the fuck alone."

"God dammit, Aaron…" his mother began a sentence she could not finish.

"Get out of here!" Aaron stood, wobbling against his sister. He turned on her.

"You…get out…get her out…I can't do this. Leave me alone!"

He never before felt so deeply the need to be heard and seen though to be seen now was the ambition of a ghost. And to be remembered was all that was left for the dead.

Aaron could not imagine nothingness. He climbed the big dune with all his effort and sat at the top, breathless and unafraid.

"It is not the sorrow of dying," Aaron said to himself as he watched high tide push the ocean hard against the dunes.

"It is the sorrow of living."

His mother was the maker of Aaron's life and he, as he always had, disappointed her. There was no comfort in that. There was no comfort to be derived from his sister or his mother, or his ex-wives, either of them, who must certainly be happy to be rid of Aaron and the memory of their useless, wasted marriages. Memories would die with him. Cold, still death felt like the wind pushing at him and his dune. Cold, still death was the only truth and for a moment Aaron took some comfort that suffering and sorrow eventually ended for everyone.

Dr. Lopez phoned the next morning. He was sympathetic but also direct. There were no more treatments that offered hope for a cure. The tumor was growing again but more critically the cancer had metastasized and invaded lymph nodes. The doctor lifted all limits on prescriptions for painkillers, including morphine if that should become necessary. These were not interventions to heal. Aaron knew the doctor was preparing him for a comfortable, if not at all comforting, passing.

"So how long?" asked Aaron. "Really…"

Dr. Lopez hesitated. He would not predict what was unpredictable.

"I think you should live as well as you can for as long as you can," said the doctor. "You should ask for what you need and receive it. As you need medical assistance, I'm always here. You should not suffer."

The afternoon brought overcast and a wet fog that chilled Aaron as he sat on the porch. His phone rang and he answered it. It was Marthe.

"I'm sorry about yesterday," she said. "I shouldn't have brought mom. She can't deal with this at all well. I'm having my own problems but they aren't yours. Don't worry, Aaron. We won't bother you again unless you need us."

Aaron heard his sister's voice, melodic and familiar. It ignited a peculiar poignancy that washed him clean of attachment. He had one foot out the door and felt so prepared to leave he resented now any need to say good-bye.

"One more thing," said Marthe. "I phoned a local hospice. It was recommended and I spoke with a nice man. His name is Kurt. He said he would phone you—I know, you probably don't want to talk with anyone. But please…he sounds like someone who knows the ropes, who knows what you're going through…please…"

Marthe's voice sounded for a moment as if she were choking as she tried to suppress an incipient groan.

"Thank you," said Aaron, momentarily softened by his sister's projected tenderness. "I'm sorry, too. I just…I mean, I can't…"

"I understand," said Marthe, not waiting for Aaron to find the end of his endless sentence. "I love you and I understand."

"I'm not goddamned dead yet," Aaron shouted defiantly at his phone. "I don't know what my sister was thinking but I don't need any help."

Aaron finished his rant and waited through the silence of his caller.

"This has to be a mistake," Aaron, finally snorted. "I'm stronger than death. I don't need anyone to help me."

"Let me leave my number, Aaron," Kurt said. "You never know… and as for your sister… I'd just say she's not trying to hurt you. She's frightened, too. She might die for you in a minute if she could."

Aaron left the cottage before sunset and climbed the big dune, his shortened breath and painful joints a suddenly fierce and imposing hindrance. Perhaps Aaron was a multitude of men, all now scream-ing at him for justice, stirring in him the anger that did nothing to ease his pain. Breathless, he reached the top of the dune from which he observed the resplendent world he was so near to leaving.

He had no grasp of what was possible or not possible. Instead, he wondered if he might make a deal. If he planted his ficus in the soil, gave up his ownership of it, set it free, would he also be set free?

Aaron did not respect a god so there was no one with whom he might negotiate his destiny. But he wanted to make a deal. He wanted desperately to reset his clock. Aaron's past became in its remembrance tighter, stronger, and more affecting. Old girlfriends, old embarrassments, isolated successes and multiple, incautious failures all returned as a deafening, humiliating score that sung out his miserable and unexplainable life.

He cried both in pain and revelation. He stood to leave and stumbled badly, hurtling down the big dune with dangerous, careless velocity. He hit the sand hard and could not stand up. How can I make a deal? Aaron asked himself. How could he erase time between his fate and the moments far behind him where his fate was conceived, grown and imprinted as the brittle and vulnerable fact of his life?

5

Aaron in his presumed multitude was not a corporation. He was a chorus that sang in secret harmony the diminished pleasure of a failing life. Increasingly he thought himself a eunuch in a harem. And he was at last being asked to leave.

The real apocalypse arrived, not with the disappearance of kingdoms, but with the loss of the body. Aaron could feel the accelerating vacancy within him. His mind's furious and frantic calls for performance were more frequently met with corporeal denial. His arms, his legs, his hands, even at times his bladder or bowels, refused to respond to his needs or desires.

When he became forgetful, when his mind no longer tracked accurately the formation and direction of his thoughts, Aaron found Kurt's number and phoned him.

"I don't know what I want," Aaron said as Kurt sat across from him in the cottage.

"I don't believe in a god. And if I have a soul, it's a goddamned manikin."

Kurt smiled.

"You don't have to believe in god," said Kurt. "But you deserve to be comfortable. You deserve to have things just the way you want them, no matter what anyone else thinks is best."

"What makes me so deserving?" Aaron asked with a twinge of sarcasm.

"Your humanity," answered Kurt. "Your good life. Your time alive and the infinite links you have with all you've touched, loved and experienced."

"I haven't had a good life," said Aaron after a long pause. "But I don't want it to end yet. I'm not finished."

Kurt offered an empathic nod.

"An end is the hardest thing to understand," said Kurt. "We so easily assume our lives are our personal property and that we'll be the ones to decide exclusively how this life is used. That's never the case, though. It can be unsettling when we first discover this."

Aaron found Kurt trustworthy. Kurt could cast attractively the strong current of a life's river toward the delta of death and an oceanic emptiness beyond.

"There is no such thing as a single human being, simple and pure and unmixed with other human beings. A personality may be a world unto itself but it keeps a company with many, many others. We have formed these relations and links since the day we were born. We are the product of countless links and exchanges."

"And what's the comfort in that?" Aaron snapped.

"Comfort? asked Kurt. "Is living comfortable? In my work I see much more pain in living than in dying."

Kurt would not probe further, at least not now. Once an identity had outlived its usefulness the only choice left was to lose it. A living being ate until it was eaten. Kurt watched Aaron struggle to find a loophole, as if winning the argument that life was unfair would extend his life through endless appeals. Though Aaron was at last breaking boundaries, freeing some of his prisoners and relinquishing his terror. It was a familiar process of breaking things down. With what time was left, Kurt hoped eventually to offer Aaron a breakthrough.

Birth was a bursting shell and Aaron could not recall his arrival anymore easily than he could imagine his departure. He was told his birth was loud and violent. He and his mother both screamed through its pain.

Aaron first asked Kurt to protect him from his mother and sister who wished to help Aaron and enlist him into their hopeful but unrealistic expectation he would be cured and survive. It was too much pressure for Aaron to bear. He often felt he must live or he would disappoint everyone who loved him. And whether he burned or simply decayed, Aaron rationalized that he was simply an error of creation.

"Then we all are," said Kurt. "We're all some kind of cosmic discontinuity and living then is not a natural state. In this vacuous, limitlessly empty universe we are most certainly the exception. Perhaps we're like a virus, alive momentarily before dying in the air or heat."

Kurt visited Aaron a few times a week. He sometimes helped him shop. He brought him books from the hospice but Aaron did not read them. Nevertheless, Aaron looked forward to Kurt's visits and, as he continued to weaken, opened more readily to the idea of dreamless time, especially a time when others might live without him.

"Do you worry about leaving something unfinished?" Kurt asked while he drove Aaron into Sebastopol to pick up a prescription.

Aaron talked about his mother, his sister, his dead father, and Madeline and her deceitful flight from him. He was sorry he had no children and had failed to love his sister's two nephews who now as adults rarely called him and never visited. He forgave his father though it was too soon to forgive his ex-wife.

"Gaps I've made and never closed," Aaron said with a lilt of resignation.

"I also worry about the mechanics," said Aaron. "What happens when you die?"

He had been reading about suicides and executions—hangings, beheadings, gunshots, electrocutions, drugs—he worried death would be painful. Would he suffocate? Would he writhe in exquisite and unbearable pain?

"None of those traumas are involved," Kurt answered. "Aaron, you've done nothing wrong. You won't be punished. We're talking only about a loss of consciousness."

Kurt said the last sense to leave appeared to be hearing.

"Music. You might want that. You might want sounds playing that give you comfort."

As Kurt drove out of the coastal hills and into the valley, Aaron shouted for him to stop.

"There. There!" shouted Aaron.

He pointed to a road sign.

"Go back. I want a picture."

Kurt made a U-turn and passed the sign, a yellow diamond board that read *Bump*.

Aaron handed Kurt his phone.

"You take it," he said as he pushed open the passenger door and crawled out to limp feebly toward the sign. Aaron stood in front, his hands shoved into his front pockets. He rocked on the heels of his shoes as if he were waiting for a bus.

Kurt framed him vertically and made several photos.

"A bump in the road," Aaron said. "The goddamned bump. Here it is."

And Aaron laughed, as if he stood at the break of a new day that had banished many shadows.

By mid-September the coast's summer fogs gave way to warm southern winds that blew Aaron toward another season and likely his last. He loved fall. It was the warmest time of the year when temperatures at the shore rose to nearly 70 degrees and every evening ended with a vibrant, tawny sunset.

Kurt visited every day now. He brought Aaron a framed print of the photo he made of him standing beside the bump sign. Aaron loved it and placed it on the cabin's long bookshelf that now also held his ficus plant, which was still his only dependent and, if he had his way, would be his only heir. For a moment he wished he were the ficus, the plant he had loved enough to take from his ex-wife and that, even if it never spoke, now loomed as a needy relation.

He laughed again at the thought of the ficus mentioned as a survivor in his obituary. The plant would need a name and Kurt thought of Fred. Fred the Ficus. He thought first he would leave the ficus to Kurt who might have a corner of an office where it would fit. Or he could ask his friend Joseph to take it and perhaps every time Joseph looked at the ficus he might think of Aaron, might reconstitute Aaron's life. Someone should do that, thought Aaron. Someone really should.

"Have you thought of writing anything down?" asked Kurt one afternoon.

"Like what?" asked Aaron.

"Some thoughts? Something others might read about you and your life."

It had been weeks since Aaron had opened his laptop. Internet service was spotty at the cottage. And he had long ago lost any interest in the news. An election was happening but he wouldn't be around long enough to vote. There was no mail he cared to read or to which he needed to respond.

"Parting thoughts?" said Aaron.

Kurt smiled.

"Something like that. Your experiences would interest others I work with. Would you consider it?"

Aaron said he would.

When Kurt arrived the next afternoon, Aaron was hunched over his laptop as he pecked stiffly at the keyboard. Yes, he said to Kurt, there were truths to tell. He had been up most of the night hoarding his life's salient moments. He wanted to pass them on, face-to-face and hand-to-hand. They were quickly and urgently important and, like him, also perishable.

6

In the early hours of a morning Aaron remembered the cubby in his cottage's attic where as a child he had hidden treasure from the beach. He thought it might have been shells, or a bright, plastic piece of rope or decorous colored glass or some other flotsam or jetsam from far out in the ocean.

Kurt arrived mid-morning and when Aaron did not answer his knock, he opened the door and found Aaron sprawled on his back in the hallway under a ladder below a hatch in the ceiling that had been roughly pushed aside. Aaron was breathing and his eyes were wide and quickly engaged Kurt.

"What happened?" Kurt asked as he tried to remain calm.

It was a problem when late stage hospice patients wanted to be left alone. Kurt could not know what he might encounter and needed to be prepared for anything. Aaron was alive and alert but once he had fallen, too weak to move.

"Long, old story," said Aaron quietly.

"Any pain?" asked Kurt.

"No…" Aaron let the answer drift out of him. "No pain anymore."

Kurt first turned Aaron over and then leveraged his lower torso so Aaron could climb slowly to his knees and, once steady, rise to standing within Kurt's strong, experienced grasp.

"Not dead weight yet," said Aaron.

Kurt smiled.

"I think it's time," said Kurt, once he had placed Aaron in the living room's large chair.

"It would be better if you'd let someone stay with you. Is there someone you trust?"

"No," Aaron responded. "No one. I don't want anyone here just to watch me fall asleep and not wake up."

Kurt was familiar with the thought of death as a kind of slumber, some state of eternal rest when, of course, it was nothing of the kind. It was the cessation of existence and experience. But the processes that now led him far away from recovery so weakened Aaron it was natural for him to imagine the need for a long nap.

Living was a journey, of course, and Kurt understood why Aaron now thought of it as something unwillingly commenced. His own body was an anchor he forever had assumed would hold him steady but this, too, was going to move and take him with it.

"The world is the home of either the dead or nearly dead and nothing else," Aaron said.

He asked Kurt to finish his futile attempt to search the attic for the contents of his childhood cubby. Kurt climbed the ladder and disappeared into the attic. Ten minutes later he returned with a plastic bag containing old rope, two shells, the broken half of a bright blue float, and a small amber bottle.

Aaron handled the items as if they were an iridescence drawn out of the void. Kurt held Aaron while he cried. The sea had bestowed its treasure, the sea that flowed in Aaron's veins and fused him with sudden and transcending marvel.

A few days passed as Kurt stayed close to Aaron, at least as close as Aaron would allow. Kurt arrived in the mornings and left after fixing Aaron a late afternoon meal.

"Don't close the door," said Aaron one day as Kurt prepared to leave. "Don't."

It was the closest Aaron came to expressing in words his fear of nothingness. Though words were now empty and corresponded only to the hollowness of everything. Words, in fact, became an inevitable problem as Aaron with each passing day and finally with nearly every hour found it harder to speak. He was present and yet also absent, his world passing irrevocably behind a veil of annihilation. And then there was a last burst of energy, and Aaron's desire to have the one last experience of everything though all Kurt could manage was a hundred yard walk on the beach and one last climb of the big dune at sunset. Ice cream, too, was among the few lasts available to Aaron though after one bite of chocolate fudge, Aaron gagged and fell asleep.

And then one morning that Kurt thought for a moment could be the last Aaron sat up in bed, his eyes wide and remarkably clear.

"I can see past the deepest sorrow," he said quietly. "My body is a rebellion against the universe."

And Aaron smiled. The hours passed quickly as Kurt sat with his quiet client before the Sand Box's wide rear window. The sound of crashing waves made a distant rhythm that seemed to soothe Aaron into a light sleep.

"See you in the morning," Aaron said after Kurt prepared him lunch and got ready to leave.

"I'll be here early," said Kurt. "Will you be OK?"

"I can still get to the bathroom," said Aaron. "When I can't do that anymore, we can start to worry."

"Sure," said Kurt who took his own comfort from nature and its laws that dictated the conservation of all energy in the universe. Death, he often thought, might be a return. Certainly it was a mystery and the denouement of every individual's journey through its limited, ephemeral passing through time. Kurt found purpose in helping others through this passage. They were all children, not simply of their mother, but of one mother that was the perpetual vehicle of matter's passage into discontinuity, into the flash of each atom's rebellion against the entropy of the growing and also dying universe.

Kurt arrived after ten the next morning to find the cottage's front door still open. He entered and called for Aaron. There was no response. Kurt entered the bedroom to see Aaron still in bed, his covers kicked half-off. He knew Aaron was dead. He walked to the bed and put his hand on Aaron's cold, still chest. He untangled the covers and spread them over Aaron's face and body. He returned to the living room and phoned the hospice to make arrangements for the transport of Aaron's remains. He then phoned Aaron's mother.

"He's passed," Kurt said. "I'm sorry, Sonia."

"And without anyone there with him?" Sonia shouted. "Why? What kind of help is that for a dying man?"

"It's what he wanted," answered Kurt. "We talked about it yesterday. Aaron had his reasons. He loved all of you. He said so many times."

"I need to come to him," Sonia said anxiously. "God…" and she began to cry, her hoarse sobs held away from the phone.

"Do you need a ride?" asked Kurt.

His hospice had an office in the city that could arrange transportation.

"How long do I have?" Sonia asked.

"As long as you want," answered Kurt. "No one's going anywhere."

Kurt meant to speak only for himself but realized later he also spoke for Aaron.

As he ended the call, Kurt heard a car arrive outside and then footsteps on the cabin's outdoor stairs. He walked to the front door to see Joseph preparing to knock on the open door.

"Dead? Oh, no…"

It was all Joseph could say. He had honored Aaron's late wish that no one any longer visit. Now Joseph regretted his obedience to a friend's last request.

"May I see him?" Joseph asked Kurt, who pointed him toward the bedroom and followed behind. Joseph approached the foot of the bed and let Kurt pass by to lift the cover from Aaron's body. Joseph stared at his friend's still and unexpressive face, its skin drained of color and no eyes open to draw Joseph into his friend's once alert countenance.

"He's gone," Joseph said quietly to Kurt before turning back toward Aaron's body.

"I'm so fucking sorry, man…"

There was no response and Joseph turned to leave the room while Kurt again covered Aaron's body and face.

Later in the afternoon Kurt was on the phone with Marthe when Sonia arrived, all of them now connected in a triangle of electronic exchange of mutual grief. Kurt put his phone on speaker so Marthe could speak to Sonia but Aaron's mother pushed past Kurt and ran up the cabin stairs.

"And the arrangements?" asked Marthe. "When will we have a service?"

Kurt told her it was Aaron's request that his remains be cremated and scattered in the ocean off Salmon Creek beach. But that's all he wanted and Aaron had been clear: he did not want a funeral.

"If that's what he wanted…"

Marthe had nothing else to say and ended the call, likely left in the void that was Aaron's legacy. He was absent now and gone from his self-made place and time. It would be possible for Sonia and Marthe to live without Aaron, though it might be harder now simply to live.

7

It is the wisdom of the body to know when it is no longer needed. The end was one last breath and no more, however labored the ones that preceded it. Each was life until there was no more life. Kurt reviewed the medical determinants of death: a stethoscope applied to the chest, a finger held over a vein in the wrist. A doctor was called to confirm that everything of Aaron had stopped, all the synapsing of electrical life at last turned off as if a switch had been thrown.

Joseph left and Kurt waited at the top of the cottage's stairs and listened to Sonia wail over Aaron's still, cold body. After several minutes through which her screams dissolved into sobs that then became whimpers and, at last, a hard, long silence, Sonia emerged from the bedroom.

"I'll never understand why he needed to be alone."

Sonia spoke as if to Kurt while looking far beyond him through the cottage window and at the distant, churning sea.

"It must be hard," answered Kurt. "Aaron did not want his death to cause anyone else suffering. I don't think he understood that what he thought were his best intentions would hurt others."

"Why didn't you tell him?" Sonia said accusingly. "Why didn't…"

"Because this death was Aaron's and no one else's. And how it went was always his choice. I know he loved all of you. He had his reasons. And you were all very kind and loving to allow this to go his way, regardless of what you all might have otherwise thought was best."

Kurt's words concealed his own concern: that for all the work he did to help the dying pass from life, he was still a virgin, still among the undead even as he studied death, witnessed death, handled death. What did he really know?

He had long ago decided to leave the mystery of death on the other side. Rather, he addressed specifically what was not mysterious: the cold, hardening body, the terms of its disposal, the necessity to celebrate in future time a person's past and finished life and to offer those close to the deceased a life-bound procedure for the organized acceptance of another's death in what was really a rehearsal of their own. Death, silence, dissolution and burial were also rehearsals for the world's presumably distant, but also inevitable and certain end. Kurt considered death one event subsumed within the processes associated with time: birthing, growing, living and ultimately waiting, waiting for an end written into the course of a life from its very beginning. The question was never whether life would bring about its death, but rather how and when?

Three weeks after Aaron's death, Kurt received a phone call from Marthe.

"Mom's died," she said coolly. "I'm coming out."

"I'm so sorry," Kurt said after hearing the surprising news. "What happened? Can I give you any help?"

"Aaron's death was too much, I guess," Marthe said, her voice quiet and remote.

"She had a stroke last Thursday and it was downhill from there. As for you, I think you've done enough."

Kurt heard bitterness in Marthe's voice and assumed it was directed toward him.

Aaron had left instructions on his laptop that included his wish that there be no service or memorial for him and that his ashes be scattered across the beach shore at low tide. From there the ocean would carry them away. He also left Kurt his photo taken at the bump in the road sign and the ficus plant Aaron had named Fred. Kurt gazed at both while speaking with Marthe.

"When would you like to scatter the ashes?" asked Kurt.

"Can't tell you now," said Marthe. "Listen, I'm in the middle of divorcing my husband. A lot's happening up here and I'm too damned far away to care much about anything else. I need to deal with mom first. It's complicated. She's supposed to be buried with Dad in a memorial park south of the City. It means a funeral at a church service and a long list of old city friends for a reception."

Kurt said it sounded like a lot of work, and he understood, but he didn't offer again to help.

"Aaron's ashes…" Kurt tried again to form a question.

"They're still in the attic of the cottage. They aren't going any-where," said Marthe.

"OK," said Kurt. "Good luck. Sorry for all you're dealing with right now. It must be…"

"It's fucked," said Marthe. "It's all so god-damned fucked up."

She hung up the phone.

Kurt tried to re-imagine how and when Aaron's ashes might be scattered. He thought it might be worthwhile to drive out to Salmon Creek, take a walk and scout locations. Perhaps the next time Marthe phoned he could offer a plan that would calm her and ease her anger. Whatever, it was clear to Kurt that Aaron's death had removed him from among Marthe's immediate priorities. Sonia's sudden passing required more time, expense and trouble. And, if she were in the middle of a divorce, Marthe had more than enough trouble of her own. The scattering of Aaron's ashes had become for Marthe just another bump in the road.

Winter rains came and, were it not for watering Fred the Ficus and viewing every day Aaron's last photograph, Kurt might have moved on from the very loose ends of Aaron's passing. His was not the first death to remain incomplete and without any memorial. Kurt frequently finished death's details when survivors could not or would not.

Kurt tried to reach Marthe again. A message told him her phone number was no longer in service. Efforts to scan an on-line directory brought up nothing and since Sonia was dead there was no one else he knew to ask.

Shortly before dying, Aaron told Kurt who he wanted to scatter his ashes, and who he did not want. His mother and sister, of course, and Joseph, his friend at work, could do it along with Kurt. Aaron pointedly did not want his nephews or brother-in-law to be present. And ex-wives were not to be told about it or where his ashes were scattered: a way for Aaron to edit his life and erase some of its pain even after death. And there would be no service. No minister. No ceremony. No encomiums or closing words by anyone.

On a brisk mid-week afternoon, Kurt left the home of a new client in Sebastopol and on a whim drove west to Salmon Creek.

He pulled up in front of the Sand Box to see a *For Sale* sign swinging from a post driven into the ground by the driveway. Kurt parked in front and walked up to see a lock box hanging from the door handle at the top of the stairs. He could contact the realtor, Kurt thought. The realtor would have Marthe's phone number. He would speak to her and offer to scatter Aaron's ashes. Kurt imagined her relief until, stepping to the back of the property, Kurt looked through the living room window of the cottage. All its furnishings were gone.

"She's not coming back," Kurt said to himself. Had Marthe ever again visited the cottage? Kurt wrestled with the difficult feeling Aaron's ashes were gone, were packed with the furniture to be shipped far away from the beloved sand dunes of his entire life, Aaron's wish for the scattering of his remains also a casualty of Marthe's choices. Kurt thought of Aaron now as not his ashes but as a life pushed to the back of a closet or resting in a basement and never released.

Until he remembered that Marthe told him Aaron's ashes were in the attic. It was the attic that for years held undisturbed Aaron's childhood beach treasures. Perhaps Aaron's ashes were still in the attic, unnoticed and out of mind. Kurt looked up and down the dirt road. No cars in front of any of the other homes. He climbed the cottage's stairs and stood at the locked door. He remembered that Aaron had trouble squeezing the deck's sliding door handle and so left it unlatched. Kurt climbed from the stairs to the deck and tried the slider. A firm, hard push cracked the door enough for Kurt to leverage it open.

He walked inside the empty cottage and stood under the attic's ceiling door. He found an empty packing box in a bedroom and positioned it under the hall ceiling, gingerly climbing onto the box to reach up and push the ceiling door away. With a carefully timed jump that collapsed the box's walls he pushed himself up and into the attic to see in a dark corner a modest white carton. He slid it out toward the light and saw its label. In sweeping, serif lettering it read "Aaron Fisk."

Later at the shore, Kurt walked to the ocean's edge and spread Aaron's ashes on the sand where a wave swept in quickly and carried them away. He retreated to sit on Aaron's high dune. Well into the night he thought of Aaron as one of his own life's important connections, one that had withdrawn as all did and would. Kurt's possession of a ficus and a photo made him Aaron's only heir. But certainly there was something more left of Aaron for someone, and for at least some amount of time, to remember. And then the dawn arrived in a flourishing burst that momentarily blinded Kurt with the stunnning brightness of the next first day of all creation.

———————————————

ACKNOWLEDGMENTS

These stories and their themes dwell on the experiences of surprise, exposure and remorse. So much of living catches us unprepared. So much of what is scary and painful also exposes us to ourselves and to others. And, inevitably, there must come those moments of remorse when we realize that what happened cannot be undone. All these stories are grown from real experiences. My characters also grow but none escapes the consequence of an unexplainable urge.
I am deeply grateful to A. Cort Sinnes, a brilliant writer whose editing raised my manuscript to a higher level of verisimilitude. His thoughtful questions and probing analysis provided critical insights that grounded my characters and strengthened the premises of their various crises. I'm also grateful to my life-long friend Rick Jevons with whom I've spent decades spinning and sharing wondrous and soulful tales.

And, of course, I am deeply thankful for my loving wife, Claire Marie Beery, whose enthusiasm and support for this work keeps my lamp burning bright.

www.ingramcontent.com/pod-product-compliance
Lightning Source LLC
Chambersburg PA
CBHW071431200726
48294CB00002B/592